MANNING WOLFE

DEAD BY PROXY

PROXY LEGAL THRILLER SERIES | BOOK 1

STARPATH BOOKS, LLC

Starpath Books, LLC
Austin, TX
www.starpathbooks.com

Library of Congress Control Number: 2023916463
Paperback: ISBN: 978-1-944225-52-0
Ebook: ISBN: 978-1-944225-53-7

Manufactured in the United States of America
10 9 8 7 6 5 4 3 2 1

1

B yron Douglas never forgot his last jury trial in New York City, not because he won, but because it forced him to become dead by proxy.

It started in the grand wood-walled and portrait-adorned federal courtroom, with Byron's client, Killian Tyrone, on trial for murder and RICO charges. The Feds were sure that Tyrone had violated several sections of the act in conjunction with the murder of one Morgan Allen White in his own home.

Voir dire went well, Byron was always good before a jury, especially when the members of the box had not yet gotten to know his client. That would change. Killian Tyrone was not a likable fellow, and the charming, well versed, and talented Byron could only go so far before the jury could see through to the rat-bastard he was representing and surmise the truth. Guilty of something, if not the crime at hand. And, surely lying.

In defending Tyrone, Byron knew he had to be especially charming and likable, not hard for the six-foot three-inch, lean barrister with sparkling blue eyes, thick dark hair, and engaging smile. He moved gracefully from one candidate to the next during the preliminary examination of the jury.

"Do you believe that you can be a fair, impartial, and objective juror in this case?" The answer was always yes and, as doubtful as it was for every person in the jury pool to be totally objective, Byron looked as if he believed and trusted the word of each one. "Thank you."

Byron knew that most criminal attorneys assume their clients are not innocent and it's their job to get them off and obtain a not guilty verdict. Byron didn't see it exactly that way. He assumed that the client was probably guilty, but he put himself in the shoes of the jury and said to his inner judge, "Prove it." Byron believed 'innocent until proven guilty' was one of the founding tenets of criminal trial law and one that he embraced fully. If he could provide any explanation or alternative for his client to be innocent, he fought like hell for that position.

Byron's view of being a trial lawyer harkened back to the days and ways of fictional Atticus Finch, real life Ruth Bader Ginsberg, and historical Oliver Wendell Holmes. He had been a disciple of justice ever since his mentor in law school had inspired him with the culture of the judicial system. Byron saw the law as did legal historian, F.W. Maitland. He often quoted him, "The law is a seamless web." Byron loved the intricacies of the history, tradition, and patriotism attached to the legal process and the way it crisscrossed into every area of the world.

Byron was not jaded or trapped into being an attorney as many he knew were, and he was not in it for the money, although that part was nice. And, he was not naive, as he was aware of severe injustices in the criminal justice system and felt improvement was needed. Byron continued to be on the playing field because he was one of the last true believers. The system was the best available right now, and he actually trusted the outcome, most of the time.

Having deceased parents, one semi-estranged sibling in California, and no current plans to marry, Byron embraced the law as his mistress and his life. He simply loved it all. As most careers went, loving it meant he was devoted to it and good at it. He never glossed over a precedent or twisted a legal argument beyond its parameters. He was thrilled every time he set foot in a courtroom to do battle for his client, guilty or innocent.

Across the aisle, the prosecutor, Sebastian Roberts, relished this chance to incarcerate another criminal. Roberts moved his short spark-plug-of-a-body, decorated with a vest and bright paisley bow tie, around the courtroom as he laid out the federal government's view of the case. He looked at Byron and his client, then back to the twelve chosen members of the jury.

"Ladies and gentlemen, I promise that I will prove in this trial that Killian Tyrone not only murdered Morgan Allen White, he did so as a part of a RICO conspiracy, involving gangster activity as defined in 18 USC Section 1961. While the Irish mob and crime boss, Tua Dannon, are not on trial here, Killian Tyrone's connection to them and his work at their behest is an integral part of this case. And, while our case is circumstantial, as we have no witness who actually saw Mr. Tyrone pull the trigger, we will show, beyond a reasonable doubt, that there is no other logical conclusion, featuring the facts, other than his guilt. Simply put, we, the prosecution, allege that Tyrone killed Mr. White, that he did so at the behest of Tua Dannon, head of the Irish mob, and we'll prove it."

Byron organized his thoughts, felt excitement tingle through his fingers and toes, and stood up at the defense table. In defending Killian Tyrone, Byron's opening argument went something like this: "Your Honor and members of the jury. Today, I'd like to introduce you to my client, Killian Tyrone, the accused in this case. Now, I know what the prosecutor said about what he did, and that is probably swirling around in your brain right now, but I'd like for you to take a step back and listen to both sides of the story before you make a decision about my client's behavior, guilt, or innocence. You also heard his inference about defense attorneys, that would be me." He smiled and the jury laughed. "I'll leave it to you to decide, but I have no intention of tricking you or trying to hide the ball."

Byron pointed at his co-counsel, Michael, a shorter, younger version of himself, but with brown eyes. "My colleague, Michael Everett, and I will present Mr. Tyrone's side of the case and, when we're finished, I'm certain that you will find him not guilty."

Byron smiled at the jury and took pride in the fact that when he won, he won fair and square, and he instilled these principles in his protégé, Michael. Byron encouraged Michael not to be blinded by the legal system, nor be immune to the tricks of the trade. Byron used the tools expertly, but he wanted to win with an equal playing field, or not at all, and the law allowed for plenty of ways to win. To Byron, what was the point if cheating was involved? That only proved he was the best cheater, not the best lawyer.

Byron moved past the bench to stand directly in front of the jury box. "Judge Linton has instructed that each of you keep an open mind until all the evidence is presented, and during voir dire I asked you to do the same. I'm asking you again now. Listen fully and then decide."

The jury seemed to pay close attention to what Byron was saying, but their eyes were on Tyrone who was sweating under his dress shirt.

As Byron returned to the defense table, he winked at Michael, who smiled. The two litigators, who weren't far apart in age, had clicked when they were introduced on Michael's first day at the firm and had grown closer as they worked together, sometimes finishing each other's sentences and often coming up with the same legal strategy independent of each other. The two men had planned their courtroom strategy in defending their client, so both knew what was coming.

Byron stood behind Tyrone and put his hand on the man's broad shoulder. "My client did not grow up with advantages and may have the demeanor of someone you might not befriend. Hell, he's not my friend, either, but I have not walked in his shoes and neither have you. Here in New York, he encountered some unsavory characters when he was just a lad. You may have heard or read about the origins of the Irish mob in Hell's Kitchen, and you may think that the same mob is still alive and active today, but all that is the stuff of movies and novels. I won't deny that there remain criminal networks around the world, but the modern-day mob is nothing like that of the stories you've read and heard. The mob today consists of businessmen in suits and ties, going to work in offices, and flying around the world on airplanes. My client is far down the pecking order of this organization in today's times, and he has no power or control over what they do. Nor is he controlled by their decision making."

Juror number three fidgeted in his seat. Byron made a mental note to have Michael look at the juror's history and try to discern why he was so uncomfortable.

Byron took a few steps closer to the jury box. "My client deserves a fair trial with a full understanding by you, the jury, of how things work in his world and what he could and could not do to promote criminal enterprise under RICO. The elements that must be proved by the prosecutor are specific. I think you'll see at the end of this trial that the burden of proof has not been met, and you'll find my client, Killian Tyrone, not guilty of any RICO activity. He's just a muck who happens to know some guys. Whether they're in the mob or not is none of his business, or ours here today.

"Next, as the prosecutor said, with regard to the second element of the charges, the murder of the deceased, this is a circumstantial case. There is no smoking gun, no witness who saw my client shoot the deceased, no CCTV footage placing him at the deceased's home."

A female member in the gallery yelled out, "His name is Morgan Allen White, not the deceased."

Just as the judge raised his gavel, Byron turned and looked at the grieving widow of Mr. White. Then, he turned back to the jury. "She's correct. Mr. White deserves our respect, and his family deserves our sympathy, but that cannot affect the verdict in this case. We must give Killian Tyrone the full benefit of the doubt. I plan to show you that he is not a murderer. He is not a mobster. He is an unlikable, and unfortunate, man who got caught in the wrong place at the wrong time, and the police grabbed him up on suspicion of association, without searching for the actual killer. Mr. White deserves better than lazy police. He, and his widow, deserve to know the truth."

During the lunch break, Byron and Michael braved the cold, took a short walk from the courthouse toward the World Trade Center Memorial, and found a seat at the Stage Door Delicatessen, an iconic lunch spot decorated with New York memorabilia and crammed with rows of wooden tables. They ordered up a pastrami on rye for Byron and a corned beef on sourdough for Michael – both with spicy mustard. They read each other's minds, each expressing the desire for a beer, but refrained because of the trial, and ordered sodas.

While they waited, they took a look at the big-screen TVs

hanging on the walls at each end of the room where ESPN was showing the latest March Madness scores.

"Looks like your Longhorns beat Gonzaga."

"Hey, sure does." Byron put up his fingers in the form of a horned steer. "Hook 'Em."

"You can take the boy out of Texas, but you can't take Texas out of the boy."

Byron laughed. "Actually, you can. Since my mother's gone, I have no reason to go there ever again."

Michael looked sympathetic.

The men had three things in common besides the law. First, both came from humble beginnings. Byron's mother worked as a maid in a hotel in Houston and brought home whatever was left in the rooms to stretch the budget and make ends meet. Byron had not seen a full roll of toilet paper in his home until he went to college. He often ate whatever packaged goods were abandoned by hotel guests, although he wasn't aware of that until he turned about eleven or twelve. For his mother's sake, as he grew older, he pretended that he didn't know, even to the day she died. Michael's mother was a domestic servant in Buffalo, New York, cooking for, cleaning up after, and taking care of other people's homes and children, until she developed Alzheimer's and had to have constant care.

Secondly, and maybe most importantly, both had absent fathers. To repay their mothers for their many sacrifices, both Byron and Michael had supported them in their later years, buying homes and providing living allowances until Byron's mother died in Houston, and Michael's went into a nursing home in the Bronx, where she still resided. Although Michael visited regularly, most days she didn't know who he was.

Last of all, they shared the love of pimento cheese, a leftover from the south for Byron and a recent discovery by Michael at the insistence of his mentor. To the disgust of Byron's girlfriend and Michael's wife, they lunched frequently on southern pâté, the orange and red mayonnaise concoction, wherever they could find it.

When the food arrived, Byron tucked a napkin into his collar, took a big bite of the fatty pastrami, and talked with his mouth half full. "Did you notice Roberts almost spilled the beans about White's three-year-old son being in the house?"

"Yep. That would have been a mistrial for sure. Judge Linton was very clear that the information about the son was to be excluded."

"I don't think he wants a mistrial any more than we do. Besides, there's no way to know if the kid saw something or slept through the whole thing. A three-year-old can't testify."

"Lucky for Tyrone, is my guess."

Byron snapped off the end of his pickle between his front teeth and crunched on it. "Right. How do you think the opening went?"

"The jury clearly likes you, hates Tyrone, and is giving the prosecution the benefit of the doubt. Juror number three is just a natural fidgeter, I think. I couldn't find anything unusual about his history. They understandably feel sorry for Mrs. White."

Byron chewed thoughtfully.

"Oh, and they love me."

Both men chuckled.

"Yeah. I agree. I'm going to have to make old Prosecutor Roberts look like he's being dishonest."

Michael took a long pull on his soda straw. "Right, or at least manipulative, without looking manipulative yourself."

Byron grunted and chewed, then put down his sandwich and rubbed his chin. "I need to discredit their first witness right out of the gate."

"How are you going to do that?"

2
———

After lunch, once Judge Linton settled himself into his robe on the bench, Prosecutor Roberts, and his minions, put on their case.

"Call your first witness, Mr. Roberts."

"Thank you, Your Honor. Today, we will show through Federal Bureau of Investigation agents the pervasive nature of the Irish mob in New York and its control over Killian Tyrone."

Byron stood. "Your Honor, Mr. Roberts already had his opening statement. Now, he's testifying. Do we have a witness coming?"

"Pontification and repetition are not welcome here, Mr. Roberts. I said call your first witness."

Roberts stuttered, then moved on. "The prosecution calls FBI Special Agent Frank Purvis." As the main witness for the prosecution, Agent Purvis's task was to provide an overview of the federal case, lay out for the jury each point that the prosecution would make via the witnesses who would follow, and connect the dots between those witnesses.

The prosecutor adjusted his lucky blue bow tie and

addressed the witness. "Sir, please state your full name and occupation."

The agent pushed up the microphone before him and cleared his throat. "Frank Purvis, special agent in charge of the FBI case against Killian Tyrone and other co-conspirators, known and unknown."

"Thank you. Now, Agent Purvis, can you tell us first about the murder of Mr. Morgan White and the evidence against Mr. Tyrone that makes you certain of his guilt?"

"Yes, the defendant had motive, means, and opportunity. First of all, Mr. Tyrone was seen in the vicinity of Mr. White's home on the day of the murder. He has prior convictions involving the same brand and caliber firearm that was used in the murder of Mr. White. Lastly, Mr. Tyrone was associated with higher-ups in the Dannon mob with motivation to remove Mr. White before he could work with my agency, as a confidential informant."

Byron stood. "Objection, Your Honor, no predicate laid as to Mr. White's plans for FBI cooperation."

"I'll rephrase. Agent Purvis, had your agency approached Mr. White to ascertain his interest in helping the FBI?"

"Yes, we had ascertained, by visual observation, that Mr. White was a dispatcher at the Dannon warehouse, sending trucks to and from delivery destinations. The legitimate deliveries masked the illegitimate ones. We needed Mr. White, among other things, to clarify which were which so that we could obtain search warrants and open the trucks that carried contraband."

"Was he open to discussing the case?"

"We spoke with him twice and were hopeful that he could be persuaded to assist us further."

Tyrone gently nudged Byron with his knee under the table.

He wrote a note on the yellow tablet before him: *Why aren't you objecting?*

Byron gave him a look that said: *Settle down. I'm the lawyer here.*

The prosecutor looked down at his notes. "Now, Agent Purvis, can you next tell us the elements of a Racketeer Influenced and Corrupt Organizations Act case and why Killian Tyrone's actions fit within that statute?"

"Yes, I can. The power of RICO lies in its conspiracy provision. The statute permits a defendant to be convicted and separately punished, as in this case, for the underlying crimes of the gang associated with a pattern of racketeering activity. It also forces convicted felons, such as Mr. Tyrone, to stay away from any organized crime gang, which he has not."

"Now, Agent Purvis, what have you concluded from your investigation with regard to Mr. Tyrone's affiliation with organized crime and how it led to the murder of Morgan White?"

"Mr. Tyrone is clearly a mobster and dangerous. He takes orders from higher-ups in the Dannon Irish crime cartel, and he carried out one such order in the murder of Morgan White."

Tyrone bristled from the top of his bald head, down his full six feet, to the bottom of his size twelve shoes. Byron stood and put his hand on his client's arm in order to restrain him as obsequiously as possible. "Objection, Your Honor. Opinion is not fact. Where's the proof?"

Byron sat and his client seemed satisfied with his attorney's vigorous attempt on his behalf. After Judge Linton adjourned for a break, Tyrone seemed calmer and under control of his emotions, but Byron could hear the tick of a time bomb in his client's chest.

When it was the defense's turn to question Agent Purvis, Byron stood and looked to his co-counsel, Michael, who handed Byron a file folder. He moved around the defense table, opened the file for effect, because he knew exactly what was there, then rolled his clear blue eyes up at the witness.

"Agent Purvis, what called your attention to my client on the date of the incident?"

Mrs. White squirmed in her seat at the use of the word incident but did not speak out this time.

Agent Purvis squirmed a little as well. "We did not identify him on the date of the murder. We found him through the investigative process."

"So, you looked for the killer and found my client. You didn't find him onsite with a gun in his hand, or handcuffed by responding police officers?"

Agent Purvis frowned. "No, we found him through good old-fashioned investigative work."

"How so?"

"As I testified on direct, we canvassed the neighborhood and discovered an eyewitness, Mr. John Didar. He reported seeing a man entering Morgan White's home prior to the murder."

"Was Mr. Didar crossing the yard? Sitting on the doorstep?"

"No, he was on the street walking his dog."

"And he reported seeing a man, at night, in the dark, at the back door of the house?"

"Yes, there was outdoor lighting in the area."

"Let's talk specifically about the lighting at the back of Morgan White's home. There was no onsite lighting turned on at the time, only street lighting one-half block from the back of the house. Is that correct?"

"Yes, but ..."

"That's sufficient, Agent Purvis. Now, there was no emergency lighting, motion sensor lighting, or even a back door light on at the time of the incident. Was there?"

"No, but ..."

"So, how did Mr. Didar identify my client?"

"Mr. Didar worked with a sketch artist, and we compared the drawing to mugshots and descriptions of known murderers, some known associates of Tua Dannon, and the cartel. We narrowed the pool of suspects and Mr. Didar pointed to your client."

"How many men in the mugshots were Irish, with Irish features, with my client's height and weight?"

"As many as we could find. They were all similar in coloring and facial features."

"Once Mr. Didar identified my client's photograph, did you indicate to him who he had identified?"

"I didn't, but I may have heard one of the police officers make comments about your client's rap sheet."

"Did you consider that to have made an impression on Mr. Didar and his possible witness testimony?"

"Not really. Besides, we had Mr. Didar come in for a line-up identification with your client in the group of possible suspects. You were there." His sarcasm wasn't lost on the jury.

"Yes, I was, and we're getting to that. First, the line-up was at the local precinct, but the police did not conduct the line-up, did they?"

Purvis obviously didn't like the line of questioning and became defensive. "The police facilitated the line-up, but it was conducted by me and other FBI agents."

"Why would the FBI be called in prior to the line-up identification of the suspect?"

"We were invited by the local police after the photo identification had given rise to the line-up."

"Even prior to knowing if there were any federal charges to

be made, you and your FBI buddies were invited to come on down to the local police station and interview a witness who matched up a drawing to a photo, then conduct a line-up?"

Purvis was obviously pissed. "Yes."

"Is that standard?"

"Sometimes. We had Mr. White under surveillance."

Byron looked at Purvis. "So, you were watching the house and you didn't see who murdered him?"

Purvis looked embarrassed. "No, somehow the killer slipped past our agents and entered the property. It must have been a professional."

"A professional? Any evidence of that?"

"None, except that he slipped by two agents."

"Are your agents professionals?"

"Yes, but they missed the perpetrator."

"Right. They could not see someone enter the back door of Mr. White's home, but an eyewitness could see him? Do I have that right?"

Purvis didn't answer.

Judge Linton looked at Agent Purvis. "The witness will answer."

"Withdraw the question, Your Honor." Byron walked back to the defense table and Michael handed him another file folder. Tyrone looked pleased. Byron shot him the evil eye and Tyrone put his game face back on.

Byron walked back to the witness box and paused for effect. "Agent Purvis, isn't it true that you were looking for a member of the Dannon cartel because of Mr. White's association with them, that you assumed the murder was ordered by Tua Dannon, and you focused only on faces that you deemed to be known associates of the cartel?"

"No, we looked first to mugshots of known criminals who might be in the area, then we looked to the cartel associates."

"Now, Agent Purvis, that's just not true, is it? The FBI was on the scene before the local police, you asked to be invited to conduct the line-up, and you had a book of photographs of possible suspects. That book of photos contained only alleged cartel members."

Prosecutor Roberts stood again. "Your Honor, he's testifying again."

"Ask a question, Mr. Douglas."

"Yes, Your Honor." Byron turned from the judge back to Agent Purvis. "Now, isn't it true that you actually made the identification fit your preconceived notion of who was responsible for the murder?"

"No."

"No? So, you were first on the scene, invited yourself into the investigation, conducted the line-up, and accused my client all without any preconceived idea that the Dannon cartel might be involved?"

"True."

"Did you look into any of the delivery patrons of the warehouse where Mr. White worked?"

"No."

"Did you look into any grievances that others may have had against Mr. White?"

"No, we didn't need to. We had an eyewitness who identified your client."

Byron looked at the jury as if to say: *You don't believe that, do you?*

"Agent Purvis, how reliable is witness identification in murder investigations?"

"It can be very accurate."

"Isn't it true that the Innocence Project has shown that misidentification is the leading factor in wrongful convictions?"

"I have no idea."

"Isn't that part of your job, to know what can and cannot be trusted in your line of work?"

"Legitimate sources are consulted and researched."

"The Innocence Project is not a legitimate source?"

"A biased source."

"Would you be surprised to learn that the Justice Department provides the background information used to compile statistics by the Innocence Project?"

"I wouldn't know."

"Okay. Agent Purvis, hasn't it been proven that in a standard line-up, the line-up administrator typically knows who the suspect is and often provides unintentional cues to the eyewitness about which person to pick?"

"That did not happen here."

"Isn't it true that eyewitnesses often assume that the perpetrator is one of those presented in the line-up and this often leads to the selection of a person despite doubts as to whether the suspect is in the line at all?"

"Mr. Didar said he was sure."

"Isn't it also true that the non-suspect fillers in the line-up often don't match the photograph by the sketch artist as closely as the suspect?"

"There cannot be exact matches, or all of them would have to be twins. By your standards, we wouldn't have line-ups at all."

"Maybe we shouldn't."

Prosecutor Roberts was on his feet. "Your Honor!"

"Watch the comments."

"Yes, Your Honor. Now, Mr. Purvis, did you confirm to the eyewitness that he had selected the correct suspect in the line-up?"

"Yes, but only after the identification."

"Don't you think that would increase his confidence that

he'd selected the right person and influence his testimony in this trial?"

"You'd have to ask him. He seemed pretty confident to me."

"My point exactly."

The prosecutor stood again.

The judge held up his hand prior to the objection. "I won't warn you again, Mr. Douglas."

"Yes, sir." Byron walked back to the defense table, smiled, and retrieved another file from Michael.

"Now, Mr. Purvis, let's turn again to the reliability of eyewitness testimony. Are you aware that over seventy percent of all convictions overturned due to DNA testing were prosecuted due to eyewitness testimony, making it very suspect?"

"Those statistics are biased and dated."

"Biased how? The number of convictions that are overturned has been calculated, the number attributable to conviction via eyewitness testimony has been calculated. The math has been done and it's seventy percent. What does outdated have to do with it?"

Purvis didn't answer. The judge started to speak.

"I'll rephrase, Your Honor." Then to the witness, "Don't cases, over the years, often cast doubt on the trustworthiness of witnesses to properly identify suspects?"

"That's ridiculous. Makes no sense."

"Actually, it does. What makes no sense is zeroing in on a small pool of suspects, influencing the eyewitness, and bringing these charges with no further corroborating information. The real evidence in this case is so scant it hardly exists does it, Agent Purvis?"

"What doesn't exist is your client's innocence. We have a witness, he identified Tyrone fair and square, and the jury can clearly see what you're doing."

Byron looked at the jury. "You overreached, didn't you, Agent Purvis?"

Purvis's face turned purple, and he began to sputter.

Before he could answer, Byron turned to the judge. "Withdraw the question, Your Honor. No further questions."

Agent Purvis left the witness stand in a huff, which was not lost on the jury. Byron had humiliated him on the stand, but Agent Purvis's testimony still carried weight as he was a veteran member of the FBI. Byron looked at the jury, but he couldn't read all of them, even with his best poker skills. A few kind expressions made him think he might be creating at least a scintilla of reasonable doubt.

The prosecution continued to put on its case, scoring points now and then. Tyrone appeared increasingly agitated as he sat next to Byron at the defense table. On more than one occasion, Byron asked for a break, proffering the need for a bathroom, in order to calm his client and admonish him about his body language and facial expression. "We get to go next, just remember that."

That seemed to appease Tyrone for a while, but as the prosecution's portion of the trial progressed further, Byron observed Tyrone's mood sully again when the prosecution called a list of witnesses from relatives of the deceased to jailhouse snitches. All testified for the government, and all pointed the finger at Tyrone, as a soldier of the Dannon Irish mob, and the murderer of Morgan White.

3

The next day, when the prosecution finally rested and it was Byron's turn to present his case, he called as his first witness, Loki Murphy. Tyrone had not given his alibi witness's name to the FBI at the time of his arrest, but by the time of his first conference with Byron, at the county jail, he had identified Loki as his drinking partner for the evening.

Byron smiled at Loki who smiled at Tyrone. "Thank you for being here today. Would you please state your full name and city of residence?"

"Loki Murphy. I live in Queens." Loki seemed to stretch to look taller in the witness chair, but he didn't have the height or swagger to pull it off. What he did have, and what made him a good witness, was a nice smile and a friendly disposition.

"Thank you, Mr. Murphy. Where do you work?"

"I work construction jobs around the five boroughs. I'm a pretty good carpenter, and contractors call me when they need cabinets, bookshelves, crown moldings, that type of thing."

"Got it. Good with your hands." Byron smiled again. "Have a family?"

"I have my mom in Queens. I live in her basement and help out with the taxes and maintenance on the house."

"Good son." Byron punctuated the testimony. "Does Mr. Tyrone work with you?"

"No, he's a dock worker. He loads and unloads stuff off ships."

"So, your relationship with Tyrone is just friends?"

"Right."

"Now, could you please tell us where you were on the night in question?"

"I was in Queens at O'Grady's Pub."

"What time?"

"From about eight thirty at night until they closed at two."

"Who was with you on that night?"

Loki pointed to the accused. "Killian Tyrone."

"The entire time?"

"Well, we didn't go to the john together, but all but a couple of minutes, yeah. Dell O'Connor, a buddy from the neighborhood, was with us."

"None of you left the bar at any time?"

"No. Not until we shut it down."

"Now, the prosecution has established, through the medical examiner, that time of death was within a few minutes of midnight. Are you sure you were with Mr. Tyrone at that time?"

"I'm sure. We threw some darts, drank some stout, hit on some pretty girls, got rejected, and left just before they locked up the doors at two." Loki laughed at his own joke. "There were lots of people there who saw us."

"Thank you." Byron let the clarity of the timeline sink in for the jury, then said, "Pass the witness, Your Honor."

Prosecutor Roberts stood and walked toward the witness box. "Mr. Murphy, are you employed by the Dannon Irish cartel?"

Loki lost his smile. "No. I work contract construction."

"So you said, but aren't most of those jobs part of the cartel business? Buildings or houses owned by the mob?"

"No way. I work hard for a good wage and keep my nose clean."

"You said you were hitting on some girls the night of the incident and that lots of people saw you. Do you know the names of any of the other people who saw you in the bar?"

"No, girls don't give their names or numbers if they don't want to take you home."

A few in the courtroom laughed.

The prosecutor kept a straight face. "Are you aware that investigators could not find a single witness who remembers seeing either you or Mr. Tyrone after ten o'clock?"

"Well, it was crowded and they were probably all drunk by then. Did you ask the bartender?"

"I'll ask the questions, but since you mention it. Yes, we did. He was a witness on direct. He remembers both of you earlier, but only you later in the evening."

"Well, he had lots of customers to serve, and we were in the back playing darts later."

"So you said."

Loke smiled. "Yes, I did."

"Did Dell O'Connor stay with you and Mr. Tyrone until the end of the evening?"

"Most of it." This was Murphy's first seemingly evasive answer.

"Do you know where Mr. O'Connor is now?"

"Nope."

"Is there a reason he's not testifying today for Mr. Tyrone?"

"I have no idea."

"And you can't think of a single reason that he wouldn't come forward and tell the court about your night out?"

Byron was on his feet. "Objection, Your Honor. Asked and answered."

Byron and the prosecutor had battled it out in chambers before the trial about the unavailability of Dell O'Connor. The prosecutor had asserted foul play in the witness's absence, and Byron asserted that there was nothing to connect Tyrone to the disappearance. Byron had won, and the judge had ruled any testimony about the absence of Dell O'Connor was to be excluded and the jury could think what they would. Now, the prosecutor was trying to bring in the absence of O'Connor through the back door with Murphy's testimony.

The judge wasn't having it. "Mr. Roberts, you're standing on shaky ground. Move on."

The prosecutor returned to the attorney table. "Release the witness, Your Honor."

Murphy smiled at Tyrone as he exited the witness stand.

A day later, Byron met with Michael for a sit rep in their office conference room. It was late and the support staff was gone for the day. It was eerily quiet with no one bustling about.

The firm was a midsize, midtown, metal-and-glass office, with respect in the legal community that provided a steady stream of referrals. Byron had joined it because he could work hard, get high-level cases, and make all the money he could ever want. He had all the support he needed and little interference once he'd proven he could take care of his clients without supervision. Michael had been assigned to him when he could no longer juggle the load on his own.

Over the last day and a half, Byron had put on the remainder of their case, consisting mostly of character witnesses and an expert on faulty eyewitness identification.

Both Byron and Michael thought they had presented a fairly good case with what little they had to work with. Tyrone's alibi witness, Loki Murphy, was his strongest defense. Loki could not be linked to the cartel by the prosecution, and he had no criminal record, so his testimony was somewhat believable. Also, Loki owned a small carpentry business in Queens, so was not the type to lie and put his life and livelihood at risk. But, did his testimony provide reasonable doubt that Tyrone had not gotten the order from his mob bosses and murdered Morgan White, as most of the prosecution witnesses had testified? Did the jury think that Murphy would lie for his friend? Trying to show Tyrone detached from the cartel had been challenging, but the prosecution had done no better proving that he was attached.

Byron stretched his arms up toward the harsh ceiling lights to release his tense neck muscles and looked at Michael. "I feel it's down to whether the jury believed the prosecution witnesses or the defense witnesses."

Michael agreed. "I observed several jurors nodding positively during your questions on direct and during cross-examination. It looked promising. I think Tyrone has half a chance at an acquittal if we're lucky."

"I agree. It's a roll of the dice, but we have a shot. I think we're finished for the night. Let's get out of here. I'm beat."

They parted in the parking garage, Michael driving home to Brooklyn, and Byron exiting to the street to catch an Uber to the gym. Neither realized they were being watched and followed.

Byron had long used exercise, especially swimming laps, to restore his equilibrium, to think before or after court, and at any other stressful time in his life. GYM, as it was simply labeled on a black and white sign, looked a lot smaller from the front than it was. In typical New York style, the double glass doors, facing 43rd Street, presented a small store front that opened to a much larger space behind. Byron went through the reception area to a room of exercise machines and free weights in a configuration aligned with upper or lower body work. At the back were twin doors to locker rooms labeled MEN and WOMEN.

Byron went through the masculine door, changed into his favorite blue Speedo, and went out the back of the locker room to the club's sparkling blue-green heated lap pool. He could smell the chlorine and feel the dampness. The rectangle was marked off with floating yellow plastic buoys that divided the water into swim lanes. He chose an empty lane, number three, dropped into the cool water, pulled on his goggles, and began to swim the length of the pool. He crisscrossed with two other patrons, a man in lane one and a woman in lane six. His progress was slow at first, then picked up speed as his breath fit with the rhythm of his strokes, while the other two swimmers finished and left.

When Byron had the pool to himself, he let his thoughts run free and the case started to work itself out in his mind. He saw the issues on both sides, the strengths and weaknesses of his position and major points of his closing argument clearly. When he'd strategized all the counterpoints that the prosecution might make, his mind let go and he went into what he called the zone. His muscles relaxed, his breathing became effortless, and his stroke automatic. When he finished the last lap, he climbed up the chrome ladder on shaky legs, out of the blue-green water.

He grabbed a towel from a rack in the corner and dried himself off, satisfied that he'd processed all the angles. *Swim-*

ming never fails me. Little did he know swimming was, and was not, going to save him.

Byron and Michael arranged a quick visit with their client in the attorney-client meeting room at the courthouse before the weekend break. Byron gritted his teeth and waited for the guard to open the door. Byron had grown weary of Tyrone's constant complaining and questioning of his expertise. Tyrone was sitting at the usual metal table, waiting for them, smiling and upbeat. The lawyers sat down and summarized the case to date and the fifty-fifty, or better, shot they thought Tyrone had to win.

Tyrone smiled even larger. "So, you think we've got this?"

Byron grimaced. "No. As I've said from day one, there are no guarantees. Maybe your chances are more like sixty-forty. We're not out of the woods yet, but I think there's reasonable doubt. Murphy did a good job with the alibi testimony and the prosecutor didn't shake him. Your character witnesses were positive, and they didn't falter in their praise of your recent good deeds."

Tyrone smirked. "Good old Loki Murphy. Out for a night on the town. Can't be in two places at one time, can I?"

"Exactly. The rest depends on the other witness's testimony seeing you near the back door of White's house and all the rest."

"But, as you told me, eyewitnesses are known to make mistakes. Aren't they?"

"Yes. It's all down to who the jury trusts more. Which witness seems more credible. Not just whether they are lying, but whether they are secure in their memory of the night's events."

Tyrone grinned. "So, you think we've got it in the bag."

Michael looked incredulous.

Byron was frustrated. "No way. I said we have a shot, but there's no telling who the jury will believe more or what they're thinking. We were lucky the judge excluded the evidence of Dell O'Connor's disappearance. It would be difficult to explain how the person who was allegedly with you and Loki during the murder suddenly vanished from the face of the earth."

Tyrone averted his eyes. "Right. Well, Dell could be sunning on a beach in County Cork for all we know."

Byron rolled his eyes. "True, he could be in Ireland, but we don't need to worry about that, thanks to Judge Linton's ruling, and he was correct. The evidence was not relevant and too prejudicial and there's no proof that you had anything to do with his leaving town."

"Good, so when do I get to testify?"

Byron scoffed. "You don't. I'm getting ready to rest our case and proceed to closing arguments."

"What is the jury going to think if I don't tell them I'm innocent? Besides, I can look them in the eye and tell them I was at O'Grady's Pub across town, just like Loki said I was."

"Maybe, but what if you get the time wrong or the dates mixed up? What if you connect the dots for them to prove the racketeering charges by your association with Tua Dannon? Can you be sure to remember every place you were on every day of the last few years? Can you swear you were never seen with cartel members?"

"I won't get mixed up and I'm good with people. The jury will believe me. I insist on defending myself. I'm innocent."

Byron scratched his chin and looked as though he'd swallowed his tongue. He could not knowingly put a liar on the stand and, although he had no direct knowledge of Tyrone's guilt or innocence, just looking at his face made Byron believe he was not telling the truth.

"I can't in good judgment let you take the stand. And, you really don't want to. It's a faulty idea all around."

Tyrone's face grew red. "You can't stop me. I know it's my choice under the law."

"That's true, but you'll be going against advice of counsel, and I strongly urge you to sleep on it. We've gotten you this far and we don't want to blow our lead. It's a bad call." Michael nodded in agreement, and both lawyers left the holding area less happy than they had been going in.

As he signed out at the guard's desk, Michael asked, "Do you think he'll insist on testifying?"

Byron took the pen from Michael and wrote his name on the sign-out sheet. "Not if he knows what's good for him."

Byron sent Michael home as he had a lovely wife, Nina, and baby girl, Sophie, Byron's goddaughter, to care for. Truthfully, Byron preferred to create his closing argument without input, at least on the first draft. He intended to rest his case after the weekend, after he'd had a chance to swim again and sleep on it. He'd send the draft to Michael for a quick review. That was the best he could do for Killian Tyrone, guilty or innocent.

4

I n court, on Monday morning, Byron leaned over at the defense table and whispered to Tyrone, "Last chance."

Michael, sitting on the other side of their client, heard the admonition and winced.

Try as he might, Byron had taken the weekend to try to convince Tyrone not to testify before closing arguments. When he would not be dissuaded, Byron had prepared him as best he could for the witness stand, asking all the questions he thought the prosecution would ask. He had drilled him hard, partly as prep and partly as a warning of what was to come, in hopes he'd change his mind under pressure. Byron was not confident that Tyrone could pull off the 'I am innocent' speech.

Tyrone pulled on his collar, wrapped in a dark blue tie, and shot a cold look at Byron. The decision had been made.

Byron stood. "The defense calls Killian Tyrone."

Judge Linton looked surprised, Michael was crestfallen, and Prosecutor Roberts hid a wicked smile, as Tyrone took the stand and was sworn in.

Byron approached his client. "Mr. Tyrone, why have you insisted on testifying here today?"

Tyrone looked at the jury. "I want the jury to know that I'm innocent. I want them to hear it from me."

"Okay, let's tell them. Where were you on the night of the murder?"

"I was with Loki Murphy at O'Grady's Pub in Queens. We were celebrating his getting a new client. Big job with a high bid. Dell O'Connor was with us and a lot of people from the neighborhood."

Byron nodded. "Did you have anything to do with Mr. Murphy's new client?"

"No. I just know Loki from around and decided to grab a stout to mark the occasion."

"Were you there all evening?"

"Yes, the drink turned into a night and we wound up staying late."

"Okay. Now, about the assertions that you are close to Tua Dannon. Are you one of his right-hand men as FBI Agent Frank Purvis insinuated?"

Tyrone shifted his massive muscular weight in the witness chair. "Not at all. I know some of the low-level guys around the shipping business who work for one of his companies, but that's hardly close, and I certainly don't kill for him."

Byron turned to look at Michael to make sure he didn't allow the jury to read his expression. He didn't trust a thing Tyrone was saying. Michael read the situation and shuffled some papers to give Byron time to settle.

"Now, Mr. Tyrone, as for the gun charge that the prior witnesses testified about. Were you arrested for using a gun and shooting a man when you were younger?"

"Yes, but I went to jail and I learned my lesson. He didn't die and I was out in a few months on good behavior."

"Do you have any guns now?"

"No. I haven't owned a gun since that conviction. I'm not allowed to have one."

"When you were arrested, were you in possession of a weapon of any kind?"

"No. And they didn't find any when they searched my place either."

Byron looked atTyrone, paused, then asked one last question. "Why should the jury believe you over all the witnesses called by the prosecutor in this case?"

Tyrone was pleased that the question he'd requested from Byron had been asked. "Because I'm innocent. I had no reason to kill Mr. White, and I have no connections to organized crime. I'm an honest, hardworking man and I don't kill people."

"Pass the witness, your Honor." Byron returned to his chair and held his breath.

Prosecutor Roberts walked to the front of the courtroom and burrowed his eyes into the witness. "Mr. Tyrone, what is the nickname that your crew calls you?"

"I don't have a true nickname, just Killian, or Tyrone, or Kel to my close friends."

"Oh, come on now, don't your subordinates call you Killer? Killer Tyrone?"

Byron stood up. "Objection, Your Honor. Asked and answered. I insist that the prosecutor call my client by his proper name, Killian Tyrone."

Prosecutor Roberts looked at the jury and smiled as if to say: *You know the truth.* The damage had already been done.

The judge cleared his throat. "The prosecution will address Mr. Tyrone by his proper name. Let's move on."

Byron showed his indignation. "You can't un-ring a bell, Your Honor; please ask Mr. Roberts to refrain from further grandstanding."

The judge gave Byron an admonishing look for trying to do his job for him. "So ordered."

"Yes, Your Honor. Now, Mr. Tyrone," sarcasm dripped from Prosecutor Roberts' lips, "you testified on direct that you were at O'Grady's Pub all evening on the night of the murder, but we know that's a lie. You left the pub when no one was looking, didn't you? You, and your buddy, were at Mr. White's home and you murdered him."

Byron stood. "Your Honor, the prosecutor is testifying again. And, he's repeatedly using the word murder in relation to my client. It's inflammatory." Byron didn't point out the breach of revealing the 'buddy,' Dell O'Connor. If he needed to, he'd bring it up later in chambers. It was very close to mistrial material for the defense. Byron didn't want a mistrial. He thought the case was as good as it was going to get and giving the prosecution time to possibly locate O'Connor would only make it more difficult to win when Tyrone was re-tried.

Judge Linton looked at the prosecutor. "That's enough, Mr. Roberts. The witness may answer."

Tyrone cast a nasty look at Prosecutor Roberts. "Which question?"

Byron gave Tyrone a look that said: *Watch the smartass.*

The prosecutor looked incredulous, first at the jury then back at Tyrone. "Do you expect this jury to believe that you were misidentified in both a sketch and a line-up?"

Byron was on his feet again. "Your Honor. Do I need to object again?"

"Objection sustained."

Prosecutor Roberts turned to the judge. "I'd like to call an additional witness."

Byron was on his feet. "Objection."

Prosecutor Roberts gestured toward the judge. "Side bar, Your Honor?"

The judge motioned to both attorneys. "Approach."

Both walked up to the bench and Roberts spoke first. "Your Honor, I have a rebuttal witness who will testify that Tyrone and Tua Dannon met regularly for drinks and dinner, and that they were more than acquaintances."

Byron grunted. "Your Honor, this person should have been called on direct. There's no one left on the witness list. The prosecution rested its case days ago."

The prosecutor looked at the judge. "Your Honor, I did not know on direct that Mr. Tyrone was going to testify or that he was going to lie. He just sat on the stand and told this court that he does not know Tua Dannon well. This witness will rebut that testimony."

Byron interrupted. "The relationship was part of the prosecutor's case before my client testified."

The judge paused for a moment, then said to Byron, "Your client opened the door with his statements about Dannon. It's rebuttal. I'll allow the witness."

Byron tried to speak again but the judge cut him off. "Return to your seats."

Byron walked toward Tyrone with dread and regret. If the jury hadn't been watching, he'd have shaken his head.

Prosecutor Roberts addressed the judge. "I have nothing further for this witness."

"Dismissed."

Tyrone was livid. He started to speak, received an admonishing look from Byron, and left the witness stand.

Prosecutor Roberts signaled to the bailiff. "The prosecution calls Ms. Jennifer Brothers."

The bailiff went to the heavy double doors at the back of

the courtroom and called into the hallway for Ms. Brothers. She walked up the aisle to the witness stand, raised her right hand and swore to tell the truth. She was a young, tiny little thing with bleach-blonde hair, wearing a suit that didn't go with the look. Byron guessed it was purchased for the occasion, possibly from a vintage store or Goodwill. A few tattoos peeked out and around the edges of her garments.

Prosecutor Roberts approached her. "Hello, Ms. Brothers. Could you state your full name and tell us where you live and work?"

"My name is Jennifer Brothers, but people call me Jenny. I live in Harlem, and I work at O'Grady's Pub in Queens."

"Thank you. Do you recognize Killian Tyrone, the defendant in this case?"

Ms. Brothers looked over at Tyrone, who glared at her. She shrunk back under his gaze.

"Yes, sir."

"And where have you seen him before today?"

"He used to be at O'Grady's Pub a lot. A few months back."

"And did you ever see him with any other person in the bar?"

"Yes, lots of women. I don't know their names."

"What about men? Have you ever seen him with any Irish men?"

Byron stood. "Objection. Leading the witness."

"Sustained."

"Let me rephrase. Who else have you seen with Mr. Tyrone, if anyone?"

"I've seen him with different men and women and several times with a man who wears very nice suits."

"If I showed you a picture of this nicely suited man, would you recognize him?"

"I think so. Yes."

"May I approach the witness, Your Honor?"

The judge nodded. "Yes."

Roberts took an eight by ten photograph from his second chair attorney, walked up, and put it on the ledge in front of the witness. "Do you recognize this man?"

Byron stood. "Your Honor, this isn't a proper identification procedure."

The judge looked at the witness and said in a kind voice, "Just yes or no, Ms. Brothers, if you know. If not, say so. There's no wrong answer."

Ms. Brothers looked at the photo. "Yes, that's the man that I've seen with that man." She pointed at Tyrone with a tiny, thin finger. "Some call him The Gaffer."

Mr. Roberts smiled reassuringly at his witness. "How often have you seen the two men together in the bar?"

"Just a few times. Maybe three or four."

"Did you ever hear the defendant call the man in the suit The Gaffer?"

"Yes, that's the only name I heard him use."

Roberts handed the photograph to the court reporter. "The prosecution places this photograph of Tua Dannon into evidence."

Judge Linton nodded. "Admitted."

Roberts turned to the judge. "Thank you. Pass the witness, Your Honor."

Byron stood and smiled at Ms. Brothers from the defense table. "Just a few questions, Ms. Brothers. When you saw the men together, what were they doing?"

"Just drinking and talking."

"Were they casual or intense?"

"Just casual."

"So, they could have met by happenstance, enjoying the same bar?"

"Objection, Your Honor. She can't know the answer to that."

"I withdraw the question. Have you ever seen my client with any other men in the pub?"

"Oh, sure. He knows a lot of people. Very popular." She smiled.

"Has he ever been in a fight or altercation in the pub?"

"Not that I know of."

"Do most of the people who patronize the pub live in the neighborhood?"

"Yes, mostly."

"And, would you think it's safe to say that they all pal around because they are neighbors, even if they don't know each other well?"

Prosecutor Roberts stood. "Objection. The witness doesn't know the statistics of the patrons in the pub."

"I think a waitress in a bar has a pretty good idea who her clientele might be."

Judge Linton turned to Ms. Brothers. "You may answer."

The witness looked relieved to have permission. "Yes, most of the people who come in live around there and I see them a lot."

Byron smiled his best witness smile. "Thank you. Now, when these neighborly people come in, do they mix it up? Chat with each other, get to know each other at the bar?"

Prosecutor Roberts stood. "Objection, Your Honor."

"Withdraw the question." Byron sat down. He'd done as much damage control as he could muster.

Prosecutor Roberts stood. "Redirect, Your Honor?"

Judge Linton looked at the large, round clock on the wall. "Make it brief."

"Ms. Brothers, when you saw the two men together did it strike you that they were friends or that they had intentionally met?"

"Objection. Ms. Brothers can't know my client's intentions or emotions."

Prosecutor Roberts looked at the judge. "Your Honor. He opened the door to this line of questioning and, as he said, a bartender of any experience can read his or her patrons. If she has an opinion about the two of them from their body language and demeanor, I think the jury should hear it."

"The witness may answer. Go ahead, Ms. Brothers, if you have an opinion."

"They were definitely more than just bumping into each other. They always met, just the two of them, and they sat in the same booth at the side of the bar every time. I thought they were friends or business partners."

"Thank you, Ms. Brothers. No further questions."

Tyrone fumed and Byron gave him an 'I-told-you-so' look.

———

Byron passed Prosecutor Roberts in the hall on his way to the courtroom the next day. Both appeared to have taken some extra time getting dressed.

"Hugo Boss?" Byron said, admiring the fabric of Roberts' suit. He didn't comment on the bow tie. "Pretty slick, holding that bartender as a surprise witness. How did you know you'd get to put her on the stand on rebuttal?"

"Oh, a little birdie told me I might get a shot at your client."

"Little birdie with a big mouth, I bet." Byron guessed his client had bragged to his cellmates about testifying and blew their shot at a surprise in court.

The prosecutor chuckled and pushed into the courtroom ahead of Byron where both attorneys took positions at their respective tables. It was closing argument day. The last shot either of them had to convince the jury of their position in the case.

As was usual, the prosecutor went first, walking to the jury box and looking at each member in turn. "Ladies and gentlemen of the jury, I won't take much of your time. You've heard the testimony in this case, and I think it's clear that Killer Tyrone has earned his name and reputation. He has shown himself to be a devious criminal of the worst sort."

Byron let him run with the smear. No sense calling attention to the moniker again. Tyrone cringed.

Roberts went on for half an hour summarizing the entire case, then began to close when it appeared the jury was losing interest. "In summary, you heard a credible eyewitness, Mr. John Didar, who saw the accused at the back door of the home of Morgan Allen White. That's opportunity. You heard Jennifer Brothers testify that Mr. Tyrone and Tua Dannon met regularly at O'Grady's Pub, and you heard FBI Agent Purvis testify that Mr. Tyrone was a known soldier in the Dannon mob. That's motive. Lastly, you heard of Mr. Tyrone's experience with weapons including a prior arrest and conviction on a gun charge with a pistol of the same caliber as that used to murder Morgan White. That's means. When you combine these facts, I believe you will find that the elements of a circumstantial case have been met beyond a reasonable doubt. Thank you."

Byron sat for a long minute, and calmed his breathing, before he walked to the jury box; he also looked at each juror in turn. "Ladies and gentlemen, when the prosecutor puts the elements together as he has, you might be inclined to believe that my client is guilty, but as we take these elements one by one, the case against Mr. Tyrone breaks down and holes in the story begin to emerge. You heard a credible witness, Mr. Loki Murphy, swear that he was with my client on the night in question. You heard the expert testimony regarding the unreliability of eyewitnesses, and you heard the prosecutor's own witness, FBI Agent Purvis, testify that the lighting at the back of the victim's home was poor. You heard Jennifer Brothers testify that O'Grady's Pub is a local hangout and that many people frequent the bar from the neighborhood, allowing Mr. Dannon and my client to cross paths."

A couple of jurors in the back row fidgeted in their seats and Byron knew they didn't buy that last point.

"Lastly, you heard testimony that my client was not found at the scene, was not tested for gun residue, and that the murder weapon has yet to be found. No physical evidence whatsoever. When you consider these facts, I believe you will find that the elements of a circumstantial case have not been met beyond a reasonable doubt. In fact, there are holes in the prosecutor's case big enough to drive a truck through. A similar story could be created with any number of people, and you would then believe that story if woven together with Prosecutor Roberts' silver tongue."

Roberts looked like he would object, but held his silver tongue, as it was closing arguments and some leeway was allowed.

"When you consider that my client was across town, has no proven connection to the Dannon Irish mob, and has not been properly identified outside of his alibi, you must find him not guilty. Even if you think he may have committed the crime, that is not enough in a circumstantial case. You may be tempted to buy into the FBI's stories about my client that they may believe to be true. However, with all the manpower and time they've had to connect him to the cartel, they have not done so, except infrequently and in passing. Before you convict my client, you must be sure beyond a reasonable doubt and, in this case, that is just not possible. Thank you."

Byron looked at the jury as he backed up a few steps.

Clearly, the tide had turned in the case and, although Byron had called several good witnesses on Tyrone's behalf, including the character witnesses from his neighborhood, Byron saw a dead end coming. They were going to lose. Tyrone was just not a person who was easily trusted and his fumbling on the stand under the cross-examination of the prosecutor had proved too much for him to juggle with any veracity. In addition, the sheer volume of witnesses called by Roberts added credibility to the government's case.

Byron knew he didn't have most of the members of the panel. The best he could hope for was a hung jury. One thousand Frenchmen can't be wrong, as the saying goes, or in this case, Irishmen.

Only one day later, jury deliberations had ceased, and Byron and Michael were called back to the courtroom. They stood before the court with their begrudging client standing beside them. It appeared as if Tyrone wanted to let his tie swallow him down so he and his huge, sweaty neck could disappear into his shirt and suit jacket.

The judge turned to the jury. "Will the foreman please stand?"

Michael held his breath. The foreman stood up, holding a single sheet of paper in his hand.

"Does the jury have a verdict?"

The foreman cleared his throat. "Yes, Your Honor."

"How do you find?'

Tyrone seemed to struggle to stay calm. Byron had coached him that the trial was not over until sentencing and the judge would not look kindly on an outburst at this stage.

Byron and Michael held onto their last smidgen of hope for a hung jury.

Prosecutor Roberts sat tall with the confidence that he'd done a good job and had presented the evidence well.

All looked to the jury foreman.

"We, the jury, find the defendant, Killian Tyrone, guilty of murder with premeditation, compounded by the RICO statute."

A whisper spread through the courtroom, like the wave at a baseball game. The judge admonished the room with a stare and the whispering ceased as all eyes turned to the bench.

Tyrone whispered into Byron's ear. "Find out who voted against me."

Byron didn't want to do it, but his client had the right to hear the count and standing in his way would only make matters worse.

"Judge Linton, I wish to poll the jury."

The judge turned to the foreman. "You may be seated. Juror number one, is this your verdict?"

"Yes, Your Honor."

"Juror number two, is this your verdict?"

"Yes, Your Honor."

And, so on down the line through all twelve jurors, each affirming that the verdict was unanimous and implying by the mere weight of the vote that Tyrone was, in fact, guilty as charged.

5

Tua Dannon, a mobster and boss of Killian Tyrone, was the one who benefited from the murder of Morgan Allen White. He had never tolerated snitches in his circle and getting rid of White was little more than brushing a fly from his expensive designer lapel. He had a long list of those he had disappeared because of their lack of loyalty. Even the slightest hint of betrayal and the name was added to the list, the appropriate thug called in to do the job, and poof, they were gone. The FBI had most of the names on the list, but every time they got close to turning someone to aid in prosecution, poof, just like Morgan White, gone.

Dannon's driver, right hand, bodyguard, and number one soldier, Seamus Devlin, looked at his perfectly turned-out boss in the rearview mirror. In the early days, Devlin had been one of the thugs who disappeared those who betrayed Dannon, but he had moved up and groomed up, now spending a substantial amount of his paycheck on his wardrobe, emulating his boss's taste, since he had none of his own.

Dannon had just received the news of the conviction of

Killian Tyrone and he was unhappy, actually furious at the outcome. He'd plowed thousands into Tyrone's defense, hiding the funds in special accounts, and it was all for nothing. Not to mention losing one of his best soldiers to prison, there was the question of further RICO prosecution by the FBI. The possibility of Tyrone's turning and ratting out the cartel was slim, as he'd been a trusted associate for years, but anyone could be compromised. Dannon had learned that the hard way.

Devlin pulled into a long driveway, lined with chain link fencing, leading to Dannon's headquarters. Although the mob members called it his office, it was actually a warehouse on the Hudson River, near shipping docks, that proved to be useful for multiple purposes. It was well camouflaged by being nondescript and rough on the outside, but was sleek on the inside in the actual offices. When Devlin pulled up to the chain link gate, two men ran out of the guard shack to open it. Devlin waited for the men to clear the gate from the driveway, pulled in, and shot up to the warehouse entrance, a large metal door in the side of a metal building surrounded by other metal buildings. Devlin opened the car door for Dannon and both disappeared inside.

The FBI task force on RICO violations had known of the office warehouse for years, but they had yet to find probable cause for a search warrant to enter the premises and look around. If they did, Dannon had protected any information they might seek behind encryption and firewalls. Anything not computerized was hidden elsewhere around town, away from the prying eyes of law enforcement. The loss of Morgan White as a possible confidential informant had been a hard blow to the feds.

After Dannon settled into his office, Devlin took the remote and turned up the volume on the television on the credenza in the corner. Dannon poured himself two fingers of Jameson

Irish whiskey and held up a glass as an offering to Devlin, who shook his head in refusal. He always refused when he was on the job, Dannon always offered anyway, knowing the refusal was coming. In fact, relying on it.

Seamus Devlin was often called Shifter, a nickname from Irish/Celtic lore. The term shape shifter had been coined over the years by victims, and their surviving families, because he disappeared people, ghosted kidnappings, perpetrated real estate violations, and conducted offshore money deals, always behind a veil of secrecy that the FBI had been unable to crack or tie to the Dannon cartel.

Devlin was more than a driver; he was one of many men behind the throne. His loyalty to Dannon had been tested over the years; he'd passed every trial and outlived multiple other associates of the cartel. If Dannon was the heart and brains of the mob, Devlin was the axe. His scheming was unsurpassed, and he insisted on being hands-on, solving any issue himself, when possible, rather than delegating to those he considered morons. He tolerated other people because they were necessary, not because he trusted their judgment or their acumen.

Both men turned to the news anchor onscreen, who was reporting on the day's events in court. "An alleged member of the Dannon Irish crime cartel was convicted by a federal jury today for the murder of Morgan Allen White, a man with possible gang affiliation, who was executed in front of his three-year-old son."

Devlin shook his head. "Idiot didn't do his homework."

"Killian Tyrone, also known as Killer Tyrone, of Queens, was convicted on several counts after a two-week jury trial before United States District Judge Leonard Linton. Tyrone was found guilty of violating the federal Racketeer Influenced and Corrupt Organizations Act, RICO, in relation to the murder of the thirty-three-year-old warehouse dispatcher."

Dannon took a long pull on his drink.

"The jury also found Tyrone guilty of conspiring to murder Mr. White, as well as committing the actual murder, both of which were performed in furtherance of the Dannon criminal enterprise. Based on these convictions, Tyrone faces a mandatory minimum term of life in federal prison, plus ten years. Tyrone is scheduled to be sentenced by Judge Linton in thirty days.

"The federal convictions came after the FBI's New York City Task Force on Violent Gangs investigated the case and uncovered evidence related to the murder and Tyrone's involvement with the Dannon cartel. There has been no indictment of Tua Dannon, as the evidence connecting him to the order of the murder seems thin at this time. Dannon is alleged to be well insulated from prosecution by a layer of soldiers doing his bidding. Prosecutors, no doubt, are hoping to turn Tyrone, or some other member of the Dannon cartel, in order to bring in the kingpin, and others in charge, for prosecution."

Dannon grimaced. "Kingpin, my ass."

"The evidence, some of which was excluded at trial, showed that Tyrone drove his car, which contained another armed gang member, Dell O'Connor, to Morgan White's home. The Dannons, as the gang has been called, were allegedly seeking to quiet Mr. White who had been working with prosecutors, or was asked to work with prosecutors, in the purported prosecution of the Dannons. According to witnesses who testified, two Dannon members, one of whom was Killian Tyrone, armed with handguns, got out of Tyrone's vehicle, and ambushed an unsuspecting Mr. White, who was at his home with his three-year-old son who may have awakened and witnessed the murder. The gang members shot Mr. White twice in the back while the victim's son may have been in the kitchen watching. Of course, the child was too young to testify at trial. Mr. White's wife was out of the home at the time.

"The murder was unsolved prior to a federal racketeering indictment that charged that Tyrone and his co-defendants were members of a criminal enterprise that engaged in murder, drug dealing, firearms trafficking, witness intimidation, and armed robbery as part of the Dannon's money-making enterprises.

"Tyrone's partner in the killing of Mr. White, Dell O'Connor, disappeared shortly after the murder and has not been seen since. Prosecutors have stated that they believe he is not missing but dead, as a result of his knowledge of Dannon's enterprises and participation in the slaying. The FBI continues to search for the body."

Dannon spoke to the reporter on screen. "Good luck."

Shortly after the courtroom loss, Byron called his car service and rode to Rikers Island in the East River between Queens and the Bronx, the 400-acre home to New York City's main jail complex.

Once inside, Byron went through the steps to clear security, and signed the register, in order to meet with Tyrone. Although he'd visited many clients at Rikers before, he threw off a shiver when he walked down the main hallway and heard the jailer's doors clank shut behind him.

When Byron entered the attorney-client meeting room, a small cold space sparsely decorated with industrial-looking furnishings, Tyrone was already seated and handcuffed to a ring in the center of a metal table. His legs were free, but the length of the handcuffs prevented him from standing if he were to try, not likely for Byron's benefit, as attorneys were hated by most of the guards at Rikers. The attendant waited for Byron to be seated, then without comment, left through the windowed door Byron had just entered. The guard stood outside for a moment, peeking through the glass, then seemed to move on.

Tyrone sported a new prison tattoo on his left arm that was still red around the edges and appeared to be healing. It was sealed in plastic wrap, making the shamrocks and Celtic cross appear fuzzy around the edges.

Tyrone smirked. "You here to spring me?"

"Yeah, right." Byron faked a laugh. "I'm here to do a postop on the trial and talk about what you want to do next."

"Postop? That's an interesting way of putting it. You thinking appeal?"

"That's up to you, but it's not likely to be granted. The judge played this one by the book, and the jury gave you a fair shot from what I could tell."

"Well, that's not the way I see it. You lost the trial after The Gaffer paid you over two hundred thousand dollars to defend me."

"No one paid me except you, and I did the best anyone could have done at a murder trial with an eyewitness. You should have thought about jail before you killed the guy."

"The case was circumstantial, no witnesses, no gun, no nada. How did the jury find me guilty?"

"You had a fifty-fifty shot or better before you took the stand, almost nil after. I warned you about that. I had you sign a waiver to that effect, if you recall."

"Yeah, you warned me alright, and covered your ass."

"I also told you to take the deal offered by the prosecutor before the trial. You didn't do that either. You made both choices against my advice."

"You should have stopped me, or at least asked me some more questions not to make me look so bad up there. You know

I couldn't take a deal. The Gaffer would never have stood for that."

"I don't work for The Gaffer, as you call him, and I don't have a magic wand. You made your bed, now you have to sleep in it. If you want the appeal, it will be another fifty thousand just to get it started, or I can refer you to another lawyer if you'd rather move on."

Tyrone looked Byron straight in the eye. "Since I'm in here for life, anyway, what's one more guy, heh? You lawyers are all the same, I'll just me buy another one. I don't need you."

Byron stood, preparing to leave. "You might want to think twice about threatening the only guy who would take your case to begin with and one that knows a lot about you."

Tyrone grasped for the only power he had left. "Maybe, but you might want to expect a visit from a few friends of mine."

Byron knocked on the door. "I'll get you a list of three good appellate attorneys. You can take it from there. I assume you're just angry and those are empty threats."

Tyrone flipped him the bird. "Assume this."

The next day, Tyrone met with Seamus Devlin at Rikers in the visiting area for high-risk offenders. There was plexiglass between them with holes at the level of their mouths, and it was assumed they were being recorded as the bright red warning signs all over the room indicated they might be. Devlin had signed in as Tyrone's cousin, Kelly Tyrone, just to minimize the ties to the cartel in the event anyone checked, but at this point, there wasn't much left to hide if the FBI decided to compare faces from the CCTV cameras.

Devlin looked slick in his Venga suit compared to Tyrone in

his prison jumpsuit. "The Gaffer is concerned about the outcome of your trial."

Tyrone appeared irate. "It's all on that asshole lawyer, Byron Douglas. I didn't want to testify and he insisted. I knew I'd get scrambled and even though I practiced, it didn't help. I think he was trying to tank my case."

Devlin perked up. "Do you have any proof of that? Double-cross is a tough pill for our friend to swallow."

"You can tell The Gaffer that there are debts to pay and that I say that lawyer is bent." Both knew this as code for Tyrone expecting Dannon to make things right because Tyrone had protected him in court.

Devlin acquiesced. "Okay. We'll gather some apples." Code for checking out the lawyer's legitimacy and, if he was found to be working with the FBI, take him down.

Tyrone pushed. "I'm serious here. If that fucker isn't dealing with the Fibbies, I'll eat my mother's Irish bonnet."

Devlin looked at the sign on the wall about monitored visits and gave Tyrone a 'watch it' look.

Tyrone wouldn't let it go. "I know a lot, remember that."

Devlin shot a cold stare at Tyrone, as cold as the bars around them.

Agent Purvis, listening in and knowing full well who Seamus Devlin was, and the code for Tua Dannon, smiled at the thought of turning Killer Tyrone.

———

Tua Dannon answered the burner phone. Devlin sat in the SUV outside the prison gates and reported on his visit to Rikers with Tyrone.

"Tyrone thinks that his lawyer threw the case for the FBI."

"Do you think he did, or is Tyrone just pissed off?"

"Maybe both, but we should check it out. At the very least, he should have prevented Tyrone from testifying."

"Get on it."

Byron knocked on the door of the office of FBI Agent Frank Purvis. Byron knew he would have to eat a lot of crow to get help from Purvis, or anyone in the agency, after the embarrassment they'd experienced at his hand on the stand in the Tyrone trial. However, he needed to make sure someone was aware of Tyrone's threats to his life.

"Enter," a deep male voice called from inside the office.

Agent Purvis sat behind his desk, with his wing-tipped shoes up on the corner, leaning back in a black mesh office chair. He did not get up to greet Byron. Neither did Agent Timothy Tyler, Purvis's protege, more like a puppy dog trailing behind him and hanging on his every word and deed.

"Hello, gentlemen." Byron extended his hand to Agent Purvis.

"Have a seat." Purvis didn't shake Byron's hand, but instead pointed to one of two office chairs arranged before his desk. Agent Tyler moved to stand in the corner behind his boss, bearing witness to the meeting. Byron assumed his role was in part to gloat and in part to guard against assertion of any possible misrepresentations in his conversation with Purvis.

Byron sat with a thud. "Thanks."

"Gentlemen and thanks? Very polite this time aren't we, Mr. Douglas?"

"It was nothing personal in court. You know I had to vigorously defend my client."

Purvis almost smiled. "Well, it didn't work, did it? He's toast. On his way to the dungeon as we speak."

Byron placed his right ankle on his left knee and unbuttoned his suit jacket. "I don't blame you for being pissed, but I need your help. If I need to apologize to get that, I apologize."

Byron guessed he had about a week before Dannon discovered that he wasn't going to help with Tyrone's appeal and send someone to find out what he might know, which wasn't much. Dannon probably wasn't sure how much Tyrone had revealed, or if Byron was the type to put two and two together. If the cartel would wipe out Morgan Allen White, they'd certainly question Byron's loyalty to Tyrone.

Purvis smirked. "You're an American citizen, you're entitled to help. What can we do for you?"

Byron uncrossed his legs, sat forward in the chair, and looked into Purvis's eyes. "I fear someone in my client's organization is planning to come after me. Tyrone all but said so when I visited him at Rikers after the guilty verdict. Since then, someone has been following me."

"Who in the organization?"

"I can't tell you that, and you know it. Any names or activities around Tyrone are covered under attorney-client privilege, but you know more than I do. Take a guess."

"And you want us to protect you from a vague threat from a possible organization by a client you almost got off for murder?"

"You know exactly what I'm talking about. Tyrone and his gang are blaming me for the verdict and may be coming after me."

"Tyrone? What happened to the attorney-client privilege?"

"The crime-fraud exception to the privilege not only allows me to report a possible impending crime, it requires that I do."

"Oh, I see, now it's convenient. How about you tell your client to turn state's evidence against that Irish bastard, Tua Dannon, then you won't have anything to worry about."

"I can't confirm that Dannon is involved in this at all, and Tyrone will never rat out anyone he's ever allegedly worked with."

Purvis took his feet off the desk, leaned forward, and rested on his elbows. "Then, what's in it for us?"

Nice guy left Byron's methodology and was replaced by astonishment. "You get to do your job."

"Protecting sleaze bag lawyers is not in my job description."

"Mine either," Timothy, the puppy, chimed in.

Byron slammed his body into the back of the chair. "What happened to my being an American citizen?"

Purvis scoffed. "I'm sure you can afford a bodyguard or two."

"You're pissed enough to let me hang to get revenge for a little courtroom song and dance?"

Purvis broke out in laughter. "Is that what you call it? Trying to get a known murderer set free to kill someone else? Maybe that someone else will be you and we'll try him again."

The puppy smiled. "That could be handy."

Byron shook his head. "I'll have to go over your head if you don't step up here."

Purvis laughed. "Go ahead. Good luck with that."

The puppy in the corner mimicked his boss. "Yeah. Good luck with that."

After Byron left Purvis's office, the agent turned to Tyler, "Looks like that conversation at Rikers meant exactly what we thought it did."

Tyler nodded. "Are you going to help him?"

"Let's watch him just in case. We might get lucky and catch someone trying to murder him."

"Maybe capture and turn the would-be assassin on Dannon's organization?"

"Exactly, if we can't turn Tyrone. I have a meeting with him this afternoon."

"Should we arrest the assailant before or after he kills him?" Tyler laughed.

"One less lawyer wouldn't bother me a bit." Purvis laughed, too.

The Gaffer, Tua Dannon, sat in his long black SUV with tinted windows, reading the daily racing form. When Byron exited the FBI building, Devlin watched from the driver's seat. "There he is."

"Bastard. Does he really think he can talk to them without retribution?"

Devlin grunted. "Or worse, orchestrate a deal for Tyrone, if Killer's decided to talk."

Dannon watched Byron hop in a cab. "Question is whether Tyrone is talking directly to the FBI and if not, how much did that loudmouth Tyrone tell his lawyer?"

Devlin put the SUV in gear. "And, if he knows anything, how much did the lawyer tell the FBI?" Devlin pulled into traffic a few cars behind Byron's cab. "I thought lawyers had to keep secrets."

"Supposedly." The Gaffer folded the paper and threw it on the seat.

Devlin looked at his boss in the rearview mirror. "Tyrone says he didn't tell him anything that wasn't about the case, and only his part in it. Nothing about orders from above. In fact, he said he told the lawyer that he didn't do the murder, so how could it be on orders from you?"

"That might be true since they didn't introduce anything but that in court on defense. Still, Tyrone is a risk. Let's handle that."

"Yes, sir. Want to keep following the lawyer?" Devlin turned the SUV at the corner behind Byron's cab.

"Let's see where he goes next."

At that moment, Byron's cab dropped him on the curb outside a building marked GYM. Dannon watched Byron go inside. "Nah. Looks like he's set for a while. Have one of the guys take over watching him and drive me to the office."

Inside the GYM, Byron swam, considered his options and safety, and decided he needed a plan. *Just in case.*

6

Byron took Michael to Smith and Wollensky on 3rd Avenue in Midtown Manhattan. The iconic restaurant was known for dry-aged beef, martinis, wine, and old-school waiters, but the lawyers were there for the off-the-menu pimento cheese as well. Classic Frank Sinatra and Dean Martin type tunes played in the background.

It was a goodbye dinner, but neither of them knew it.

Byron ordered a bottle of red, and Michael flipped through the menu. "We don't usually celebrate after we lose. What gives?"

Byron smiled. "This time we do. How's my goddaughter?"

"Pulling up on the furniture. Toddling all over the house. Growing like a weed. I've got new photos."

Byron closed the menu. "Break them out. I never get tired of Sophie pics. I miss seeing her."

The waiter poured the wine and both attorneys ordered New York strips, black and blue, with sides of steak fries and pimento cheese.

"Nina says you have to come over before Sophie's suddenly a teenager."

"Oh my. Short-shorts, giggling, and boyfriends."

Michael sipped his wine, a moody dark red cab sav. "Don't remind me. Thank goodness I have a few years to get used to the idea."

Byron flipped through the pics on Michael's phone, commenting and smiling, until the steaks and sides arrived.

"You look sad, bro. She'll still remember her favorite Lovie Byron. We'll have you over soon. You can bring Giselle if you want."

Byron smiled. He knew Nina had never approved of his dating Giselle, his girlfriend of over a year. Thinking of her only added to his melancholy. He took a bite of steak to hide his sadness. "Love you, man, you and your whole family."

Michael laughed. "Don't get all mushy on me, Byron. Just kidding. We love you, too."

Byron hung his head.

Byron's estimation that he had a week before a retaliation strike from Tyrone's gang proved to be wishful thinking. His hopes that the FBI would have a change of heart proved fruitless as well. And, to make it even scarier, the people following him were getting more obvious by the day. Byron guessed this was to threaten him further and limit his ability to meet with the FBI.

Byron was in the lobby, on his way out the door of the building that housed the law firm, chatting with Michael, when he heard a loud vroom. The Harley Davidson motorcycle, the driver all in black, pulled up to the curb and put a bullet through the glass door as Byron ducked and glass shattered all around him. He fell to the floor and made himself as small and flat a target as he could. The motorcycle fled as other office employees shrieked and ran.

Shocked, and covered in glass, Byron checked his arms and chest to make sure he wasn't hit. He looked over at Michael who lay on the floor by the shattered glass door. Byron stayed low, crawled over to Michael and took his pulse. It was faint, but still there. Shaking and fumbling, he reached inside his breast pocket for his cell phone to dial 911, then took off his jacket and used it to press on the wound on Michael's abdomen. Several people in the lobby, hiding behind walls and in elevators, also dialed 911, then began filming the scene.

Byron laid his head on Michael's chest to hear his heartbeat, but hearing nothing, began CPR. As onlookers gawked and filmed, he finally realized his friend was gone. After Michael was taken away in the ambulance, Byron told an NYPD officer what happened. Other officers interviewed witnesses who offered the video footage and confirmed Byron's version of events.

Byron sat on the side of a planter and tried to make sense of what just happened and why. The heavy fog of realization spread over him as he came to terms with his guilt in Michael's death, and the pain he was about to cause Nina and Sophie. The baby would now grow up without a father at the hands of her godfather. Byron remembered the oath he took on the day of her baptism, to be there for her no matter what. "Will you care for her, and help her to take her place within the life and worship of Christ's Church?" He had sworn the oath with every intention of carrying out his promise, and now this. He could not have hurt her more.

He stood and his chest spasmed so hard he grabbed onto a nearby wall to keep from collapsing to the floor. He wished he could go back and protect them all better. He could have warned the firm's security. He could have told Michael to be careful. He could have done a lot of things. *Too late.*

When his legs were steadier, Byron went over to the officer who had taken his statement. "The family should be informed, as soon as possible. We're close. I'd like to go with you."

The officer radioed his superior and permission was granted. Byron left the scene on a sad errand to Michael's home, widow, Nina, and innocent little Sophie.

After Byron failed at his task to comfort Nina, and made sure she was not alone, he asked the notification officer to drop him at his apartment. He was still trembling from the trauma of telling Nina that Michael was gone and didn't trust himself to get home without assistance. He looked down and realized he'd added to her trauma with the glass cuts and blood on his hands.

Byron jumped out of the officer's car, yelling over his shoulder as he bolted toward the doorman and into the lobby. "Thanks." In unison, both the doorman and the patrolman said, "You're welcome."

Byron rode the elevator up to his apartment, fumbled his keys, finally got the door unlocked and went inside, securing the lock and deadbolt behind him. He sat on the end of his bed for over an hour as the adrenaline subsided and he came to grips with the fact that Michael was gone, and he wasn't going to make it out of this one with his courtroom banter and lawyerly charm. He'd felt threatened in the past few days, but now he was terrified. Byron curled up on his bed and felt the loss of his friend. He wept for the first time since his mother died. After the waves of grief gave way to numbness, he finally fell into a fitful sleep.

When Byron awoke, he took a moment for self-pity. All of that work. Undergrad and law school at Columbia, clerking for a nasty judge he could barely tolerate, years as a junior partner to make partner, and now, an Irish gangster was going to snatch it all from him along with his last breath. He knew the bullet that took Michael was meant for him, and the killer most assuredly would try again. The realization spun in his brain like a top that began to wobble as he felt the full-blown terror of his vulnerable state. They would come for him again. He was sure of it.

He had a short window of time to make his decisions and he had to be very careful and secretive. He would attend to arrangements for Michael's funeral, then execute his plan quickly. No one could know. Not his sister in California, not Michael's widow, not his office assistant here in New York, nor his poker buddies and colleagues.

He was on his own. If he revealed his plan, someone could intentionally or accidentally leak it, or worse, another soul could die.

7

Tyrone worked out every day at Rikers in the yard surrounded by other cons vying for the same weights and bodybuilding equipment. Today was like every other day, the yard crowded and stinking with sweat and aggravation. The frustration level among the inmates was high with the group because it was comprised of those with nothing to lose: lifers and convicted murderers.

Inmates who'd not yet been to trial or those with shorter or less violent sentences were scheduled for the yard on alternate days. Guards were relaxed and more at ease on those days, but not today. Today, they watched the lifers and murderers like hawks with one hand on their billy clubs and the other hand ready to grasp their radios.

Tyrone looked around. This was the nasty bunch, but that didn't disturb him at all. He was known as one of the meanest 'mutha' fuckas' in the group, and definitely the best connected. His reputation as one of The Gaffer's soldiers gave him priority in line, caused those with lesser venom to skirt him when he swaggered by, and afforded him protection from rival gangs. Usually.

Today, Tyrone's luck and influence had run out. The worm had turned and The Gaffer had placed a bounty on this soldier in the furtherance of self-preservation. In short, he didn't trust the mean 'mutha' fucka' anymore and had called 'time's up.'

Rad and Bruno Portensky, brothers, and a couple of Eastern European human traffickers, had landed in Rikers about a year apart on the same charge of murder in the first. Rad had killed a security guard in a shoot-out and Bruno had murdered a pregnant woman, the wife of a rival who'd double-crossed him in a prostitution ring bust. The brothers had nothing to lose, both serving life sentences, but a lot to gain in terms of reputation and perks from The Gaffer via the prison pipeline. The brothers didn't share a prison cell, so their only time to talk and cook-up the details of their endeavors was in the yard and during mealtimes. They'd been making plans for the past few days for this event. They actually were looking forward to it.

At exactly three o'clock, the guards ghosted the yard inmates by going inside the building early for the shift change. The riflemen, looking down on the yard from the guard tower, appeared to take note, but took no action, probably assuming there was a good reason for the guards' early absence, or maybe they were in on it.

Rad and Bruno each picked up a twenty-pound barbell with fifty pounds of weights locked on. Each removed the weight on one end, leaving a long mental rod with a disc on the other end.

Rad swung first, hitting Tyrone in the back of the knees as he was lifting a barbell with a hundred pounds over his head. Tyrone fell to his knees dropping the weight and breaking his wrist in the process. "Aargh."

Bruno followed up with a blow to the kidneys causing Tyrone to faceplant into the gravel of the yard. Blood flowed from his split lip and the side of his face onto the ground as Rad raised his barbell weapon above his head and came down on Tyrone's skull, finishing him off.

The riflemen in the tower peppered the gravel all around the lifting area with bullets as a siren went off. Guards came running. "On your stomach. Down everyone. On the ground."

Too late for Tyrone. Rad and Bruno had already dropped their heavy weapons and fell into prone positions amongst the prisoners, hiding in plain sight. The tower guards would later say they weren't sure exactly who the perpetrators were. "They all look alike in their prison garb from up high in the watch tower." Fingerprints discovered later on the barbell weapons added information to their prison files, but what more could you do to a lifer in a state without the death penalty? Why burden the public with the cost of a trial when the 'mutha' fucka' they killed probably deserved it anyway. Maybe someone would charge them later.

For now, the most that could be done was a long stint for each in solitary, which the brothers happily served in exchange for the payments their families had received. As each was led away from the lunchroom to the hole, Rad said to Bruno. "See you on the other side."

Bruno grunted, then smiled.

———

Byron planned to go to his weekly card game, partly to appear normal and partly to make some extra cash. He was going to need a lot of dough for what he had planned. He was pulling cash out of his business and personal accounts in small amounts, but he didn't want a huge singular withdrawal to call attention to himself. He was hoping that if anyone looked at his accounts later, they wouldn't be on notice that he was doing anything out of the ordinary at first blush.

He took a cab to the card game, as always, but this time, he got out a few blocks away and stayed in the shadows of a doorway, watching the entrance to the card room, until he was fairly certain no one was watching or waiting for him.

Once inside, he felt somewhat safe, as several judges and other attorneys had security guards accompanying them. Tough men in dark suits had become almost a fashion accessory, as those participating in the criminal justice system in New York added bodyguards. If Byron's plans didn't go well, he would have to hire security help as well, but he didn't want anyone witnessing his movements for now.

Byron sat at his usual round table of fellow legal colleagues. He actually enjoyed the company of most of them. He'd known most his entire career in New York. "Deal me in."

The dealer slid cards around the half circle. "Sorry to hear about your friend."

"Thanks. I'd rather not talk about it." He said it loudly because he wanted the entire table to know the subject was off-limits.

The dealer sent another round of cards to each player. "Sure, Byron." The group stuck to playing and talking about superficial things for a while.

Within two hours, Byron was up by over three thousand dollars, most of it from Judge Kenneth Stratford, a magistrate he didn't respect or admire. He'd been in Stratford's court several times over the last few years and had found that the judge had little real knowledge of criminal law, allowing himself to be swayed by the most persuasive attorney arguing the case, usually the prosecution. It didn't bother Byron a bit to take a few grand off the old man. It also didn't bother Byron that his buddy, Larry Johnson, took a few bucks out of the pot as well. He'd miss Larry, but not as much as Michael.

As he studied the next hand, Byron absentmindedly scratched his chin, realized he was showing his tell, and gently moved his hand to his lap. No one seemed to read the behavior. A prosecutor, smoking a fat cigar, who'd taken advantage of Stratford's lack of knowledge on several occasions in criminal trials, sat next to the judge and provided another thousand or so in losses to others around the table, mostly to Byron. The prosecutor glared at Byron just as he'd done in court over the years. "Guess we wasted all those tax dollars trying Killer Tyrone for nothing."

Byron smiled. "Your side won this time, but there's always a next time." *I wish.*

Judge Stratford laughed. "No next time for that client."

Byron jerked his head up. "What do you mean?"

The prosecutor tapped ash into a heavy, smoky-brown glass ashtray and joined Stratford in the good laugh. "You haven't heard?"

"Heard what? I'm not representing him on appeal. I'm no longer his attorney of record. No reason for him to call me."

"He won't be calling anybody anymore. Couple of inmates took him down in the yard yesterday." The prosecutor folded, spinning cards as he tossed the losing hand into the center of the table. "What a coincidence that your law buddy is killed and then Tyrone. What do you think of that?"

Byron blanched but hid his distress. "Fold." He felt perspiration trickle down his back. He took the moment as the hand played out to calm himself, inside and out.

The prosecutor frowned and the dealer began to deal another round. "Dead as a dumbbell."

The judge kept laughing. "With a dumbbell."

Byron sat with his poker face on while the others played out the hand but his mind was reeling. If they took out Tyrone, it wasn't him who sent the motorcycle goon after him and killed Michael. It must have been Tua Dannon, The Gaffer, who was trying to keep him quiet. He was in deep shit with the big boss now and he'd have to step up his timeline.

Byron won the next hand when he laid down a full house, kings and sixes, and said, "Full boat."

The judge laid down a pair of aces. "Damn, you got me again."

Byron faked a smile. "Shuffle up and deal. I'll give you guys three more hands to win your money back, then I'm out of here."

Time to hurry up the plan.

8

The next day, Byron swiftly walked several blocks from his apartment to the busiest nearby intersection and disappeared into a throng of bustling New Yorkers and tourists. He monitored the activity around him but never stopped moving. He dropped down into the subway entrance, went through the turnstile, and caught a train. He got off at the next stop where he hailed and took a yellow taxi to Diver's Depot on Lafayette Street, all the while watching to make sure he wasn't followed.

He entered the dive store and found an entire section of scuba gear, flipped through some cheap merchandise, then perused a high-quality black neoprene wetsuit, with matching booties, gloves, and hood. A male clerk came over to assist him when Byron started pulling expensive gear from the racks.

The clerk was enthusiastic about the wetsuit's capabilities in cold water. "This one is treated with blubber technology like the Navy SEALs use. You can swim the English Channel in winter and never feel a thing. See how lightweight it is? Like a second skin."

Byron squished the thin spongy fabric of a sleeve between his fingers. "Just doing a little scuba diving in the Caribbean."

"Then this is probably overkill."

"I don't like being cold," Byron lied. "I'll try it on."

After struggling into, then out of the suit, in a dressing room provided for that purpose, Byron came out in his street clothes with perspiration on his upper lip and forehead.

"What do you think?" If the clerk noticed his sweaty face, he didn't mention it.

"I'll take the set and that black canvas bag over there." Byron handed him the gear and took out his wallet.

"Do you have a dive knife? Never go down without one."

"Yeah, but I'll take a new one." He walked over to the display case and pointed to a row of knives all with colorful handles. "I like the Spyderco dragonfly 2 Salt Lockback. Give me the ankle scabbard for it as well."

The clerk appeared delighted, probably calculating his commission on the purchase. He held up the knife in two colors. Byron pointed at the bright neon yellow one.

"How would you like to pay for it?"

Byron pulled out a wad of bills. "Cash."

The next day after work, Byron took a cab to a men's Big & Tall store and went inside the double glass doors. He looked behind him to make sure he wasn't followed, but missed Devlin's soldier who was tailing him and reporting back to The Gaffer and Devlin that Byron was out shopping.

"What can I help you with?" A beautiful amazon-sized woman in scant sports shorts and a NY Yankees crop top greeted him. She sized him up and down, obviously waiting to hear why such a slim man was shopping at Big & Tall.

"I need a birthday gift for my dad. I'm thinking of a jogging suit to encourage him to get in shape. He's a big guy, about my height, six-two, but has about ten or twenty pounds on me."

"That's what we're here for." She pulled a bright blue hoodie from a rack and showed it to Byron.

"Let me try on the top. I think I can tell how much bigger it needs to be." He took off his suit jacket, pulled on the sweatshirt, and zipped it up. If it had been a whale, it would have swallowed him.

"What do you think?" the clerk cooed.

"This might be a bit too big and too bright colored. Let's go one size smaller and in black or dark blue, and do you have these jogging pants in a dark color without the reflecting stripes down the legs?" Byron pointed to the garment on the rack.

"Sure do." She pulled the requested items from an adjacent rack and placed his selections by the cash register. "Anything else?"

"Could I see some lightweight jogging shoes, size twelve, wide?"

The woman went behind an opening in the wall and came out with two boxes of shoes. When she flipped open the box tops, she revealed one pair with reflective strips and the other pair plain black. Byron selected one of the plain shoes from the box, balanced with a hand on the counter, bent his knee, and measured the sneaker against the bottom of his size eleven Oxfords. The running shoe was a bit longer and wider than his dress shoe.

"These should work."

"If not, just bring them back and we'll swap them out for you."

"Thanks. I'll pay cash." *I won't be bringing them back.*

71

That night, Byron left his walk-up in a dark navy pullover, pants, and sneakers, all bearing no visible branding. His oversized sunglasses covered most of his face.

He kept his head and eyes downcast, especially when crossing streets, passing banks, and in the path of visible cameras. He avoided the subway and walked the length of Manhattan Island until he reached Wall Street.

Byron frequently checked back over his shoulder and jaywalked a couple of times into crowded sidewalks. Devlin's man couldn't keep up with Byron on foot. He lost him about three blocks down Broadway. Byron was free to move around unobserved.

Acting like a tourist, Byron entered the Staten Island Ferry terminal. He waited in line to board the ferry through the Whitehall entrance on the New York side. He snapped pictures on his phone of the shoreline, terminal entrance, ferries, seating areas, boarding protocols, and security guards as he listened to tourist announcements over the loudspeaker.

"The Manhattan Island Ferry runs between Manhattan and Staten Island in upper New York Bay. It's been operated by New York City Department of Transportation since 1817. It takes twenty-five minutes to cross, and because it's free, and beautiful, it's one of the most visited tourist sites in the city. The boat you are boarding is the *Spirit of America Ferry*. The hull is built from the steel out of the World Trade Center buildings post 9/11."

He followed the crowd to board the ferry and once on, found an inside seat on the port side of the boat and waited. In a few minutes, an ordinary-looking man in a New York Jets cap sat down beside him.

The stranger leaned toward Byron and asked in a low voice. "You looking for some help?"

"Are you Lyle?"

"That'll do. Did you bring the photos?"

"Yes." Byron pulled an envelope from his hoodie pocket and handed it to the stranger. "The name has to be spelled exactly as I printed it on the card I included."

Lyle put the envelope in his pocket without looking inside. "No problem. Money?"

"It's in the envelope with the pictures, plus ten percent extra, as agreed, for rushing it."

"Meet me back here, same time day after tomorrow."

"I'll be here or I'm dead and you can drop it overboard."

Lyle paused only slightly. He was accustomed to working with people in dire straits. "I understand."

When the ferry docked on the Staten Island side, Byron waited for the man, calling himself Lyle, to exit, then left the boat himself with a throng of tourists and commuters. He removed two phones from his pocket and chose the burner phone in lieu of his regular phone which he dropped back inside his pants. As he exited the terminal, he activated the screen, opened the Stasher app, flipped through the nearby options, and followed the walking directions for a couple of blocks until he found the address he was seeking. A small shop selling weather radios, cameras, and other miscellaneous electronics displayed a small sign in the window: *Luggage Storage*. He snapped a picture of the store front with the address, and the luggage sign, but did not go in.

He walked north down several streets, peeking into alleys but rejected each in turn as they were busy with workers and trucks. He returned to the store and started in the other direction. He walked two doors down, then turned into an alley just west of the store and snapped more pictures of a row of dumpsters and a loading dock that was empty except for weathered crates and empty cardboard boxes. No one was around, which wasn't surprising since it was narrow and smelled like rotten vegetation and urine.

"Perfect," he whispered to himself.

Byron had been using temporary bodyguards, referred by Judge Stratford, to accompany him to and from his office and to court. He had told the judge he was worried because of Michael's death, which was true. Mostly, Byron had to buy time for a few more days while he waited for Lyle to get his new credentials finished and delivered.

Byron arranged to meet with Giselle, his girlfriend of about eighteen months, at the Second Avenue Deli, the best kosher deli in Manhattan in Byron's opinion. He gave strict instructions to the bodyguards to stay completely under the radar, outside and out of sight. He couldn't risk Giselle asking questions about his security. Although she did know about Michael's death, she didn't know that Byron was now sure he was the intended target.

Byron chose the deli because he didn't know when he might be eating pastrami on this level again and ordered his last favorite meal like a man going to the gas chamber. It felt like that to Byron. The end of life as he knew it. He hadn't done any real legal work in days and hadn't seen Giselle but once since Michael's funeral. He hadn't wanted her in the line of fire in case things went south again.

As he ate his lonely meal, he chastised himself. Why didn't

he fight back? Why didn't he think up a clever way to outsmart his adversary like they do in the movies? Why didn't he put on a cape and fly around Manhattan, making it safe for all mankind? Byron had thought for hours on just this topic. He had gone through a mental list of options as he swam, sat in his office, and lay awake at night. He saw this as his only option. He didn't think he was going to survive any other way. The die was cast.

Giselle broke his concentration when she floated into the diner in a white peasant blouse, a pair of tight jeans, and high-heeled leather boots that made Byron wish he'd arranged the meeting in his apartment for a last tryst. He had eaten his big, stacked pastrami on rye with lots of Swiss cheese before she arrived and was just finishing his last potato chip when he saw her. She was a vegetarian and he knew she wouldn't approve of his dietary choices, leather boots aside. He wanted to totally immerse himself in the experience of the brined and spicy beef without reprisals or indigestion.

He was going to miss her, but truth be told, he and Giselle probably would have split anyway, as they'd been coasting for months. He knew it was cowardly, but he orchestrated the split in public, just to make sure there wasn't a scene he couldn't control.

Byron rose from the table and pulled out her chair, smelling her long blonde hair as he did so. "You look great. Smell good, too."

Giselle took her seat and Byron resumed his seat across the table and smiled.

"You ate?"

"Yeah, I got here early, but let's get you something." Byron knew she wouldn't eat. Rarely did in a place like this.

"I'm good. Not hungry. I'll have a cup of coffee."

Byron signaled the waiter, got her coffee, then picked a fight in a way only couples that had known each other for a long time could. Just a look or the wrong word, and there it goes. Byron didn't want to do it, but he didn't want her in the picture, for his sake and hers.

"Are you heading back to Detroit for Mother's Day?" Hometown and parents all in the same sentence. That should get the tension going.

"No, why would I?"

"Just thought maybe you'd want to see your parents. It's been a while, hasn't it?"

"You're one to talk, when was the last time you saw your sister in California, or even spoke to her?"

Byron rolled his eyes at her and smiled with a face that said it all. That did it. Pushed her right over the edge.

"You know, I'm tired. It's been a long week and I've barely seen you. What are we doing here?"

"Yeah, I've been tied up at the office since the trial, and I know we haven't been on the same page for a while. I wanted to talk to you about what's next." He let that sink in and hoped she'd get the hint and get out ahead of him. It worked. He felt like a heel, but better to let her think it was her idea. He knew she'd feel a lot better later if she called the shots and broke up with him.

She looked at him and mentally crossed over. "I've been meaning to talk to you about that as well."

And there it was, he didn't really want it to end, but felt he had no choice. She didn't flare up in anger, but snipped at him a bit, did the dirty work of breaking off the relationship, and left him sitting with an empty plate of breadcrumbs, half a beer, and her untouched coffee.

When she walked by the bodyguards, they snickered at what they had witnessed, until Byron appeared ready to go.

9

Byron withdrew money from his personal accounts until he was down to less than five thousand in each one. He didn't want anyone to be alerted to his withdrawals, so he left enough money in the bank to allow for doubt in an investigation, which would certainly ensue.

The firm's office manager kept a close watch on the office accounts, so he couldn't withdraw from those, as much as he wanted to, without attracting her attention, not to mention breaking the law. The office manager didn't have knowledge of or access to his slush fund and it was well hidden offshore, a trick he'd learned from representing some of his shadier clients. The money was his, not the firm's, so it was none of her business.

He communicated with defendants who had court appearances coming up soon and delayed two trials for several months by chatting up the judges and calling in a few favors. He left a couple of lunch dates and meetings on his calendar so that it wasn't too obvious that he was clearing his schedule.

The next night, while the firm was quiet, he shredded documents for hours until the two bodyguards started yawning in the reception area. He had them accompany him to his apartment, where he paid them, thanked them, and dismissed them for good, stating that he felt the danger had passed and he no longer needed protection. He felt the risk of going without the guards was worth it. They hadn't seen everything he was doing, but if they witnessed much more, they might put two and two together and figure out his plan. Byron hoped that if the two were called in for questioning, they would affirm that he had been mistaken in letting them go so soon.

After they left, he cleaned out his files at home until the wee hours. He checked his mental list to make sure everything sensitive was disposed of, then fell into an exhausted sleep full of bad dreams on sweaty sheets.

Byron, feeling a bit naked without his bodyguards, retraced his steps from his apartment to the busy intersection, same as the day he'd gone to Staten Island. When he was sure he'd shaken off any possible followers, he headed south. It was a lovely New York day, but Byron did not feel the sun on his face.

He carried the large black canvas tote he'd purchased from the scuba shop. The bag was on his back with his arms through the handles, creating a backpack. It was stuffed almost full and zipped shut, with a small combination lock holding the zipper pull against a ring sewn into the canvas for that purpose.

He arrived at the ferry terminal, boarded the next boat, and settled the bag next to him in the same seat he had sat in two days before. Lyle, again wearing the New York Jets cap, sat down beside him and handed him a large manilla envelope with a metal clasp holding the flap shut.

Byron took it and gave it a shake. "Is it all here?"

"Yep. Passport, driver's license, two prepaid credit cards, and a bus pass. All with your pic and new name just as you printed it on the card."

Byron detected a bit of sarcasm but blew it off. He opened the clasp and took a quick peek inside, then handed Lyle the balance of the money owed. Ten seconds later, Lyle was walking down the aisle toward the back of the ferry where other passengers gathered to exit.

"Thanks," Byron mumbled as he took a credit card with his new name from the envelope and his burner phone from his pocket. He programmed the name and number into the Stasher app then replaced the credit card in the envelope. He pulled the canvas bag into his lap, rolled the cylinders on the combination lock, unzipped the bag's opening, and placed the manilla envelope deep inside under the clothes, shoes, and few toiletries. He re-locked the bag, re-hoisted it on his back, and moved toward the exit as the boat docked and passengers began to stream in every direction through the ferry terminal.

Byron left the terminal through a side exit, taking a new route through Staten Island, and located the electronics store he had found and photographed when he'd visited before.

This time, when Byron crossed the street to the electronics store, he walked inside. It would have been easier just to get a locker at the bus station, but if something went wrong, that's the first place they'd look. He got the burner phone out of his pocket, opened the Stasher app with his new alias and credit card programmed in, and went up to the counter, where he addressed a wiry brown man with Indian features and a Mumbai accent.

Byron smiled. "I found you on the Stasher app. I'm visiting

from Boston and I'm going to travel around New York for a few days. I'd like to store my bag here until I get ready to move on." Byron had prepared his lie in advance; it seemed to bore the clerk who took Byron's phone and scanned the pertinent information from the app into his computer system.

"Show the QR code in the app when you pick up the bag. Your locker number will be automatically registered. You can pay then, based on the number of days we store your luggage. There will be a small hold placed on your credit card."

"Okay." Byron passed the bag over to the clerk, his hand seemed to take on a mind of its own and held onto the strap until the man pulled it free, tagged it, and placed it in one of several metal lockers lining the wall behind the counter. When the clerk closed the locker door, it made a whirring sound and clicked into secured mode.

Byron took note of the locker number, just in case, took a deep breath, and turned to leave the store and the bag behind. "Thanks."

10

Byron caught a bit of luck when the Weather Network announced a weather bomb brewing along the Pacific Coast. He turned up the volume on the television in his bedroom. Onscreen, a muscular Seattle reporter, wearing an all-weather poncho, stood in a windstorm holding a microphone and yelling at the camera. "A furious storm unleashed from a bomb cyclone over the Pacific Ocean slammed ashore today in drought-plagued Northern California and the Pacific Northwest, blasting a wide swath of the West Coast with heavy rain, damaging winds, flooding, and mudslides. Over 160,000 homes and businesses in California, more than 170,000 in Washington, and over 28,000 in Oregon are left without power. Two people were killed when a tree fell on a vehicle in the greater Seattle area. Flooding across the San Francisco Bay Area closed streets in Berkeley and inundated the Bay Bridge toll plaza in Oakland. By late morning, Mount Tamalpais, just north of San Francisco, had recorded a half-foot of rainfall during the previous twelve hours. The storm is expected to sweep across the Midwest and onto the East Coast by early evening tomorrow. New York and New Jersey are bracing for the onslaught."

"Handy," Byron said to the reporter onscreen. It was a day earlier than he'd planned for, but he could make it work. He watched the updates while he packed and mentally adjusted his departure time to coincide just prior to the storm's arrival. He tried to keep his mind on his actions and force the doubt from his mind, but it crept in with each move he made.

What will the future hold? Can I pull this off? So many moving parts. What if they catch me before I get everything in place? Am I a fool to think this will work?

The next day, as the storm brewed, Byron shaved, dressed, and took a last look around his apartment. He took nothing with him, not even his toothbrush. The few photos he cherished, one of Sophie with her parents and one of himself with his mother and sister when they were teenagers, were in his canvas bag in the Stasher storage locker. Leaving his apartment was tough, as he'd worked hard for his belongings and had everything just the way he liked it.

As distressing as it was to abandon his home, nothing pained him like leaving his chosen profession behind. The night before he'd gone to his office one last time and double-checked everything. He'd finished shredding a final few documents and swallowed the bitter pill of knowing that he'd probably never stand in his office again, or a courtroom. He had wanted to ask the building's security guard to put him in a cab, but he was worried that the request would be remembered after he was gone, so he crept out the side entrance and rushed into an Uber he'd arranged to pick him up.

He was tired of the cloak and dagger and ready to release

the constant burden of acute vigilance. Looking over his shoulder, changing cabs, hiding under a ballcap or hoodie, and looking into every shadow was wearing him down. Adrenaline fatigue had set in, not to mention the lack of sleep and horrific dreams he experienced each night.

Byron harbored no hope of working things out with the cartel, and with Tyrone dead, he had no real contact there. He couldn't just walk into Tua Dannon's office and say, "Hey, guys. I don't know a thing." He was sure he'd never walk out of there alive.

The Irish mob had outlasted many administrations of city government, union presidents, and lots of lawyers. Byron didn't deceive himself with thoughts that the Dannons would just disappear from his radar and allow him to eventually return home with all forgotten and forgiven. Michael was gone, Tyrone was gone. That was proof enough that he was not safe. Not in this lifetime.

Byron dressed in layers to stay warm and pulled on the oversized jogging suit he had professed to buy for his father's birthday. He put the oversized running shoes over his webbed swimmers, pulled on yet another ballcap, and headed toward the door for the last time. He took one last look back, stepped over the threshold, and closed the door behind him.

Devlin, on The Gaffer's orders, was staked out on the corner opposite Byron's apartment in the company SUV. He was driving, as he liked to be in control, while two soldiers, Jim Breslin and Declan Cronin, were in the back seat and heavily armed. The plan was to catch Byron on the sidewalk and gun him down as a statement to any who would go to the FBI and rat out the cartel. The plan had not worked when Michael was killed. Maybe they'd do better this time.

Devlin watched Byron run across the street, just as the light changed, and into a crowd of raincoats and umbrellas, making it difficult to see him after the initial identification.

Breslin was getting restless as he held the Sig Sauer MCX Rattler in his hands. His own personal defense weapon, or PDW, as he called it. "Where's our boy headed? Looks like he's gained some weight."

Cronin, holding another Sig Rattler, sat at the ready. "Yeah, and he seems to be in a hurry."

Devlin spotted Byron, as he jumped into a cab. The mobster made a quick U-turn to follow, amidst blasting horns and shouting drivers. The SUV trailed along behind the taxi, waiting for an opportunity to present itself for the ambush, until it stopped, and Byron climbed out near Battery Park. Devlin couldn't catch up but sighted him quickly walking south toward Wall Street and the Staten Island Ferry and made haste to follow. When Byron crossed into the ferry terminal, Devlin pulled over to the curb and yelled into the back seat. "Go after him, and don't come back until he's dead."

Breslin and Cronin dropped the heavy weapons, and both tucked a Glock 19 into their waistbands at the small of the back. Rain pelted harder on the two as they exited the SUV and ran for the terminal entrance after Byron.

Byron was aware that the two men were chasing him, although he didn't know their names. He was hoping his luck would not run out as he stood in line to board the next ferry to Staten Island. Armed policemen were visible around the terminal. The two thugs behind him seemed reluctant to call attention to themselves in the crowded area and waited in line like good little tourists. When Byron boarded, they followed him on.

Byron worked his way up the stairs to the very top of the brightly painted orange ferry and leaned against the rail on the side. He could see the outline of the Statue of Liberty in the distance amidst the fog and rain, her raised copper hand holding a lighted torch.

Byron looked back, saw the two men approaching, and took a deep breath. He climbed up on the rail and prepared to jump into the icy March water of the Hudson River below when Cronin grabbed his hooded jacket to pull him back. Byron fought to release himself from Cronin's grip when Breslin put his foot up on the rail ledge and grabbed Byron around the waist. Both gangsters grappled with Byron's torso. Other passengers noticed and began to call out for help. Some shot video on their phones. Byron turned, wrapped his arms around Breslin's neck, and stretched into a sideways Esther Williams' synchronized dive over the rail of the boat. The splash was high and loud, even in the pouring rain. "Man overboard."

Cronin peered over the side, scanning the surface for the two, as the ferry horn began to blow the distress signal and slow down, but it took a while to come to a complete stop and turn. He could not see the two men in the water below.

Byron freed himself of Breslin in the fall and stripped, underwater, as quickly as he could. First, he ditched the over-sized jogging shoes, then the hooded jacket. He wriggled out of the heavy sweatpants, letting the garments fall to the bottom of the river, leaving him in his sleek warm wetsuit. He came up to the surface for air, saw the back end of the ferry, took a big gulp, and began to swim for the Statue of Liberty. He was not visible to Cronin or the passengers in the gray rain and dark water as the ferry pulled farther away toward the Manhattan terminal. He didn't see Breslin. His plan was to hang out and then hide out on Liberty Island to catch his breath until the rescue efforts subsided. After dark, he would sneakily swim over to Long Island.

Byron had only gotten a few strokes in when he felt a jerk on his ankle. He looked back to see Breslin holding onto his web-footed bootie and treading water with his other arm. Byron could not break free from the strong Irishman and wrestled against Breslin, who held on tight.

"Let go, you bastard."

Breslin swam closer, grabbed Byron by the arm, turning him until they were face to face, and both went down. The men, still attached, struggled to the surface for air; Byron kicked at Breslin and missed. Breslin pushed Byron below the surface, forcing him to take in a mouth full of water. He resurfaced. Breslin held on fiercely and pushed Byron's head below the water once more. Byron struggled underwater until he thought his lungs would burst. He reached for the scabbard on his ankle, released and pulled out his dive knife, and stabbed in the direction of Breslin, who immediately let go.

Byron was not sure if, or where, he had punctured Breslin, but he didn't stop to find out. He was now closer to Staten Island than Liberty Island, so he swam to the Staten Island side of the river and hid between several anchored boats a few yards from the ferry terminal while he caught his breath. Despite his blubber technology wetsuit, his teeth were beginning to chatter.

Byron did not know that rescuers had secured a flotation device beneath Breslin and hoisted him onto a rescue boat. It took them only seventeen minutes to pull him from the water, but it was too late. Breslin was shivering from hypothermia and disoriented. Later, doctors said that he might have survived the knife wound to his ribs if he hadn't been slowly freezing to death. He was unaware of where he was or what happened when he was taken to the hospital and subsequently pronounced DOA.

For hours, rescuers swept the river in search of Byron, but without success. Later, Cronin, from his jail cell, reported to lawyers for Tua Dannon and Devlin that both Breslin and Byron were dead as a result of the struggle in the icy water. He was sure that the freezing temperature could not be survived. The lawyers relayed the message to their true clients, who planned to let Cronin take the fall for all of it.

Byron pulled himself up on shore on the Staten Island side of the river and found a secluded spot to change. He stripped down to his T-shirt and running shorts and retrieved his burner phone from a waterproof bag. He left the wetsuit hidden at the shoreline. He was dry, but it was still cold, even in March, so he began to jog in his web-footed booties into Staten Island under cover of darkness.

Byron's research, as he planned his faux death, had shown him that people had been committing pseudocide since the dark ages in order to escape from service in war and other undesirable roles in society. He remembered studying, in college, the faked death of Joan of Leeds, an English nun, who in 1318 escaped her monastic life by constructing a dummy of herself, which fooled her sister nuns, who buried it in holy ground. The only reason she was found out was that they later dug her up to move her into unholy ground by order of the Archbishop of York. Joan was found later, alive, in another town and living with a man.

Of course, Byron had read about and watched the fictional death of Juliet of *Romeo & Juliet* and Gregory House of the TV show *House*, along with thousands of others determined to escape their intolerable situations by faking their deaths. Byron had learned that most pseudocides involved insurance fraud or some type of money scheme. He would not benefit financially in any way from faking his death. Just the opposite. As it unfortunately happened, he was leaving his prosperity behind and running for his life.

Byron reached the electronics store where he retrieved his canvas bag using the phone app with the locker number and payment method programmed into it. He took the canvas bag around the corner into the alley with the smelly dumpsters, found a crate to stand on while trying to stay clean, and changed into jeans and boots from the bag. He hid the web-footed booties in one of the dumpsters, pulled his baseball cap down low, and headed out of the alley toward the New York Transit Yukon Bus Depot to what he hoped was safety.

11

Byron pulled a Tom Sawyer and attended his own funeral. It was just too rich, and he couldn't resist. It also allowed him to say goodbye, although secretively, to those he would miss. Lastly, it would give him information on whether the Dannon cartel had actually bought his disappearance and whether they'd be coming after him.

He had hidden out, until the funeral, near the Brooklyn Public Library, where he'd set up a short-term Airbnb under his assumed name. He was able to do research online on the library computers and had found several articles proclaiming his death.

"No one could have survived in the icy water of the Hudson this early in the spring. Although the body of criminal attorney Byron Douglas was not found, authorities are convinced that he did not survive the fall from the ferry. The heavy storm activity contributed to the inability to locate the corpse."

Byron shivered at the memory of the icy water and the word 'corpse.'

"His memorial is set for Wednesday at three in the afternoon."

Although he was a lapsed Catholic, Byron had continued to donate to St. Jerome's and was still on the membership role, so that's where the firm held his funeral. Byron perched quietly in the bell tower above the sanctuary with a pair of tiny binoculars. He looked down on the scene with complete confidence that he would not be noticed. His disguise was a nun's habit. His fine features passed for a woman's and the rest of him was covered in black. He couldn't hear the service, but he caught glimpses of it through the stained-glass windows.

Since there was no body, it was more like a memorial than a funeral. Giselle was there, as was Michael Everett's widow, Nina, and a few attorneys from his firm. In the back by the side exit were FBI Agents Frank Purvis and Timothy Tyler. *What a joke!* Byron knew they were there to spy on possible activity by the cartel and not to honor him. They also had agents out front, watching those in attendance who came and went.

Father Samuelson oversaw the service and introduced the speakers. A nice eulogy was given by his former managing partner from his law firm who gave a short speech on what a great lawyer Byron was and how much he'd be missed around the office.

"On behalf of our friends and the firm, we thank you for coming today as we honor Byron Douglas. The condolences and prayers are appreciated at this difficult time. Your presence here shows the impact Byron had on the community. He was a fine lawyer and friend. His talent was recognized by all who knew and worked with him, and his charity work with the Innocence Project is a wonderful legacy to his memory."

Unlike Mark Twain's version, where the entire town turned out for a sad and tearful farewell to Tom, Byron's funeral was sort of a letdown. His own sister didn't even attend and, with his parents deceased and his best friend recently buried, only Nina Everett wept. Byron wasn't sure whether it was for him or her recent loss of Michael. Probably a combination. Sophie, his goddaughter, was not in attendance, of course. Nina would soon find out from Byron's executor in the firm's wills and estates department that Sophie would inherit the bulk of Byron's remaining assets, including the value of his partnership in the firm, after fifty thousand went to the Innocence Project.

He recognized no one from the Dannon cartel and saw no one who was a stranger to him, so he felt confident that he had pulled off his pseudocide with some measure of success. When the service started to wrap up, Byron felt a strange letdown. He wondered if his life was really all that important after all. Maybe it wasn't worth saving. He'd caused two deaths in the last few weeks. What gave him the right to live? Survival instincts kicked in, however, and Byron slipped out of the bell tower and onto the busy New York sidewalk before Father Samuelson finished the final prayer.

He saw them outside the side door. In addition to those who appeared to be FBI agents, Byron spotted two men in sharkskin suits, a shiny fabric often preferred by the Italian mob, but apparently catching on with the Irish. Were they on to him or just making sure he was really dead? Not taking any chances, he picked up his pace and turned down the street. Still dressed as a very tall nun, he walked to the Port Authority, the busiest terminal in New York, changed his clothes in the restroom marked *Family*, and emerged as a construction worker, complete with stained jeans, a Home Depot cap, and paint-splattered steel-toed boots. He watched carefully to make sure he wasn't followed, saw no one watching for him, and caught the next bus west. By the time he rolled across the New York state line and into Pennsylvania, he was almost ready to face his uncertain future. Almost.

On his way west, Byron had a two-hour bus stop at the Greyhound Airways Transit Center in Memphis, Tennessee. He used the time to locate and walk the six and a half miles to the Memphis Public Library on Poplar Avenue. He entered, got the lay of the land, and found a free computer in a long row of people using them. He logged into the internet by peeking at the kid's library card sitting next to him, as the young man also logged in. Once online, he searched for Declan Cronin. He found an article about the fight on the ferry, the death of Jim Breslin, and his own presumed drowning.

Byron skimmed through a few more articles stating basically the same things until he found what he was looking for. Declan Cronin had been arrested at the terminal when he exited the ferry. There was a picture of Agent Frank Purvis and Agent Timothy Tyler taking Cronin into custody. A quote from Agent Frank Purvis indicated that Cronin's known associates were in the Dannon cartel. Byron laughed at the irony. *He must have been really disappointed when Cronin wouldn't flip on Tua Dannon or Devlin.*

Cronin had ultimately been indicted for attempted murder, carrying an unlawful handgun, and being a public menace. He never went to trial. The reporter suggested that the attempted murder charge would have been difficult to prove, so prosecutors had pled him down to the handgun charge. He was sentenced to Rikers for one year, three years' probation, and a one-thousand-dollar fine. Nothing too challenging for someone with Cronin's background.

He can do that standing on his head.

Byron, now Clark Kensey, according to his passport, credit cards, and bus pass, crossed nine states on the bus and arrived in Reno, Nevada, at around midnight three days and four hours later. One could not go much farther away from New York without driving into the Pacific. He was dressed in slacks and a golf shirt.

Clark was booked into a medium-priced hotel he'd selected because it had a large pool, long enough for swimming laps. His cover, if anyone asked, was that he was a real estate developer looking for possible properties to purchase. No one asked.

He knew he was taking a chance, being in a town known for gambling, but he also knew that the Irish mob was more particularly situated in Las Vegas, about a seven-hour drive across Nevada, located at the bottom tip of the state. With his new beard, mustache, and dark makeup, utilized until he could get a tan, he felt fairly safe.

As soon as Clark checked into his room, a small studio with a queen bed, tiny sofa, and kitchenette, he fell onto the bed and sank into the mattress. His fatigue was so great, but worse, the room was so cold. There was nothing there that reminded him of himself. The shiny surfaces and fake art felt heartless and distant.

As the frantic nature of the trip began to fall away and the trauma of the escape subsided a little, the realization that he was all alone and could never see his friends or family again swept over him. He lay on the bed and grieved the loss of his former life, his friend Michael, and his very being, as he'd known it. He eventually pulled an edge of the bedspread over him and didn't move for twelve hours. There was no one there to tell him that he was mumbling in his sleep.

When he awoke, Clark unpacked his Speedo and went for a swim to clear his mind and body of the sleep and the travel. He needed to stretch out his bunched muscles, digest all that he'd been through to get to Reno and plan his next moves. He'd left New York with only a short-term plan. It was time to start looking further down the road, especially at the number of resources he had at his disposal and how long they would last.

Clark swam and thought things through as he always did in the water. He was reluctant to spend a lot of his cash, or pull any out of his overseas bank account, until he could get a bearing on how much running would cost and how long he might have to do it. He had chosen Reno because it offered a way to earn money via gambling, his second-best skill for bringing in income, and his winnings were not likely to be traced as long as he stayed under certain limits.

Clark knew he would be on camera almost constantly, so his first order of business was to plan a wardrobe of disguises that he could easily put together with items purchased from thrift stores and neighborhood malls. He would not gamble until he was sure that his appearance was altered in such a way that he would not be recognized by anyone who happened upon him or observed him on CCTV.

Clark's first shopping stop, wearing his construction worker outfit and baseball cap, was a Goodwill Outlet on Oddie Boulevard. It smelled like stale clothing but was very organized. He had left the nun's habit in New York and decided not to assemble any female costumes as he would be required to speak when gambling. It was too risky with his deep baritone voice and bobbing Adam's apple. It hadn't been that much fun being a nun anyway, too much bulky fabric.

He found low magnification reading glasses and bought a half dozen in different shapes and colors. Next, he purchased a bold Hawaiian shirt, a straw Panama hat, two more baseball caps, a selection of shirts and jeans in ordinary styles, and two pairs of slightly worn shoes. It felt good to be busy.

He ran by a dive shop and bought two new scuba knives, the Spyderco dragonfly 2 Salt. One, neon yellow, like the one he'd lost in the Hudson River, and another in dark blue that he folded and slipped into his pocket. His reasoning was that he would not get away with carrying a gun around, but he needed some form of protection, and he was comfortable with the scuba knives from his diving days.

His next stop was a costume shop he'd found online on the iPad that had been packed in his canvas get-a-way bag, registered to Clark Kinsey, of course. The shop's clerk assisted him, as she hummed along to piped-in showtunes, with several types of makeup, wigs, and facial hair, including Elvis-style sideburns. His cover story for the clerk was that he was a stand-up comic and used the costumes in his act.

He ran through a Target store last and grabbed an assortment of hair dyes and bleaches, scissors and clippers, and a nice electric razor. He went through the men's clothing and added a couple of plain blazers and khaki pants to his basket. He spotted a wooden walking cane and threw that into the mix as well, before he checked out at the register.

He took his haul of disguises and paraphernalia back to the hotel and laid them out on the bed where he assembled over a dozen combinations. He felt safe in his selections, both that he could put them on alone and that he would not be recognized in them.

Time to take a test run.

Clark took a seat at the Silver Dust Casino at a Texas Hold'em table indicating a minimum bet of one hundred dollars. He stacked his chips before him and acknowledged the other four players without making eye contact. Of course, he didn't look like Byron. Clark looked like an IT guy or computer geek: horn-rimmed glasses, khaki slacks, and a blue and black V-neck sweater with an argyle pattern. He'd gelled his darkly died hair forward to look like it had been cut with a bowl on his head. He'd kept his dark stubble but had trimmed it short and neat.

No one seemed to particularly notice him. Although he was anxious, he kept his poker face on and nerves in check. He knew he was taking a chance, as all Reno casinos were removed but not totally disconnected from the New York Irish mob and Las Vegas System, whether directly through ownership or by association through other gaming houses and players. He took the chance because he needed money, and he was also craving the game.

Clark knew that the root cause of gambling addiction started at an emotional level, wherein addicts used gambling as a means for coping with daily life stressors and pressures. Although he admitted to himself that gambling did soothe his frazzled nerves, in a different way from swimming, he had not crossed over into admitting addiction because he felt it was not an obsessive behavior.

He considered poker a skill, not a game of luck, and had studied all the greats over the years. His idol was The Texas Dolly, Doyle Brunson, who was also a Texas boy. Where Byron had grown up in North Houston, The Dolly was from Long-worth, a small town between Fort Worth and Lubbock. Byron had read Brunson's strategy book, *Super/System*, and autobiography, *The Godfather of Poker*, dozens of times. His copies had been highlighted to the point of few lines left that were not yellow. He assumed someone had cleaned out his apartment by now and donated the books to a worthy cause or tossed them out.

Byron knew that poker was more about the players than odds. He understood people and used the same skills at the gambling tables as he did in the courtroom. Just as he adjusted to a prosecutor's game and the faces of the jury, he adjusted his poker play to his opponent's, whether aggressive or conservative, until he felt the moment was right and he made his big move. His method had never failed him, although he'd lost his share of hands, but the method held true today, and he won more than he left on the table.

He had developed his skills when he played in Houston with his school buddy, Quinton Bell, for over five years. Quinton was reckless and often bluffed with a losing hand, but Byron had learned quickly that poker was a game best played with discipline and honed skills. When he and Quinton parted, each to their respective undergraduate schools, Byron to The University of Texas and Quinton to the University of Houston, Byron worked on his game as much as he did on his bachelor's degree. When he saw Quinton on the occasional weekend at home, when he visited his mother, he won more hands than his friend and often picked up the tab for dinner. He did so partly because some of the money he'd won was Quinton's, and partly because of all the meals Quinton and his family had fed Byron when they were growing up.

When each graduated from their respective colleges, they went to different law schools, Byron to Columbia in New York and Quinton to Levin at the University of Florida, his father's alma mater. Byron had further refined his playing methods and paid his way through law school with poker, rather than waiting tables or messengering packages around New York. The Texas Dolly had done the same, putting himself through graduate school in Abilene, Texas, by playing poker. Neither

Byron nor the Dolly had student loans to repay. Byron was an avid fan of the game, an excellent player, and if he faced the truth, in love with poker—it was his only true vice and love, besides the law.

Across from Clark, at the Silver Dust, was a strawberry blond kid of about twenty-five or thirty who played an aggressive game. He bluffed, raised, let out heavy sighs when he lost, and annoyed the other players at the table when he loudly ordered the cocktail servers to bring him another drink. Clark suspected that it was all an act and that the kid was crazy like a fox. Clark and the kid had almost an equal number of chips before them as the other players' stacks dwindled. Some of the losers had folded and left the game when they began to bleed heavily. The dealer showed no preference to any players, but both the house and Clark clearly kept their eyes on the blond.

Clark grew fatigued from fighting the kid, watching the room to make sure he wasn't recognized, and being hot from the disguise. He colored up, asking the dealer to give him thousand-dollar chips in exchange for all of his one-hundred-dollar chips, so it would be easier to carry. He went to the teller to cash in with over five thousand in winnings. Not a bad night for an IT geek.

Clark looked back at the kid on his way out. He was still grinning and winning.

12

Clark hid for a while in Reno, sleeping most of the morning and playing poker at night. In the late afternoons, he swam and worked on his tan, growing darker by the week until he had an immigrant look about him. His clear blue eyes betrayed a foreign heritage. His dark chin stubble grew to a full-grown beard and his hair got shaggy. Exotic and mysterious, but understated as well, he blended right in with the Hispanics and Latinos who made up over thirty percent of the population of Reno.

After a month, he had a routine. He had been the computer geek several times, plus a Hawaiian shirted tourist in a Panama hat, a frail older man with gray hair and cane, the real estate developer in a navy blazer, and the scruffy construction worker in boots, jeans, and a baseball cap. Sometimes he did combinations, but these were his standard disguises. He liked the outfits best that included a cap, and almost always wore a pair of glasses or sunglasses. This worked well while playing poker, as most serious players hid their faces in order to disguise their tells.

Clark rotated casinos so that he would not run into the same players in his different disguises, but when he did cross paths with a familiar face, he didn't think he was recognized. About six weeks into his routine, he was in the Nevada Diamond, a casino known for loose slots, playing Texas Hold'em, as usual, when the strawberry blond kid from the Silver Dust sat down. This time, his hair was more a ginger color and he had a strong Irish accent. Clark was sure he had not missed the Irish connection the first time they'd played. *What was this kid up to?*

The kid played aggressively, just as he had the first time, but he occasionally had a serious look on his face when he studied Clark, who today was wearing the Hawaiian shirt and Panama hat.

The kid raised the pot and looked at Clark. "Didn't we play at the Dust?"

Clark folded his hand and averted his eyes. "Maybe, I've played there. I don't remember." Clark scratched the whiskers on his chin.

The kid shook his finger at Clark. "Yeah, we cleaned the table, were about even, then you left."

The dealer paid out the last hand and Clark tossed his ante in the pot for the next round.

"Could have been." Clark looked at the dealer who began to deal.

The kid had a crazy laugh and wild eyes. "Have you played much in Vegas? I got kicked out of a couple of places there, so I diverted to Reno for a while. Let things cool down, so to speak." He laughed again as he focused his gaze more intently on Clark's face.

Clark pushed his glasses higher up on his nose with his index finger. "Not in a while."

"I knew this guy in Atlantic City who looked a lot like you.

He was younger, but you remind me of him. I got kicked out of a few places there, too."

The dealer started looking around for security. What had this guy done to get kicked out of so many places?

Clark didn't respond as he studied his cards. He finished the hand, tossed a chip to the dealer as a tip for a job well done, and stood up. "That's it for me. Thanks."

The dealer acknowledged the tip, and the kid grinned as he watched Clark walk away toward the teller.

Clark took the long way from the casino, back to his studio, on foot. He felt for the dive knife in his pocket as he stopped to look behind him every few blocks. He hadn't been paranoid for a few weeks and had begun to let his guard down. He regretted that now. Was this blond kid attached to the Irish mob? The Gaffer, Tua Dannon? Anyone from his past life?

It was inevitable that he would run into someone eventually if he continued the gambling life. Even if they weren't connected to New York, regulars were going to gravitate toward the same tables where he played. Should he shop for another round of disguises? Had he worn out his welcome in Reno?

If he stopped playing poker, he would have to eventually dig into his offshore money. He promised himself that he would not touch that stash unless he had to flee the country and live abroad. It gave him a sense of security, however small, that he had a backup plan.

He locked and chained the door behind him in his studio, laid down on his bed, looked at the ceiling, and contemplated his next move. Where could he go for help? Not his sister in California; she could be trusted not to tell anyone, but after the initial meeting, how could he interact with her? They didn't have much in common, now that their mother was gone, and what would be the point of bringing her into harm's way? He didn't want to be responsible for anyone else. What if the cartel hadn't bought his death and had an eye on his closest living relative? If he didn't show up there, he hoped they would eventually leave her alone, if they hadn't already.

Clark knew that Nina, Michael's widow, would help him in New York if he asked her, but that would put him right back in the lion's den and place Nina and Sophie in danger. Maybe Giselle, if she would even talk to him, but that, too, involved returning to New York.

He thought of his attorney friend, Quinton Bell, his schoolmate and poker buddy from his childhood in Houston. Clark had no idea where Quinton might be but felt he might trust him if he could find him. At least no one would think to look for him with Quinton. Maybe nothing would come of the encounter with the blond kid. Maybe he was spooked for nothing.

Byron, as Clark, missed the practice of law. Every day. He'd wake up in the morning and, before he remembered that Byron was now dead, he'd return to the excitement of an anticipated trial before a jury that he would expertly sway to his point of view. He missed New York and his life there, Giselle, his friends, the firm, his poker buddies, and even the doorman of his building. He loved poker, but he loved the law more and it was gone from him. He wanted it back. He wanted to know someone and have someone know him. He finally fell asleep in a fit of dreams of being chased through a zoo by unidentified animals with gnashing teeth.

The next morning, Clark peeked around the blinds and watched out the window for over an hour. There was no sign of the blond kid or anyone watching his studio, but he was nervous, and he'd made a decision. He knew it was only a matter of time and that he'd overstayed his reprieve in Reno. He put on his construction disguise and used the app on his phone to arrange an Uber. He did a quick check around the room to make sure nothing connecting him to Byron remained. He grabbed his backpack, what he called his go bag, that he kept loaded with his new passport, cash, and his current phone, as he always did when he left the room to go out. He pulled the ballcap low over his eyes and exited the room quickly when he spotted the Uber pull into the parking lot.

Clark went to the downtown Reno Library on Center Street and passed a plaque at the entry declaring it to be on the National Register of Historic Places as the Washoe County Library. He concealed himself in the stacks while he watched for anyone who might have followed. Seeing no one, he took a seat at a computer next to a young woman wearing far too much perfume and opened up a browser on the internet. The strong fragrance calmed down, but re-bloomed each time the woman stirred in her seat. Clark looked around for a less aromatic spot but found none unoccupied and soldiered on.

Clark searched for 'Quinton Bell, Houston, Texas, attorney.' What came up was dated about three years previously. Quinton had apparently joined Mandell & Grossman, a firm in Florida, after he'd graduated from law school. The list of lawyers at the firm did not show him as a practicing attorney at present, but there was no record of why he'd left or the exact date of his disengagement. Clark considered calling the firm, but not wanting to leave a trail, he scribbled the firm name and phone number on a scratch pad with a stubby pencil, provided in a cup by the library. If he changed his mind, he could call them later. He searched the State Bar of Florida and found no current license for Quinton Bell.

He looked around the web for Quinton, searching all manner of interests: attorney at law, University of Houston alumni, Florida alumni, wedding announcements, obituaries, etc., but found nothing on his old friend.

The search did show a Sirus Quinton Bell as a sitting judge in Houston on the Criminal District Courts. He was located downtown at the Harris County Criminal Justice Center on Franklin. Clark was surprised, as he knew Sirus Bell was Quinton's father. Clark assumed Judge Bell had passed away by now, or at least retired from the bench, at the ripe old age of seventy-eight. There were photos of the judge at the ballet and symphony fundraisers, with different beautiful women on his arm. He was apparently still active in the Houston and State Bar of Texas and spoke at conferences regularly on various criminal court and legal matters.

Clark had always liked Mr. Bell, as he'd treated Byron as an equal to his son, even though Byron was far below them in society. He had been on scholarship at Kinkaid in Memorial, just west of downtown Houston, where Quinton also attended.

Clark searched for Sirus's wife and Quinton's mother, Anna Thurston Bell, and found an obituary dated three years ago, about the same time as when Quinton had left his law firm in Florida. Clark wondered if there was a connection. He searched Houston resources thoroughly, in hopes that Quinton had returned there, but found only vague references to him from years before. Clark was just about to give up and logout when he found a short article in the *Houston Chronicle* dated three years back indicating that a Quinton Lamar Bell, street name Q, had been arrested and convicted of drug sales and use. He was identified as the son of local Judge Sirus Quinton Bell, reportedly sent to a rehabilitation facility in lieu of incarceration, and disbarred by the State Bar of Florida.

A mugshot from Harris County, Texas, revealed a disheveled and angry-looking Quinton with a tattooed *Q* peeking out of his T-shirt along his collarbone. Clark searched the archives of the newspaper but found nothing further. He checked the criminal incarceration records for Harris County and Texas in general but did not find a Quinton Bell currently in any Texas correctional facility.

Clark was just about to escape the cloud of perfume from his computer neighbor when he saw them. Two men, dressed in sharkskin suits, no ties, shirt collars open, who appeared to be searching for something or someone amongst the stacks and around the periodicals section. Clark ducked behind the computer screen and looked toward the exit but knew he couldn't make it there without being seen by the men. If he stayed where he was, they were going to find him on their rounds.

In desperation, Clark turned to Perfume Girl. "I'll give you fifty dollars if you'll distract those two men over there in the dark suits so I can get out the door. I owe them a gambling debt and they'll beat the shit out of me if they find me."

The girl looked at him for a moment. "Make it a hundred and you've got a deal."

Clark peeled off five twenties from his folded cash and laid it on the desk. "Done."

As the girl walked over to the two men and dropped a stack of books on the floor in front of them, Clark cleared his browser. When she smiled and leaned over to pick up the books, revealing a nice set of probably fake breasts, Clark made his way, unseen, to the nearest exit.

Clark knew better than to go back to his studio. By design, he had all of his essentials in the day pack and the disguises, probably no longer useful at this stage, were certainly not worth the risk to recover them. He regretted leaving the second scuba knife behind, but he'd have to make do with the blue one in his pocket until he could pick up another one. He couldn't imagine any way they'd found him other than following him from his room. How had they found his hotel? The blond kid? Someone he'd played poker with? *I may never know, and what difference does it make?* The main question was whether they were sure it was him, or just checking out a tip of a possible sighting. *Wishful thinking?*

As he headed to the bus station, he dropped Clark's phone into a trash basket. He didn't dare use Clark's credit cards, so he paid cash at the bus station for his ticket and watched his bus from the window to see if the driver was checking identification before allowing passengers to board. He was not. Clark tossed his credit cards, driver's license, and passport in a large trash can, and Clark was over.

Byron, now unnamed, boarded the bus without any ID at all, but that seemed a better risk than being identified as Byron or Clark in case the two suited men came asking. Why hadn't he arranged for a third passport and driver's license? He kicked himself for the two days and four hours it took to get to Houston.

While traveling south, he found a lone payphone at a bus stop in Albuquerque, New Mexico, and called Quinton's Florida firm using the number from the scrap of paper from the library in Reno. The receptionist would not reveal much about Quinton, other than to say that he was no longer with the firm and that he had indicated a return to Texas after his mother had passed away. The receptionist knew of no one at the firm who kept in touch with him, was very busy, and had to go.

Byron picked up another burner phone during a layover in the Texas Panhandle, called no one, and slept off his nervous exhaustion on the next leg of the trip all the way to Houston.

The first thing Byron wanted in the South, besides safety, was pimento cheese. Embarrassed by how much he loved it, but unable to deny the craving and the memories it brought of his mother, he left the bus station in downtown Houston and took a cab to the Fourth Ward. Byron needed new identification, and a place to stay, but he was starving and logistics would have to wait.

Byron walked through the area known as Freedmen's Town National Historic District, dating back to Juneteenth, in 1886, when blacks congregated and flourished in the area. He strolled down the surviving narrow brick streets past the remaining cottages and by the former site of the historic Bethel Baptist Church, now a grassy park after a fire in 2005 took the building. It was a lovely Texas spring day. He continued on to the adjacent area filled with restaurants and bars and found his old favorite restaurant, Fourth Ward Soul, and ordered a big fat pimento cheese sandwich, made of untoasted white bread, extra mayo, and a cold beer. The restaurant smelled like fried chicken and grease. The pimento cheese was just as good as he remembered, and much better than the New York recipes.

Fortified with the southern fare, satisfied family memories, and cold suds, he took out his new burner and started searching the internet for Judge Bell's office. If the judge didn't want to help him find Quinton, he might have to split town, but he'd be no worse off. He remembered the judge fondly, but also knew he'd always been a stickler for following the rules. It was a long shot, but what else could he do?

He dialed the number for the Harris County Criminal Justice Center, asked to be put through to Judge Bell's office, and held his breath.

13

Judge Sirus Bell walked into the Hot Cup Coffee Shop a few doors down from Fourth Ward Soul Food. Byron sat at the Hot Cup, drinking coffee, and waiting for him in a green vinyl booth in the back. For such a thin, gray, and aged man, he wore power like he wore his expensive suit, cufflinks, and purple silk tie. When Judge Bell walked up to his table, Byron stood and offered his hand. Judge Bell blinked for a few seconds while Byron was left hanging. The judge seemed to digest the truth of the phone call he'd received, took Byron's hand, and used it to pull him close in a big bear hug. Byron let out his breath and hugged him back, as small tears formed in the corners of his eyes. When they released, Byron, looked away to hide his embarrassment.

After they were seated, Judge Bell said, "I can't believe it's you. I read that you died in a drowning in the Hudson River."

"No, I'm still around. Barely. So much has happened, I don't know where to start."

The judge continued to stare at Byron. "Start at the beginning, I cleared the rest of the day."

"First, did you tell anyone in your office I was here?"

"No, no. I wasn't sure it was actually you. I thought it might be a practical joke."

"Thank goodness for that. I need to fly under the radar until I decide what to do next."

The judge signaled the waiter for a cup of coffee. The server arrived with a second mug and a pot and filled both men's cups. As nutty roasted steam rose to their nostrils, the judge took a careful sip. "Okay. Let's hear it."

Byron spent over an hour telling the judge about losing Tyrone's trial in New York; the Dannon cartel killing his best friend and protégé, Michael; the threat to his own life and the FBI's refusal to help; his pseudocide in the Hudson River; hiding out in Reno and gambling until he was possibly identified; tossing his false documents, and ultimately his trip to Houston. When the tale was complete, the judge, who had been sitting forward in rapt attention, slammed his back against the bench and let out a long whistle.

"My God."

Relief poured over Byron as he looked into the judge's eyes and saw compassion, not rejection.

"I was hoping to find Quinton and ask him for help, but the trail went cold when I spoke with his old firm in Florida, and they said he no longer worked there."

The judge saddened. "I'm afraid I have to tell you that Quinton is dead. I have no proof of that, only reports from a gang he wound up with, using the name Q Ball. He just couldn't stay away from the dark side. Drugs, lowlifes that go along with that lifestyle, and no sense of self-direction."

Byron put his hand on the judge's arm as it rested on the table. "I'm so sorry to hear that. How did Quinton go from being an attorney to joining a gang?"

"One word: meth. After his mother died, he started using

heavily. Apparently, he'd started the habit partying in Miami, and it only got worse. I brought him back here, put him into rehab, tried to help him all I could, but he refused to be saved."

Byron couldn't respond, he was so shocked.

"He was arrested as Q Ball after he started selling for the gang. Q, can you imagine? What a nasty tattoo and moniker. I bailed him out of jail, pulled some strings with the local prosecutor, and put him in rehab again. He ran away from the facility at Lake Conroe, and I've not seen him since. Twenty-five thousand for each thirty-day program and he runs away. I hired a private investigator who told me the gang's information on the street was that he had come back to Houston. He reportedly was selling again for a while, got totally lost, and died. Overdose. I couldn't even have a funeral."

"Awful. He was always such a sweet, fun-loving guy."

"Fun might have been the problem. Apparently, it wasn't depression, or work, or even heartbreak that got him started. It was just trying the meth and instantly liking it. His doctors told me it's highly addictive and that the withdrawal is hell."

Byron teared up again. "I've heard that from several clients in the past."

"I'm sorry. I know you two were close and, on top of all your problems, now you've lost your childhood friend."

Byron couldn't respond without bursting into tears, so he sat mute.

"My biggest regret is that I didn't let him go to prison. If I hadn't bailed him out, he might still be alive."

"You can't blame yourself. There are so many drugs in prison, addicts always find a way to get them. He may have met the same fate either way."

"Yes, but still. I miss him all the time. Looking at you reminds me of him. You look like brothers."

Byron put money on the table for the coffee. "Let's walk."

The judge stood and they left the coffee shop and stretched their legs with a stroll through the neighborhood decorated with large shade trees and occasional graffiti murals drifting over from Graffiti Park. Neither spoke for a long time, both apparently thinking of Quinton and his sad ending.

The judge broke the silence a few blocks later. "I want to help you. What do you need?"

"Thank you, Judge. I hoped you might say that. I need a place to stay for a while and then some new credentials. I don't dare travel under my real name, and I'm afraid Clark Kensey had to be left behind in Reno."

"How about money?"

"I have cash left from my poker winnings, but I'll have to eventually earn an income of some sort." He didn't mention the offshore plan B account.

The judge stopped walking and turned to Byron. "I still have the beach house down in Galveston. After the traffic clears and it gets dark, I'll drive you down there and get you set up for a few days while we figure this out. No one will know who you are. If someone asks, just say you're my nephew, Jonathon, visiting for a few days."

"Thank you. Thank you," Byron said as relief to have a direction to go in swept over him.

After dark, Judge Bell drove Byron, for about an hour, out the Gulf Freeway and across Galveston Bay to the Gulf of Mexico. The Bells' beach house was a three-story Victorian residence, originally completed in 1892, in the east end historic district on Galveston's Seawall Boulevard. It was a National Historic Landmark, one of the lucky ones, that had survived The Great

Storm. Mrs. Bell had restored it, back in the day before she became ill and passed. It was a real beauty in white wood and stone with blue trim. It featured stained-glass windows, rare woods, exotic marbles, with painted murals and ceilings. She had revived impressive fireplaces and added luxurious furnishings.

Byron had visited the house with Quinton, many times in their youth, and he remembered it well. The boys had crabbed, fished, swum, surfed, girl watched, and both lost their virginity with big-haired Texas blondes on the beach about three-hundred feet from the house. As Byron remembered his friend, he was ashamed that he had lost touch and let him go so easily. He swallowed a big lump in his throat and once more felt the guilt and regret of what might have been if he had acted differently.

The judge used his laptop on the kitchen island to arrange a grocery delivery from the nearby Kroger and a beer, wine, and liquor delivery from Spec's.

Byron smiled. "I can't thank you enough."

"Now, none of that. I want you to be safe and comfortable until we can figure out what to do next. There are clothes in my closet that might fit you. There are probably some of Quinton's things left in his room. Why don't you sleep there or in the guest room on the second floor. Both are equally comfortable. I'll be back tomorrow, and we'll figure out what to do next. I wouldn't answer the phone if I were you."

"Oh, right, let me give you my burner number." Judge Bell handed him his phone and Byron typed in the number with the name Quinton's friend as the ID. "See you soon?"

"Soon."

That afternoon, Byron boiled up a pound of shrimp with a box of Louisiana shrimp boil spices that he found in the grocery delivery. The briny aroma permeated the entire house. He cooled the shrimp down in the freezer, then ate with his hands, peeling and dipping each one in turn into a spicy red horse-radish sauce. He washed it all down with a cold Gulf Coast IPA, then wondered what to do next.

Byron remembered that he and Quinton had gone out on a gambling ship several times when they were staying at the Galveston house and perfecting their poker games. He used the judge's laptop, went online, and researched Jacks or Better, the only gambling ship that he remembered departed from Galveston and had allowed them to drink underage. It was still there. The 155-foot yacht listed table games like poker, blackjack, baccarat, and roulette, as well as hundreds of slot machines and video poker games. He checked the times, found a 6:30 p.m. departure on Friday nights. He headed to the dock, grabbed a beer, and waited for the ship to open up.

Jacks or Better was docked at the pier on Galveston Bay. Byron, wearing a loud Hawaiian shirt, khaki shorts, and Islanders ballcap, all from the judge's closet, bought a ticket and climbed aboard just before the gangplank was pulled in. He found another cold beer and the buffet table where he sat and snacked on seafood dip and crackers, in order to kill time on the trip out to international waters. Most tables were full of passengers doing the same thing, and a brief perusal revealed no one who appeared familiar or threatening.

A few guests had to exit the room and visit the side of the boat when the ship hit a patch of rough sea. Byron had accli-mated long ago with his swimming and just didn't seem to get seasick.

After the yacht anchored offshore and the gambling began,

he peeked around the tables and slot machines and sought a seat at the Texas Hold'em tables. He was almost salivating; he was so ready to hold some cards and stack some chips.

The dealer said, "Ante up," and the game began.

Byron observed the other players for the first few rounds as he placed small bets. Once he got a bead on each player, he began to play in earnest and the stacks of chips before him multiplied. He never left the table and was disappointed when play ceased and the ship set sail again for shore.

Around midnight, the ship docked back at the pier in Galveston and the guests, along with Byron, disembarked. He was about three thousand dollars up for the night, but most importantly, he felt calmed and comforted. He had really missed the game, but taking a chance like this one might not be something he could or would do often.

Yeah, right.

Judge Bell returned from Houston to Galveston and took Byron out to Gaido's for lunch and a strategy session. The elegant seafood restaurant had opened its doors to the public in 1911, and since then had been applauded for fresh coastal classic seafood and an unsurpassed view of the Gulf of Mexico. After they were seated, ordered, and were served huge platters of seafood delights, including shrimp, oysters, red snapper, and crawfish tails, Judge Bell picked up his fork and looked at Byron.

"I've been contemplating your dilemma. There are many ways that you could go with this, and I have an idea."

Byron popped a shrimp in his mouth, swallowed, and said, "I'm all ears."

The judge paused until Byron looked away from the food and at him. "I think you should become Quinton and hide in plain sight."

Byron almost choked on an oyster. "What? I can't be Quinton."

"Why not? Prodigal son returns. Turns over a new leaf. Starts life down a different path."

"But he's dead. And we're so different and I don't know anything about his life for the past few years, I'm ashamed to say."

"I can fill you in. I've thought about nothing else since I left you here. You're close to the same height and build, exactly the same age, and you both have backgrounds in the law. With a few tweaks, you could even look something like him. I think it's doable. No one will suspect. There was never a body and no funeral or memorial. Anyone who heard of his death will assume they were mistaken, or the police got it wrong."

"I'd trip up a thousand times in the presence of anyone who knew him. I wouldn't know what to say or where to start."

"Think about it. Quinton had changed so much in the last few years. He hadn't been seen in Houston for a long while by anyone but me and his gang, who ultimately got him killed. He was never a member of the Texas Bar. Miami is twelve hundred miles away. No one in his firm there even bothered to follow up when he left."

Byron popped another shrimp in his mouth and thought for a moment as he enjoyed the sweetness. "Where would I say I'd been all this time? It's crazy."

"Addiction to meth. Finally kicked it in rehab. I'd confirm that I'd assisted in getting you clean, as if we'd been in contact recently, and I just wanted to make sure you were healthy before we told anyone you were still alive. Blah. Blah. You get the picture."

"What would I do? Sit around Houston, do nothing, and call myself Quinton?"

"Of course not, Son."

Son? Son? The judge had never called him Son before.

"Then what?"

"You can clean up some out of state issues and transfer in under Quinton's Florida law license, make nice with the State Bar of Texas, and get your credentials here as Quinton Bell. I can pull some strings to speed things along. No one would ever know because you, as Byron, are dead."

"Quinton is dead too, and he was disbarred in Florida. I checked. And, worst of all, I saw his mugshot. He was a convicted felon."

"A mere technicality. Once it's established that you're off meth for good, all will be forgiven. We say it was mistaken identity that Quinton was dead, or lies from the gang, or whatever yarn we want to spin."

Byron laughed. "Technicality? Off meth? I have never tried meth and I was certainly never in a gang."

"You, as Quinton, I mean."

Byron had to admit to himself that having Judge Bell take such an active interest in him was flattering. His absent father had left a hole that he had never managed to fill, although his mother had tried. Having Judge Bell, who Byron had always thought of as the perfect father to Quinton, caring for him and his situation plucked at his heart strings. "I don't know, Judge."

"Just think about it."

"This seems too farfetched to work. I don't really look like him."

"No one has seen him in years, and that mugshot shows how much he'd changed. He looked old and haggard; we bring you in as the reinvented version. We make a few adjustments to your hair, glasses, maybe a nose job. Nothing too painful or drastic."

Byron couldn't swallow, so he reluctantly gave up on the seafood and put down his fork. "But, Judge."

"You have a better idea? You want me to help you get another fake passport so you can live alone in cheap hotels and try to make a living gambling, while you hide out and forsake your chosen profession? Yeah, I checked. You were really good at trial work. Awards, accolades, big fees for your firm. Things that Quinton never mastered. You gave that all up. Tell me you don't miss it and want it back. And, Houston is an international city with global importance. You can choose one culture, mix and match, or enjoy them all."

"I know, and I can't tell you that I don't miss the city life. In all honestly, I miss it every single day."

"Let's try it. We'll tell no one. If it doesn't work, we'll abandon the idea and try something else before we go too far down the road."

Byron sat quietly looking out at the Gulf and thinking of how much he missed the law and his life in it. If he ran away again, he'd be alone forever. No one would ever really know him. This was the last stop. Here was a father figure wanting to help him. Wanting to make him part of his world. Wanting to give him a new life. "Okay. Let's give it a go."

Judge Bell beamed with pride at the son he always wanted.

Judge Bell went into a frenzy of activity to set about the task of changing Byron into Quinton. He shipped dozens of packages to the Galveston house from Brooks Brothers, Joseph A. Bank, Nordstrom, UnTuckit, Mr. Porter, Zappos, and Amazon. The new Quinton was close enough in size and build to his dead son, and the judge assumed Byron's extra two inches in height was nothing anyone would notice.

Byron signed for all the packages, with in indecipherable squiggle, and felt a bit like Julia Roberts in *Pretty Woman*. He unpacked the clothes and hung them in Quinton's room but slept down the hall in the guest room at night.

Next, the judge made a reservation with a plastic surgeon in the Medical Center in Houston and filled out the paperwork for Quinton Bell. He and Byron went to the appointment together and told the medical staff that he wanted to refresh his face and modify his nose. The judge had a blown-up picture of Q's nose without the rest of his face showing. Byron said he liked it and wanted a nose like that. It was the only part of their faces that was drastically different. Slimming Byron's Roman schnoz down and cutting back the tip was all that was necessary to make them nose twins. The surgeon's esthetician injected filler into his cheeks and jawline to make his face a bit fuller. The rest could be explained as the result of a long relaxing stay in rehab.

After the surgery, while the nose was healing, Judge Bell went down to Galveston most evenings after court, with photos of Q to share with the new Quinton. The judge told him stories and described Mrs. Bell's funeral. The new Quinton took notes on everything from the date Q had moved to Florida, the names and locations of the rehab facilities, Q's favorite movies and music, and the Houston women he'd dated before he moved.

There was one girlfriend who stood out above the rest. Joanne Wyatt and Q had been tight, and it had apparently broken her heart when Q moved to Florida and did not invite her along as live-in, fiancée, or wife. By then, Q was on the meth and didn't care for anyone but himself and his habit. Judge Bell brought a picture of her, and the new Quinton put it on the bathroom mirror so that he could memorize her face. She might not recognize him if they met by chance, but to pull it off, he must recognize her and then convince her that he was Quinton with information only Q would know.

The judge also brought forms every few days, that they filled out, to start the process of having the new Quinton admitted to the Bar in Texas. He also brought pre-typed letters for Quinton to sign for sending to the Florida Bar and Levin Law School requesting the necessary documentation of his work there. They were leaving a trail, but so far, it was a logical one with all the return documents going to Quinton Lamar Bell at the Galveston house.

Unbeknownst to the new Quinton, the judge had ordered, via a hefty bribe, some phony docs from the last rehabilitation facility stating that Q had completed his rehab, had been back for periodic check-ins, was cleared as a clean and sober functioning member of society, and could hold down a job with responsibilities without cracking up. He'd lied to the director of the facility, telling him that Q had gone cold turkey, was back, and was restarting his life. The facility's director didn't totally believe it, but he took the money anyway and provided the requested documentation.

Once the bandages were off, Judge Bell took Byron to a fancy hairstylist and makeup artist in Houston and had his beard removed and hair colored, slightly lighter. She styled it to look like Q's law school graduation picture, short and neat. It was the last look most people in Houston had seen of Q. The stylist showed the new Quinton how to further accentuate his cheek bones, with a tiny bit of concealer, in such a way as to enhance their prominence. She stepped back and looked at her work.

"Do you want me to show you how to hide the scars around your nose until they fade?"

"No need. I won't be going out until they're pretty much gone."

The judge piped up, "Anything left will just look like a bar fight. Tough guy."

Both men laughed and the judge paid her handsomely to keep quiet. Why it was a secret, or his name, she would never know, but they gave her the returning from rehab story, just in case.

The two men also visited an upscale optician on West Gray near River Oaks in Houston for very expensive glasses, like Q wore, but with minimal correction. It was uncanny how much the new Quinton looked like the photo of Q, just a bit older. When they compared the face in the picture to the new Quinton, both men were impressed with their handiwork.

Byron, as the new Quinton, began to believe that he could actually pull it off, make a fresh start, and have a life after all. He went along with the whole program for a while. *In for a penny, in for a pound,* he convinced himself. That was until the judge showed him Q's mugshot, as a refresher, and pointed out the tattoo of the Q on the neck, peeking out from the T-shirt.

"No. I'm not getting a tattoo of a Q on my neck. No."

"It's the last evidence that you're actually Quinton. All of the gang knew he had it. It won't show under your suits or most shirts. It'll just be an identity confirmation device if someone comes looking, especially law enforcement."

Byron put his foot down. "No. I will not be branded with a Q."

The judge looked surprised. "You had your nose changed, but you will not have a tattoo?"

"Correct."

"Then how will you explain its absence? Your life may depend on it. What if someone checks for some reason?"

"I don't know, but I'm not doing that. This is where I draw the line." Byron had been feeling his own identity slipping away step by step under Judge Bell's direction and this was the last straw. He felt he had to have some control over the situation, even if it was minimal.

The judge thought for a few minutes, rocking gently back and forth, as he did on the bench when contemplating a court ruling. He put his arm around Byron's shoulder in a fatherly way. "Okay. How about a scar that looks like tattoo removal? Very faint, like a wide scratch. Just enough to convince someone who doesn't look too closely."

"How big?"

The judge held up his thumb and forefinger about an inch apart.

"Okay. I can live with that and then we stop. When my nose has finished healing, we begin to introduce me to a few people and see if it works. Nothing else to my body or my mind. I'm full up of Quinton, or should I say Q?"

"Agreed. Let's take you for a test run."

The next day, a storm kicked up in Galveston like nothing Byron had seen since the Staten Island ferry and his fake drowning. He watched it ramp up then fade out, leaving a strong wind blowing inland from the Gulf of Mexico. The weather transported him back to his childhood days with Quinton and all the fun they had growing up together.

Byron went out the kitchen and through the garage to a storage room that he and Quinton had used to store their skateboards, bicycles, and surfboards. Amongst a net of spider webs was an old surfboard that Byron had used many times. He pulled it out, wiped the dust off with a rag he grabbed from a workbench along the opposite wall, and carried it into the garage. It was a 1980s Thruster Redux shred sled originally designed by Ken Bradshaw, a native Texan turned Hawaiian big wave charger. It was probably worth a small fortune to collectors these days on eBay. Nostalgia, then excitement swept over him.

Byron went back inside and smeared his new nose and neck scar with big globs of zinc oxide, changed into a pair of Quinton's bright orange board shorts, and went back out to the garage. He picked up the board and going barefoot, carried it down to the beach, by the pier, along the seawall.

About a dozen local surfers were running with glee into the water with their boards, like a band of escapees going after freedom. Byron ran across the sand and into the water behind them. He swam out easily, sat on the board in the trough, and waited for the right wave.

As he watched the waves roll by, he thought about Quinton. Would his old friend begrudge him the use of his name and identity? What had he thought about Byron over the years and their lack of contact? Had it even mattered to him? Would it matter now? He wasn't here, so Byron knew he'd never be able to ask him. He caught the next wave, and several after that. He had a private memorial for Quinton, remembering with each ride to the shore their closeness in youth, the fun they had shared, and the losses they didn't.

Byron remembered the way Quinton had shielded him from the snobs in high school at Kincaid and around Houston. He remembered Quinton's generosity and how he'd included him in every event and even lent or gave him clothes so he would fit in. Byron looked out at the ocean and thanked his friend for all he had done and all he was doing now to make his life better.

By the time the sun was setting, Byron was ready to be Quinton for good. He dragged the board to the beach and left it there as he swam way out into the blue water of the Gulf. He closed his eyes, dove deep into the water, baptized himself anew, and came up Quinton.

14

The new Quinton's first test was with the judge's lady friend, Ophelia Jamail, known as Silver, who the real Q had only met twice between rehab stays. Quinton, at first, thought her name made her sound like a hooker. She was actually a silver-haired, well-respected wills and estates attorney, working of counsel to a boutique law firm with three other women partners and a handful of associates. Silver's signature was her exquisite wardrobe. She was often seen stepping into the elevator, at the downtown office building where her firm was located, wearing a tasteful hat over her silver bob and a Chanel or St. John's suit.

Silver met Quinton and Judge Bell for dinner at Armandos upscale Tex-Mex. The restaurant was near Silver's home, and not far from the judge's high rise, both in River Oaks, a leafy residential area filled with palatial homes, elite townhouses, and skyscraping condos. The men were already at the table, surrounded by art and white tablecloths, and both stood when Silver joined them. Margaritas were ordered along with chips, salsa, and queso to get things rolling.

Judge Bell raised his glass. "To new beginnings. Salud."

All three clinked glasses and began to relax. Quinton observed the representation of extreme wealth around the room and thought to himself: *If we pull this off, it will be because of all this money and these connections.*

Silver looked at, who was unbeknownst to her, the new Quinton and smiled. "It's good to see you again. What has it been two or three years? Your father tells me you've been staying in Galveston at the beach house."

Quinton smiled back, still adjusting to his new nose and eyeglasses. "Yes. It's good to see you too. It's been great to have the ocean air and fresh seafood. I feel like a new man."

Judge Bell grinned. "It's been a real pleasure having him home again."

Silver smiled. "Of course, Sirus. I'm sure you've both missed each other very much."

Quinton held his poker face, but scanned Silver's to see if he could pick up any clues of mistrust. *So far so good.*

"I've missed my dad, life in Houston, work, everything. It's really good to be back."

Sirus held up three fingers to the waiter for more drinks. Quinton shook his head. "One's my limit for a while." Then he turned to Silver. "I'm easing back into drinking, and no drugs of any kind. I'm sure the judge, I mean Dad, told you. It's okay to talk about it. I'm being drug tested twice a week."

Silver smiled. "I'm very happy for your restored health."

The judge picked up his menu to hide his lying eyes. "We all are."

The three ordered chile rellenos and enchiladas with various sides, including rice and beans. While they waited for their food, they changed the conversation to what Quinton might do next.

Silver nibbled on a tostado chip. "Do you have a plan?"

"I miss practicing law. I'd like to find work if and when the State Bar of Texas allows me to practice. If they won't give me a license in reciprocity with my Florida license, I'll have to re-take the Bar here, or find another way in."

"The Florida Bar restored his license there after a round of forms, medical records, and character witnesses. Now, it's just a waiting game to see if Texas will recognize his license there and grandfather him in here."

Silver smiled at Sirus. "With your connections, I doubt that will be an issue. Let me know if there's anything I can do to help."

Judge Bell smiled at her. "Well, now that you mention it, I was hoping Quinton might be able to find a job with your firm. I know it's all female partners, but he plans to work hard and has no problem taking orders from women." The judge laughed.

Quinton laughed too, although he hadn't taken orders from anyone, male or female, in a long while. "It's true. I know I'll have to start at the bottom just like any other associate and prove myself."

"The State Bar will move much more quickly and favorably if we can show that he has a job lined up and that he has a licensed attorney willing to supervise his transition. I can't do it because I'm a sitting judge, not a practicing lawyer."

"So, you've plied me with two Margaritas and bribed me with Mexican food. I've been ambushed." She laughed. "We have several male associates working at the firm, but I need to think about whether we can add another employee right now."

Sirus took her hand. "Please give it some thought, Silver. We don't need an answer right now. Will you talk to your partners at the firm? Just the promise of the position should do for the Bar. He could start any time, even a few months from now, if necessary."

Quinton was embarrassed beneath his poker face. He hadn't had to go hat in hand, for work, to anyone in a long while and it made him feel like a newbie attorney fresh out of law school. The whole situation was awkward for him, but hopefully it would get easier as he became more and more accustomed to being identified as Quinton.

Hopefully.

Silver asked Quinton to join her at the downtown offices of the law firm of Jamail, Powers & Kent on the fortieth floor of the Texas Bank Building. As the senior member, Silver had transitioned into a role as 'of counsel' to the firm, which meant that her name was to the right of the other attorneys on the firm's letterhead, a position of stature, and she could work on what and when she wanted. Her primary function was that of rainmaker using her connections, status in the legal community, and social skills to bring in clients and maintain the ones they had and wanted to keep. She had founded the firm over twenty years ago as a boutique trusts and estates planning firm, but had expanded it over the years to a general business law practice by adding two partners, along with associates, paralegals, and other support staff. It was a hopping place, full of activity on most weekdays and some weekends, housed in downtown Houston in one of the bigger bank buildings, a client of the firm.

Quinton entered the corner conference room, consisting of two walls of glass and two walls of bookshelves, with a large white marble conference table in the center, surrounded by black mesh swivel chairs. Two well-dressed women stood at the window, enjoying the view of downtown Houston and The

Galleria, a second business center and shopping area on the 610 loop, just west of town, in the distance.

Silver pointed to a credenza built into one of the bookshelves with coffee, tea, and muffins. "Coffee?"

They both poured a cup, and Quinton was introduced by Silver to Maureen 'Mo' Powers, a University of Texas School of Law graduate, who specialized in litigation in the area of energy law, most particularly oil and gas, wind energy, and riparian rights. Her stable of clients consisted of energy companies from Mexico and the US to Canada, and around the world. She shook Quinton's hand. "How the hell are ya?"

"Good to be here and nice to meet you."

Next, he met Elizabeth 'Buffy' Kent, a retired nun who'd left the convent, and, good Irish woman that she was, had gone to law school at the University of Notre Dame. She eventually specialized in business, corporate, and international finance. Buffy, with her paralegal, Angela Critch, represented some of the world's largest banks, corporations, and executives. Buffy's clients trusted her implicitly, and her well-deserved reputation brought in the big dogs from companies around the planet. "Welcome."

"Thanks."

Neither of the two women had ever met Q. With the approval of her partners, Silver planned to add Quinton in a new division, general litigation and criminal defense. They had located space one floor below, on thirty-nine, that could be easily connected by an internal staircase as well as the elevator in the lobby. As Quinton sipped his coffee, and smiled at the three accomplished women, he was proud to be with them, but at the same time, wondered if they would approve of him, and if so, if it would last. He would not be a partner but would head up the litigation division with supervision from the three partners in the firm. For a while, he would take on various types of litigation matters, with heavy emphasis on criminal law, since that was his specialty, although they didn't know that. By the time all the coffee was drunk, and a few jokes exchanged, the two partners joined Silver in approving the plan for Quinton to come on board.

Now to execute and make it work.

The State Bar had accepted Judge Bell and Silver Jamail's recommendations that Quinton be licensed and allowed to practice law in Texas, grandfathered under his Florida license, for a probationary period. He would stay in good graces with the Bar as long as he remained at the firm of Jamail, Powers & Kent, for at least a year, under Silver's supervision. He was also assigned a State Bar mentor, Bob Sanders, more like a liaison, who kept track of Silver's reports and Quinton's drug testing, which was now down to once a month. Of course, the new Quinton had never failed a drug test, or even taken one, but both Silver and Sanders assumed he was recently rehabbed. After the year ended, if Quinton stayed clean, he could apply for full licensure and autonomy.

Bob Sanders was a good fit for Quinton. He was not a micromanager and had a quick wit and happy disposition. For a lawyer, he was damn jovial. He made no bones about the fact that he was a recovering alcoholic and had even written a couple of books about sobriety. In a sea of women, it was also good for Quinton to be around some testosterone every now and then, even if they couldn't grab a beer or a scotch after work. Coffee worked just fine.

Quinton enjoyed practicing law again, although he kept a low profile with the firm to start. He was the only litigation attorney and was sharing an assistant with an associate attorney on the fortieth floor until he had enough business to warrant his own. She spent mornings upstairs and afternoons downstairs working with Quinton. He had a lot of autonomy in the cases he accepted and the running of the space on the thirty-ninth floor that the firm had rented to accommodate his hiring. He was not a partner and, therefore, had to email a brief synopsis to all three partners of his intention to take a case. So far, they had yet to withhold approval except for one instance where there was a conflict of interest with another client already in the firm. So far, Silver had brought in all of his clients, as they involved white-collar crimes with very little drama and workmen's compensation cases involving firm clients. He settled most of the files with probation or plea bargains resulting in short stints in federal prisons and small financial arrangements. Quinton and Silver slowly adjusted to being around each other, and they actually developed a sort of friendship. She seemed to accept him as Quinton and eventually acted as if he was a full-fledged attorney, with autonomy, as her own life became busier, and Quinton colored within the lines.

Quinton longed to get back to the gritty cases he'd enjoyed defending in New York and, since he was expected to build up his client list, he went down to the criminal courts building one afternoon and signed up to do court-appointed work. He introduced himself to a couple of judges who were more than happy to have another qualified attorney actually wanting to do low paid criminal defense work and take the raunchy cases. It was a slow transition, but he became more comfortable answering to the name Quinton Bell, got to know the courts and judges, and began to butt heads with the prosecutors, reading their styles and abilities to actually give them a run for their money in negotiations.

He'd yet to have a full-blown criminal trial and was

chomping at the bit to find a client who wanted to go to court rather than plead out or settle. Those feelings were mixed with the knowledge that a criminal trial would bring media and public attention to his name, face, and cover story. Still, he was craving the courtroom spotlight.

He didn't have to wait for long.

After growing tired of the hour-long commute each way from Galveston and staying over frequently at Judge Bell's place in River Oaks, Quinton found a one-bedroom condo, with a small home office, in a high rise near the Rice University campus and the Houston Medical Center and moved in over a weekend.

He leased a small Audi SUV, with the help of Judge Bell and his new IDs, to accommodate the short drive to the office, but planned to find something to buy, if the charade worked and he remained Quinton. He had to admit that it was fun driving again, after his long stint in New York without a car, but he did not enjoy the traffic. Fortunately, it was a straight shot down Main from his apartment to the firm.

His other major purchase was a new MacBook Pro and a TUMI briefcase to carry the laptop back and forth to work. He had a desktop PC on his credenza at the firm, but he preferred to have his laptop, his new passport, and other essentials with him at all times, probably a habit from his running days in Reno.

He had a sofa and bed delivered from a furniture store in The Galleria and brought most of his new clothes and belongings up from the Galveston house. The rest of what he needed, he ordered online from Amazon, Target, and Pottery Barn. He didn't have a doorman in his building to handle the packages, so he often returned from work with boxes stacked outside his door.

He had lunch with Judge Bell at least once a week, and usually drinks on another night as well. The judge beamed with pride when Quinton called him dad or referred to him as his father in the presence of others. The judge seemed very comfortable with the situation and introduced Quinton to everyone they encountered. The prodigal son, returned. Quinton began to wonder if the judge ever thought of Q or the fact that he was not really his son. The feeling of being handled was getting a bit old, but he was grateful. He vowed to try and create more of a life for himself apart from Judge Bell.

Quinton joined a gym on the edge of downtown, up the street from his new firm, with an Olympic sized swimming pool and a bunch of tennis courts. Houston had a lot more space than New York for the bigger pools, and he was thrilled to have a place so close by to workout and decompress. His law practice was less stressful than in New York, as he had fewer cases and none that were high profile, but his daily life was more complicated. He wasn't worried about running into someone who would recognize him as Byron, as he had been gone from Houston for a long time, and his face was changed, but he was constantly on alert for someone who knew the old Q well enough to blow his cover. So far, as he resettled into Houston life, he'd only met acquaintances of Q who had no reason to doubt him. He didn't plan to hang out with the drug gangs, so he was not likely to run into anyone who really knew Q in the years just before his death. Judge Bell had paid off all of Q's old debts to the drug gangs when Byron first became Quinton, so he hoped that kept them at bay.

One day, Quinton had to run into the bathroom at a restaurant, to text a name to Judge Bell, after he'd been introduced to an attorney at a litigation luncheon who'd actually known Q.

The judge told Quinton the lawyer's wife's name, Julie, and his area of practice, real estate, and that was enough to satisfy the conversation that continued upon his return to the table.

Today, when he went to the gym for a swim, he had his first real test. Joanne Wyatt, Quinton's former lover and only serious adult girlfriend, walked by him in the reception area on his way out. She was headed to the women's locker room, and, in her workout clothes and long blonde ponytail, he almost didn't recognize her from the photo he'd moved to his new bathroom mirror.

"Joanne? Is that you?"

She stopped and searched his face, trying to place him. "Yes?"

"Don't you recognize your old boyfriend? It's me, Quinton." He laughed and ran his fingers through his mane. "It must be the wet hair."

She looked puzzled. "Quinton?"

He pulled her in for an awkward hug and when he let go, she seemed to adjust a little to his presence and said, "Wow, you really look healthy. Fit too."

"I'm clean and have been taking better care of myself. I've moved back to Houston and am practicing law at Jamail, Powers & Kent."

Joanne studied him. "I hadn't heard. Good firm."

"It hasn't been long. Dad is helping me. After I got settled, I was going to give you a call and catch up."

"Catch up? After all that went on between us?"

"I'm sorry, Joanne. It was the drugs, not you. I wasn't myself."

"You're still not. You seem so different."

Quinton laughed. "Good. I needed to change, and I have. The rehab helped me sort myself out. Swimming keeps me sane." Quinton pointed toward the pool area. "You, on the other hand, look wonderful. Really." Her eyes were as green as emeralds, and he understood immediately what Q had seen in her. He'd been looking at her picture for so long, he'd developed a crush that was fortified in her actual presence.

Joanne looked confused. "Thanks."

Quinton watched her face to see if she would accept him. Not wanting to give her too much time to evaluate him, he said, "I better get going. I'm late. I'll give you a call soon. Take care, Joanne."

"Right. You do that." She tossed her ponytail and continued toward the locker room.

15

Joanne Wyatt was a Houston socialite from a family of women with similar qualities. Her grandmother, and namesake, had been on the social register for over fifty years before her death. The matriarch had singlehandedly supported and brought in every benefactor of the Houston Downtown Sculpture Garden, and her granddaughter was following closely in her footsteps. Great effort was spent on appearance and all were svelte, highly groomed, and decked out in exclusive designer apparel from stores that wouldn't dare sell the same dress to more than one Houston woman. Most shopped at Neiman Marcus at The Galleria or flew to New York twice a year to purchase updates to their wardrobe.

Joanne had studied abroad at Sorbonne University in Paris and still had a slight lilt to her accent. The mix of aristocrat and Southern Belle in her voice was both charming and captivating.

Judge Bell had loved the idea of his son marrying Joanne and was not only heartbroken, but enraged beyond measure, when Q had dumped and mistreated her as he spiraled into drug use and abuse. Joanne's sentiments were closely aligned with Judge Bell's. Maybe it was the fact that no one ever turned down Joanne Wyatt, or that she deeply loved Q, but she never stopped carrying a torch for him. She had heard the news that he was dead, possibly by overdose, but since it was never announced officially by Judge Bell, and there had been no memorial service, she had not found closure around the relationship. It was humiliating to her that he had dumped her and shameful that she didn't flip him the emotional bird and move on immediately, but she could not.

Running into Quinton like that at the gym had totally unnerved her. She'd gone into the locker room as if she was getting ready for her workout, but after giving him time to leave, she slipped back out to her car in the parking garage for a good cry. She wondered if she'd hear from Quinton, to catch up, as he'd so flippantly promised, but wouldn't hold her breath.

Surprisingly, a few days later, contact came not from Quinton, but from Judge Bell. "Hello, Joanne. Sirus Bell here. I was told you ran into Quinton at the gym last week."

"Hello, Judge. Good to hear your voice. Yes, it was quite a shock. I barely recognized him. He seemed so different. He even sounded different."

"He's changed a lot since he cleaned up his act and started working with Silver Jamail's firm."

Joanne hid her suspicions behind her good manners. "So he said. What can I do for you?"

Judge Bell was not put off. "I thought we might be able to meet for cocktails and dinner."

"I don't know, Judge. Things didn't end well, as you know, and I've moved on," she lied.

"I know there's a lot of bad blood between you two, but a little dinner and conversation can't make it any worse, can it?"

Joanne paused to think. "Maybe, but I learned the hard way not to trust a junkie."

"Then don't trust him, trust me. I'll make sure he behaves himself, and besides, I'd love to see you."

"Let me think about it. I'll let your assistant know my available dates if I decide to join you."

Judge Bell stayed upbeat. "I hope you will. I think you'll be glad you did."

Quinton, Joanne, Sirus, and Silver met at Rainbow Lodge, a forty-year-old restaurant in the Houston Heights, with veteran cooks and celebrated service. It was housed in a one-hundred-year-old log cabin which was a comfortable, yet refined, setting for succulent wild game, seafood, and steaks. Two onsite gardens provided seasonal harvests and herbs to complete the menu.

The judge and Silver arrived early to have cocktails with Joanne before Quinton joined them. When the three were seated at the four-top by the window, Judge Bell assured Joanne, "He's not late. I told him to come at eight thirty. He doesn't know I wanted to warn you about the effect the drugs have had on him. He has some patchy memory loss from the time of the drug use and may not remember everything that occurred between the two of you."

Silver joined in. "We wouldn't want you to think Quinton was being disrespectful if he forgot something that you deem important. The specialists at the rehab center said that he truly may not recall many things that occurred during the time from law school graduation until last year."

The judge agreed. "Of course, you know, he was the sensitive type from a young age. The pressure of the Florida firm and the loss of his mother were the last straw. I didn't know what he was up to in Miami, with the drug usage, or I would have stepped in earlier."

Silver punctuated the sentiment. "I've been working with him for months now and he really is a good man. He's handled all the cases I've referred to him with aplomb and skill."

Joanne seemed skeptical. "I don't know. He was pretty brutal the last few times I spoke with him, then he ghosted me with no explanation."

Silver was sympathetic. "That must have really hurt, but you surely saw some good in him or you wouldn't have loved him."

Joanne averted her eyes.

Judge Bell stretched his arm across the table and put his hand on Joanne's. "Please give him the benefit of the doubt just for tonight. After this, we'll leave you alone if you want."

Unbeknownst to Silver, Judge Bell was using her to assist with Quinton's coverup, by taking advantage of her good nature and willingness to help them both. He had filled her head with information before the meeting, knowing she wouldn't be able to resist supporting Quinton as she did. By the time Quinton arrived, Joanne had been marinating in tequila and goodwill served up by Silver and Judge Bell. She was primed to enjoy the evening, if not forgive him. A little.

When Quinton arrived, wearing his newest jeans, cowboy boots, and a crisp white shirt, under a navy blazer, Joanne almost gasped. She'd always had a soft spot for the quasi-cowboy look, and with his newfound health and workout regime, he was truly breathtaking to look at. But it was more than that. There was an aura of confidence about him she'd not witnessed in him before, a depth to his persona that was enticing. He even seemed taller and had a swagger she'd not experienced in him before.

Quinton joined the table with hugs and well wishes all around. He knew it was a risk to see Joanne for any length of time, in the event that she brought up past experiences he was not privy to, but the judge had twisted his arm, and Quinton had to admit he was desperately curious about the type of woman Q would date and possibly marry.

It was awkward for a few moments, but then the four fell into a camaraderie built on their history in Houston and Galveston, knowledge of the same people around town, and desire to put the past in the past. Quinton was at his most charming, treating Joanne as if she were a juror he must win over while at the same time mesmerized by her green-eyed beauty and elegance.

Judge Bell was beside himself watching the two interact. He was finally getting the son he had always wanted: polished, intelligent, respectful, and successful. If he was lucky, he might get the daughter-in-law, too.

16

Q uinton waited for the criminal courts to appoint him to a case more challenging than drunk and disorderlies, domestic violence, burglaries, and petty larceny. Although his work at the firm was rocking along, he grew a little bored as he settled further into Houston life. He craved the excitement of the courtroom and all that went with it.

Although he was glad to have a new life, and grateful that he had people around him who seemed to care, he felt like an imposter on the inside and was never totally comfortable in his own skin. He sought cases that might turn into more challenging courtroom trials but had not been able to manifest more than a few hearings and one- or two-day trials.

After hanging around the courthouse for weeks, Quinton was finally assigned a case by criminal court Judge Robert Blaylock. Judge Blaylock ran the courtroom through his bailiff of seven years, George Grant, a retired cop, like a military operation with no excuses for tardiness or inefficiency. Both men were fit, clean-shaven with short hair, and had a militant posture.

Quinton was in the courtroom for a hearing on a motion to dismiss a burglary charge for the son of one of Silver's clients. A bunch of high school kids had gone partying at a neighbor's home while the neighbor was out of town. It turned into being one of those wrong place at the wrong time situations. Quinton was able to show through the doorbell video recording that his client was there, and intoxicated, but did not take anything from the house. Judge Blaylock gave the client a second chance by dismissing the charges after a strong admonishment that the kid would not receive another break in his courtroom, or any other in Harris County, and he better mind his p's and q's.

The kid's parents thanked Quinton profusely and quickly pulled their son out of the courtroom before the judge could change his mind. As Quinton packed his briefcase, he thought, *Another success, but how boring.* He could do dismissals, like this one, in his sleep.

The judge looked around the courtroom and his eyes fell on Quinton. "Mr. Bell. Do you have a moment?"

"Yes, Judge Blaylock. What do you need?"

The judge gestured to Bailiff Grant to give Quinton a thick file. "I'd like for you to take on another case if you have time."

Quinton's eyes lit up, but he kept his face calm.

Bailiff Grant handed Quinton the file with a knowing wink. Quinton flipped open the file. "Sure, Judge. What's the charge?"

The judge seemed apologetic. "Drug deal gone bad and murder charges."

"Murder?"

The judge continued. "The defendant is in the holding cell. He's about to be arraigned. You can go back and talk to him, and we'll take a plea. After that, you can look into it more carefully and see if you can help him out. If not, let me know and I'll assign it to the public defender's office."

Quinton snatched up his briefcase and started toward the

door to the holding area. "Yes, Your Honor. I'd be happy to assist."

Quinton went to the holding cell and read the name of his new client from the file he'd received from Bailiff Grant.

"Is Dione Arthur Owens here?"

A huge black man, more muscle than fat, who must have played football somewhere along the way, answered. "I'm Owens. Who are you?"

"I'm your court-appointed attorney. We have about ten minutes to decide on a plea and appear for your arraignment. After that, we can meet for a full debrief and you can decide if you want to hire me."

The big man looked suspicious. "I don't have any money."

Quinton was accustomed to that. "No problem. I'd be paid by the county."

Owens looked Quinton up and down. "Is this the day I get one of those stupid cheap-ass court-appointed attorneys who can't make a living except off the government?"

Quinton stared at Owens. "No, this is the day your luck has changed for the better, and you'd best not blow the opportunity."

"Well, in that case, call me Dart."

"Dart? Is that your gang name?"

"Sort of. It's a combination of Dione and Arthur. Dart."

"Okay, Dart. Let's stick to Mr. Owens for purposes of the arraignment. The only words I want you to say out there are 'not guilty.' Got it?"

Owens smiled. "Not guilty."

Quinton, back in the courtroom he'd just left, stood at the arraignment with his new client who was charged with drug trafficking and murder. Per Quinton's instructions, Owens pled, "Not guilty." Judge Blaylock accepted the plea, and the prosecutor left before Quinton could get a word with her.

Quinton, standing at the defense table, asked Bailiff Grant for a quick moment with his client.

"Just a short one, Mr. Bell."

Quinton turned to Owens. "I'll be out to see you tomorrow at the jail, and we'll see what I can do for you. In the meantime, don't speak to anyone, especially other inmates or on the phone."

Owens studied Quinton's face. "Your name's Quinton Bell? You don't remember me, do you?"

Quinton realized it must have been gang or drug related and searched his mind for a quick reply. "No, I don't, but as you probably know, I was out of it most of the time I was around the drug scene."

"Yeah. How you a lawyer now?"

Quinton laughed for effect. "I was a lawyer before; I just didn't tell anyone."

"What happened to that Q on your neck, Q Ball?"

Quinton was starting to squirm. He pulled his collar away from his neck and showed the faux tattoo removal scar. "Scraped it off. Never did like it."

"Hmm." Owens studied him further. "I guess I'll see you tomorrow."

When Quinton researched the jail rules and procedures the next day, he was shocked at the statistics his client was facing. According to information released by the Harris County Criminal District Courts, there were about fifty thousand active cases pending in the district attorney's office. There was a backlog in the criminal justice system, with most of those cases being more than a year old. The delays resulted in leaving the accused who were seeking answers and resolution hanging for extended periods of time. Those who were later found innocent were particularly harmed.

Part of the reason for the backlog was Hurricane Harvey, a category 4 storm that had hit Texas and Louisiana, and the later pandemic. The hurricane had seriously damaged the Criminal Justice Center, forcing its closure for some time for repairs. Since normal court proceedings did not take place during that time, delays were caused which were still impacting the schedule years later.

Quinton could see that he might get bail for Owens, if it weren't a murder case, if for no other reason than to keep the population down. No way the DA was going to let Owens out, even if he could make bail, which Quinton doubted. He understood why so many defendants pled out. If the infraction was minor, they might serve more time waiting for trial than the actual sentence imposed by the judge. That left some with a record who were actually innocent.

He considered Owens' options as he drove to the county jail, went through the usual time-consuming steps to see his client, and finally sat with Dione Arthur Owens in an attorney interview room about two hours later.

"Hello, Mr. Owens. I guess if you want me to advise you, you best tell me what happened."

"Hey, Q Ball. Call me Dart."

"We won't be using that name again. My name is Quinton or Mr. Bell, and if you want me to represent you, treat me with respect, as I am treating you. Now what happened?"

"I killed the guy. That simple. Flat out coldcocked him and

he whacked his head against the table on the way down and bled out."

"Why would you do that? Hit him."

"He was trying to take the drugs and the money. We had a deal, and I was not going back to the boss man emptyhanded. He'd kill me for sure."

"Who'd kill you?"

"The man I work for. He sent me with the drugs and I was supposed to bring back the money, but this guy, Jug, he tried to trick me and keep it all. I done it a dozen times before and always got the scratch. This time, the mutha' fucka' Jug wanted to keep it for some reason."

"Okay, I'm getting confused. Let's slow this down. What is Jug's real name?"

"Don't know. Only know Jug."

"Who did you work for that sent you with the drugs?"

"I ain't tellin' you that, White Boy. Besides, you already know him."

"Let's pretend I forgot. Remind me."

Owens tried to stand up but was jerked back down by his handcuffs looped through a ring on the metal table. "Hell, no. I ain't sayin' that name out loud in here."

"Okay. Okay. Let's leave that for later. Start at the beginning and tell me everything that happened from the time you picked up the drugs and left for the drop with Jug. You can leave out the names."

Owens told a long and detailed story about where he went to get the drugs and where he went to drop them off to Jug. Quinton took extensive notes on a yellow legal pad, filling several pages. Finally, Owens got to the part where Jug got the bag with the drugs inside.

"I set the bag on the dining table and he opened the bag and checked the drugs, just like he always did. But this time, he handed the bag to his man, ChoirBoy, called that because he walks around singing all the time. Anyway, ChoirBoy took the drugs out the back door to the car and I asked Jug for the money."

"So, you were left alone with Jug?"

"Right. So, I say where's the money, bro, and he say he don' have it."

"What happened next?"

"I say I have to get the money or no drugs. Then he pull out a big fat black shiny gun and shove it in my face."

"A pistol? Did he fire the weapon?"

"Nah. He just say, "I ain't got the money. He start backing up to the door with the gun on me the whole time."

"What did you do then?"

"I kicked the dining chair at his knees and when he stumbled, I grabbed the gun. He held onto it for a while, but he couldn't shoot me 'cause his finger ain't on the trigger."

"Okay. How did you get the pistol away from him?"

"I was stronger than him. Jug was a little short mutha' fucka'. So, I jerked it away and it fell on the floor. Then, I cold-cocked him before he could bend over and pick it up."

"How did he fall?"

"He fell back and hit his head on the dining table. It was one of those big rock slab jobs with edges that looked like a beaver ate it out of the quarry pit."

"Natural edge stone?"

"Yeah, natural."

"What did you do then?"

"I picked up the gun and ran out the back. ChoirBoy was in the car with the engine running so I just stuck the gun in his face and made him give me the drugs back. I never saw no money, so I guess he really didn't have none."

"What did you do with the gun?"

"I threw it in Buffalo Bayou on my way back to Channelview. That's where the boss was waitin'."

"You're going to have to eventually tell me more about the gang and the boss."

"Oh, yeah? Back in the day when you be druggin', you gonna tell about him?"

Quinton opened his mouth, then closed it.

17

Q didn't want his old gang to know he was in Houston, partly because he was trying not to use hard drugs, and partly because he owed several members money. He knew some people thought he was dead and was ashamed that his father probably thought that, too. Q had been in such a fog of drugs for so many months, he hadn't considered what it might have done to his few remaining friends and family until he went cold turkey and cleaned up. He'd gone through withdrawal on his own once before and it didn't take, but this time, he'd had the help of a friend, a group, and a sponsor and it seemed to be working. So far.

Q had run into his new support group in a somewhat lucid moment at an AA meeting in New Orleans. He was practically living on the streets and had hoped for a cup of coffee and maybe a donut or two when he popped into a Catholic church for the Friends of Bill meeting. By the end of the night, he was fed, spiritually nourished, and given a warm coat by a woman at the meeting named June Graves. June and her husband found him a temporary shelter to stay at and eventually brought him to live and work on their shrimper, docked near St. Bernard Parish on Highway 46 on the Gulf of Mexico.

They knew, at the time, that he was still using and would steal to get the drugs or money to buy them. They took him far enough offshore that he couldn't swim to land and get drugs, fed him fresh seafood, and dunked him daily in the salty, healing water until he became human again and his brain began to function somewhat normally. It wasn't easy, but he'd gotten over the hump with their help and was ready to start again. He wanted his own shrimping boat, saw it as his only way to stay clean and sober, and knew what he needed to do to get the cash for it. Houston held the answer, hence his visit.

Q also wanted to see Joanne Wyatt and apologize to her. He needed to make amends with her under step nine of the Alcoholics Anonymous program. She was the only person that he felt he owed an apology. His soft spot for her had never hardened and, if he was going to go straight, he wanted her blessing. He had no notion that she would ever take him back, but it would be enough to have her forgive him and possibly be his friend.

He also wanted to settle some scores with a few members of his old gang, especially the one called Redeye, who'd nicknamed him Q Ball, tricked him into the tattoo on his neck, and forced him to sell meth in order to keep his own habit alive. He'd never forgive Redeye and, as far as he was concerned, step nine did not apply in this instance. Giving him the nickname Q Ball, as in 8 ball, had scarred him for life.

Q's plan was to contact his father on the sly, to try to make nice if it would help, borrow some money that he would never repay, and then slip back out of town to the bayou. The judge had never refused him, and he hoped he would help him out again. And, just in case, he had the extra leverage he needed, a challenge to his father's reputation in the Houston social scene and legal community. It was his ace in the hole if the old man didn't put out.

Lastly, his old buddy Byron had to be dealt with. He'd done a little research before leaving New Orleans for the visit and found that someone was impersonating him, practicing law, and visiting with dear old dad. Did Byron really think he could get away with impersonating him? How dare he. After all he'd done for poor little Byron growing up, he would betray him by using his name and law license? He knew deep down that Byron always wanted to be him. He never had the money, the houses, the father, and all the trappings that made Q's life better. Looked like he decided to just steal it.

If the judge wouldn't help him out with all the cash he needed, he would force Byron to assist. The threat of letting the Dannon gang in New York know where Byron was hiding in plain sight would be enough to force some dough out of him. When Q had seen the online news sites, he'd done a little research about Byron's disappearance in New York and had put two and two together.

Byron couldn't be Quinton without the judge's help, so maybe he'd milk both of them. Threaten to reveal Byron to the Dannon gang and threaten to out his father to the Houston legal community. He had all kinds of ammunition to get what he wanted. Maybe he'd get a really fancy shrimp boat.

Q checked into the Top Value Motel, on Highway 69 between Houston and Missouri City, and slept for almost ten hours. He had been traveling and not eating very well since he'd left the boat and Louisiana, and it was exhausting. He was also dodging law enforcement because he'd jumped bail when he'd originally left Houston and wasn't sure if he was still wanted. He didn't know if, or how, his legal problems had been resolved by the judge and the new Quinton, but something must have been arranged since Byron was practicing law under the name of Quinton Lamar Bell. Better to be safe until he knew for sure that a return to jail wasn't in his future.

When he finally woke, he placed a few calls to shocked recipients. Meetings were arranged and venues set, and Q set about the business of facing old ghosts, asking for forgiveness from Joanne, and settling scores with others. One at a time.

18

Judge Bell was disturbed at three in the morning by his cell phone. It was not entirely unusual for a criminal courts judge to get a middle of the night call, but it had been a long time since the last one. The judge was actually lying in his bed alone, having a restless night, and still awake when he answered the phone. "This better be good and entirely necessary."

The voice on the other end was a deep baritone sprinkled with Louisiana hot sauce. "Judge Bell, it's Detective Clive Broussard."

The judge recognized the Cajun accent. "Yes?"

"I'm at the Harris County morgue and I have a John Doe here with your business card in his pocket. His ID says he's Quinton Lamar Bell, but we called your son, Quinton, and he's on his way down here, so we know it's not him."

"Oh, Lord. I'm on my way. Tell Byr... I mean Quinton to wait for me before he goes in to ID the body. I'll try to reach him on the phone on my way."

"Okay, Judge. I'll wait for you here."

As the judge dressed, his phone rang again; it was Quinton. The judge answered. "I just got the call. You on the way?"

"Yes. I'll swing by and pick you up. Do you think it's Q?"

The judge juggled the phone while pulling a shirt over his head. "I can't imagine that it's anyone else."

"Holy shit!"

Judge Bell and Quinton entered the morgue and signed in as father and son. They were escorted into the cold metal room of the dead and directed to stand near a wall of what appeared to be large metal file cabinets. Each drawer pull was labeled with a name, several of them *John Doe*. The orderly pointed to one such sepulcher and pulled it open. A lifeless body drained of blood lay in the drawer covered with a white sheet up to the chin.

"I'm sorry to have to tell you that the body was mutilated. I can't pull the sheet down any farther."

Judge Bell drew in the smallest amount of air that whistled between his teeth as his eyes fell on his only son. He was almost unrecognizable, but he knew it was him. The new Quinton looked down at Q, his childhood friend, whom he'd been impersonating for months and shivered.

"May we have a moment," Judge Bell said to the attendant.

"I'll be right outside. Detective Broussard would like to speak with you on your way out."

The judge nodded. "Of course."

Quinton froze.

"Stay calm," Judge Bell said as he put his hand on Quinton's shoulder, looked down at Q, and teared up.

Quinton teared up as well. "I should be comforting you. Are you okay?"

Judge Bell shook his head. "I think so. There's time for that. Right now, we need to decide on a plausible story and both of our accounts better match."

Quinton recoiled. "What story? They'll find out it's Q and I'll be revealed. I'll be dead in less than a week. New York may be across the country, but it's a small world when someone wants you badly enough."

The judge stared down at his son, then looked up at Quinton. "Not if you're already dead."

"What do you mean?"

"I'm the only judge in this district. If I identify this body as Byron Douglas, you're dead for good and your career and life as Quinton will go on as it has been."

"But, Judge."

"No one will question me. They haven't so far, have they?"

"No, but how can you continue the charade after what's happened to Q?"

"I can't bring him back. I have a son, and it's you."

Quinton's eyes welled with tears as he looked at the judge and down at Q's lifeless body. "This is a nightmare. You're so calm."

Judge Bell dropped his shoulders. "We thought Q was dead before. Now, he really is. I've been living with his absence for a long time."

"But, who killed him? How can we find out if no one knows who he is?"

"We may never know, but we can guess. The old gang finally caught up with him."

Quinton nodded. "I thought you paid them. What about the tattoo? What about fingerprints? What about DNA?"

Judge Bell examined a cleaned, bloodless wound on the

side of Q's neck. More like a large gouge. "No tattoo, but he still has his fingers."

"So, fingerprints."

"Leave the rest to me. If anyone asks, you and I were together last night working at your office. Other than that, we don't have to reveal anything else."

"I wasn't at my office all night."

"I'll alibi you as being there. We were going over the Masterson case file. You say the same thing."

"Alibi? Masterson, right. I will. I can. But, Judge, are you sure? It's your son."

"I'm sure."

Judge Bell and Quinton found Detective Clive Broussard in the break room down the hall. The judge introduced the officer. "This is my son, Quinton. Quinton, this is Detective Broussard."

Quinton shook his hand. "We spoke on the phone. Thank you for checking on me before you called the judge."

The judge nodded. "Yes, thank you. It's a big enough shock, but that would have been worse."

Quinton looked away.

Broussard sipped from a vending machine cup of coffee with a full house, aces and eights, printed on the side. "Don't mention it. Doing my job. Any idea who the body is?"

Judge Bell nodded. "Yes, it's Byron Douglas, a childhood friend of Quinton's."

Quinton froze.

"Why would he have Quinton's ID and your card?"

"The card is simple. We've known Byron since he and Quinton were in junior high school. The ID is a mystery."

Broussard looked at Quinton. "Do you have your ID?"

Quinton took his wallet out of his jeans pocket and opened it. He removed his driver's license with his new photo and new address and handed it to the detective who took a picture of it with his phone.

"He was registered at a motel out near Missouri City, as Elvis Presley, paid cash, and the receptionist didn't ask any questions or ask for ID. It's that type of place. No calls from the room and no cell phone."

The judge nodded. "It's all so shocking."

"Any idea who might have wanted to kill him?"

"No. Like I said we hadn't been in touch in a long time."

Broussard turned to Quinton. "How about you?"

Quinton shook his head. "No idea. How did he die?"

Broussard handed the ID back to Quinton. "Gunshot wound in the back. Went through to his heart. Probably never saw it coming. I'm sorry to have to tell you that the body was mutilated. There were pieces of flesh carved out of his neck and calf."

Quinton looked at the judge who blanched white. "We were told."

"The room was wiped down, no prints at all. The guy in the room next door heard the gunshot and banged on the door. By the time he went to get the manager at the office, the killer was gone and took some of the flesh with him. Maybe a trophy, maybe to prove the death if it was a hit. If there was a cell phone, took that too. He or she probably wasn't finished. The neighbor may have interrupted the killer."

The judge seemed calm. "How awful. No one saw the shooter?"

"No witness that we can find." Broussard opened his notebook and checked the time of death. "Just for the record, where were you around ten last night?"

Judge Bell looked at Quinton. "We were in Quinton's office reviewing a case."

Quinton affirmed. "Right. The Masterson files."

Broussard made a note. "How late?"

"Probably finished up around eleven thirty or twelve. Sound about right, Dad?"

"Yes, Son. That's about right."

Broussard flipped closed his notebook closed. "I'll be in touch after I have time to investigate further."

"I'd appreciate that."

Quinton dropped his head in sadness. His childhood friend was really gone, someone had mutilated him, and now his real life was over too. No more Byron. On top of that, he'd just lied to a police detective, and he had no idea how the judge was going to hide Q's identity and protect him.

Judge Bell had Quinton drive to an office supply store for an ink pad and white card and took a set of the new Quinton's fingerprints. The ink smell reminded him of the print in law school books.

"What are you going to do with those?"

"I'm not sure yet. I need to get home and think."

After dropping the judge at his high-rise condo, Quinton drove home to his apartment. He felt that he was drowning in the details of his disappearance and now Q's murder. Had Q Ball's old gang really caught up with him? Had they removed the tattoo they'd bestowed upon him in some kind of loyalty ritual? What was cut from his thigh? If it was established that the body was Byron Douglas, Detective Broussard would not be looking at Q's old gang for the murder and would not find the real killer. Didn't the judge want the killer found? What about justice, or even revenge?

How deep would Detective Broussard go? If he believed the body was Byron's, would he research the Dannon cartel in NYC and chalk it up to that? But it couldn't have been the Dannons because Q was not Byron. Even with the plastic surgery, The Gaffer's henchmen would not have mistaken Q for Byron. Would they? The judge had been so calm and sure of himself that it had given Byron a feeling of security, but at the same time, a queasiness that the judge had lost his sense of reality. Was the death too much for him to handle? Was he drowning in grief and unable to see how his complicated tactics might cost him his career and Quinton's life? How could he take the news of Q's mutilation with such stoic resolve? Had he convinced himself that Quinton, not Q, was really his son? He was getting dizzy trying to puzzle it out as he took a shower and dressed to go to the office. When he turned the key in the lock of his door to leave, he saw that his hands were shaking.

Judge Bell sat at his desk, rocked back and forth, and pondered what to do next. He had not been required to send the new Quinton's fingerprints to the State Bar of Texas along with the application for licensure, but the Florida Bar did have them on file. The judge had hoped no one would ever research them, and so far, they had not, and why would they?

The real risk was that Q's fingerprints were the same fingerprints on file from Q's drug arrest. When the body was processed and fingerprints taken at the morgue, they would match the ones on file and prove that the body was the real Quinton. It was standard practice to take the fingerprints and run them through a database for use as identification, as well as create a record for future crimes or investigations. When that was done, Quinton's arrest record would be there and the fingerprints would match.

Judge Bell needed Byron's prints to be substituted for Q's, and he had to swap them before they were scanned into the system or it would be too late. Luckily, the ID found on the body had provoked an identification at the morgue from both Judge Bell and Quinton. That would do for the time being for law enforcement, but not for the medical examiner, which would probably happen the next day.

The judge had to hurry, and he had a plan. He always had a plan as he saw his power as paramount to any obstacle and wielded it to his advantage whenever necessary. He also had a habit of doing favors and keeping a list of those owing him favors in return. It was like having an address book of IOUs.

He called in one of those favors by contacting a tech in the district attorney's IT support office. A young man he had shown mercy, and let walk on a hacking charge years before, was now in a job that allowed him entry into all kinds of databases that the judge liked to secretly access from time to time. This would be the biggest favor to date, but he knew the hacker wouldn't ask any questions. The judge had too much power over him, and the hacker's moral standards were low anyway. Plus, he needed the money. He always needed money.

Detective Broussard arrived the next day at Judge Bell's office in the Harris County Criminal Justice Center. The judge escorted him in, offered coffee, showed him a chair, and asked about the investigation. "Thank you for coming by. I really appreciate the update, Detective."

Broussard sipped the coffee and looked at it as if anything without chicory was a second-class brew.

"Glad to, Judge. I ran down Byron Douglas from his days in New York. He was last seen in the Hudson River after an altercation on a ferry headed to Staten Island." Broussard gave the judge the basic facts surrounding the disappearance in New York. "Law enforcement reported he was declared dead."

The judge sat down in his desk chair. "I had heard some of that. So, how did he wind up here?"

"We can only assume he came here to hide. Houston is a city known to him, big enough to get lost in. Maybe he planned to try and get help from someone he knew. But that's just a guess."

The judge waited.

When the judge didn't respond, Broussard continued. "He did have your business card. He hadn't contacted you or your son?"

"No. Quinton and I had lost contact with him when he left for law school at Columbia. He stopped coming back here when his mother died. He has a sister in California. I called her this morning to let her know of his passing. She had been notified of his death in New York as well. Needless to say, she was confused and distraught. His law firm and friends in Manhattan had a memorial service for him."

"I guess I'll contact her about the body after the autopsy."

"I wrote down her contact information here." Judge Bell handed him a page from a notepad with his monogram, SBL, engraved at the top. "She's asked me to handle the cremation and ship the ashes out to her. You can verify that with her, but she's already called the morgue to let them know. The autopsy is complete, and I released the body to Height's Mortuary on Washington."

Broussard looked at the note. "That was fast."

"Efficient. I think she'd like this craziness to come to an end as quickly as possible. What mourning she did for him was already done."

"That leaves a lot unexplained. Maybe a few too many coincidences?" The look on Broussard's face said that he thought something fishy was going on.

"Yes, Detective, it does leave us with many questions, but I don't know what else to tell you."

19

In the days that followed Q's death, both Judge Bell and Quinton had expected a follow up visit from Detective Broussard, but none came. After a few days, they stopped holding their collective breaths and got back into their routines as much as possible. Murder in Houston was not unusual. With over five hundred homicides a year, plus those in the outlying counties, the police had their hands full.

In the meantime, Judge Bell had a full criminal docket to dispose of. For Quinton, it was time to put his attention on the Dart Owens murder trial.

Quinton knew he needed help to try the Owens case and had been flirting with the idea of bringing on Maureen Powers, one of the partners in the firm, as second chair. After some coaxing from Quinton, Mo, as she was called by friends and colleagues, agreed to give it a try. She made it clear that it might be a one-off for her, as she'd done a lot of litigation, but never any criminal work, and that the other firm partners would have to sign off on it. Hence, another meeting in the firm's conference room on the fortieth floor.

Quinton made his plea. "I can't try a murder case on my own and no judge will allow it. If something happens to me, the trial will end and the prosecution would have to start over. There has to be at least one other lawyer who knows what's going on." Quinton didn't share how precarious his situation could become at any moment.

Silver was quiet for a beat, considering the firm's position. "Do we have a conflict with the client in any way?"

Mo fielded the question. "This is a court-appointed defendant with drug and gang relations. None of our clients are even part of his world, much less in conflict with it."

"His full name is Dione Arthur Owens."

All shook their heads. No one recognized it.

Buffy turned to Mo. "Do you want to do this type of legal work? You've never shown an interest before. We could allow Quinton to hire outside counsel to assist him."

Mo looked pensive. "I think I'd like to give it a shot. Seems interesting, and I can juggle my regular clients with the help of my assistant and a few associates.

As the matriarch of the firm, Silver called for a vote. "Okay with everyone if we try this out with Mo as second chair?"

"Aye."

"Aye."

"Aye."

"Let's give it a shot. Quinton, I'd like to have an update email every week. Please copy all of us."

"Will do."

Mo took a deep breath and let out a sigh. She looked nervous or scared, Quinton wasn't sure which.

Quinton searched high and low for a technicality with which to exonerate Owens. He and Mo tossed around several legal strategies and applied them to the case in hopes of discovering a get out of jail free card.

Quinton started down the list. "Under Texas criminal law, there is a concept called fatal variance, whereby the proof must be identical to the charges. In many cases, the Court of Criminal Appeals has declared the evidence insufficient to support a conviction for something as meaningless as the written charge against the defendant having the wrong name of a store or bank, or the wrong street address of a crime scene."

Mo looked astounded. "You're kidding."

Quinton shook his head. "No, I'm not, and, because of double jeopardy, cases such as these cannot be re-tried, even when the defendant is caught in the act. Often, the perpetrator of a crime goes scot-free when mistakes are made by prosecutors."

"A loophole I'm not so fond of."

"It is what it is."

The two compared the charge to the information provided by Owens and found it to be sound. Mo shook her head. "No luck here."

Quinton agreed. "Too bad."

Mo remembered a few things from her criminal law class at The University of Texas. "How about violation of his rights? Did they do anything that would allow us to exclude the evidence and may be useful to get the charges dismissed?"

Quinton considered. "Good idea, but Owens wasn't at the scene at the time of his arrest. They came after him later and Mirandized him right away."

"No illegal search?"

"Nope, the crime scene was accessed through the landlord of the building and with permission."

"How about coerced confession?"

"Owens clammed up and asked for a lawyer. He didn't give them anything at the time of arrest."

Mo was running out of what she remembered from class. "Was the arrest legally effective?"

"They had enough probable cause to get a judge to sign off on an arrest warrant, and with Owens' fingerprints all over the place, I don't think we can challenge probable cause in the arrest. We could move to dismiss the charges, but I think we'd just aggravate the judge, and we'd fail anyway. We don't have an alibi because he was there. We can't incriminate someone else, or introduce an alternate theory, because he told us he did it."

"Can we try to plea bargain? Maybe make a trade for information on his drug boss without admitting guilt?"

Quinton scratched his chin. "He won't even tell me his name, although I think I've deduced who he is. Owens is not going to rat him out, even if he's convicted of murder. He says he'd be dead either way."

"Okay, then what?"

"I guess we'll have to try the truth?"

"And what is that?"

"Self-defense. There were only two people in the room. Jug's buddy, ChoirBoy, had gone out to the car to get ready for a fast getaway with the dope and possible cash. Our client says he pushed Jug away to protect himself when they quarreled, causing him to fall and hit his head."

"Isn't that risky? Will a jury really buy that?"

"Only one way to find out."

20

At the firm, Quinton's assistant buzzed his intercom and announced, "Joanne Wyatt is here to see you."

He pulled his feet off his desk, sat up, and straightened his tie. "Send her in." Quinton smiled just thinking of her as he walked around the desk toward the door. He still wasn't entirely sure she was buying in on the whole story about Q, but he was sure that she liked him. A lot. He liked her too. A lot.

She walked through the door in a navy knit suit with a chain at the waist, looking like a million bucks, which was about a twentieth of what her trust fund was worth. The blonde curls must have cost a couple of hundred, just for the haircut, not including the streaky highlights that created sunshine sparkling around her head like a golden halo.

He started to compliment her until he saw the look on her face—pure rage.

"Was it you?" Joanne asked as she rushed toward Quinton.

Quinton took a step back. "Was what me?"

She beat her fists on his chest. "Did you kill him?"

Quinton recoiled. "What? No, of course not."

He closed the door to the outer office and turned back toward Joanne.

She pounded on his chest again. "I know you're not Quinton. He told me when he called that you were impersonating him."

Quinton held her back by the shoulders so he could look at her face. "Q called you?"

Her story came out in a gush. "Yes, he told me you were acting the part to avoid some crazy Irish people in New York. I know it was his voice. His old voice. Not your new smooth shtick. He said he wanted to make amends. Something about a ninth step. He swore me to secrecy until we could meet so he could explain. We were supposed to get together, but he never showed."

Quinton mumbled, "I can explain."

Joanne continued her rant. "Some detective with a Cajun accent called this morning. He said Byron was dead and wants me to come in for questioning."

Quinton was startled. "I had no idea Q had called you or anyone."

Joanne's eyes were flashing. "He was a liar, you're a liar, Judge Bell and Silver Jamail are liars. What a bunch of crooks."

"Joanne, I swear, I didn't mean to hurt you. I wanted to get closer to you, but I couldn't tell you the truth. Not yet. Only Judge Bell knows. Silver thinks I'm Quinton. She didn't know him well before, so it was easy to fool her. I'm so sorry. I should have told you. I should have known you were too perceptive to think I was Q."

Joanne spat words at him. "Well, perceptive or not, look where it's landed me. This Detective Broussard has asked me to come in and he thinks I know something, or worse, that I killed Q. How am I going to explain this without making it sound like I was in on the whole thing with you and Judge Bell?"

Quinton tried to take her hand. "Let's calm down and try to reason this out."

Joanne would have none of it. "Reason? Reason? Isn't that fraud or something close to it?"

Quinton gulped, making his Adam's apple move up and down. "What did you tell him?"

"Nothing. I just set a time to see him today at 4 p.m. in his office. God knows I had motive to kill Q. I had badmouthed him all over town. It was no secret I was angry at him. I may have even said I wanted him dead."

"Does anyone else know about my not being Quinton?"

"No. I don't know whether to say I never knew Byron, or it's really Quinton who's dead and I helped you fool everyone. Should I say I don't know a thing and lie to Broussard? What if they show me the body? I can't look at it. I can't. You're the criminal defense lawyer. What do I do?"

Quinton turned the guest chairs so they faced each other. "Please, let's talk this through."

Joanne begrudgingly flung her designer purse on the desk and sat down with a thud. Quinton sat in the other chair, his knees touching hers, and leaned forward in earnest.

"First of all, the body, as Byron, has been cremated and the ashes are in transit to my sister in California, so you won't have to see the body. The judge contacted her, as next of kin, and took care of it for her. She knows nothing of the whole mess. We're not close, but I don't want her at risk from these Irish thugs Q told you about."

Joanne calmed down a notch, took a deep breath, and expelled the air in a jagged shudder.

"Next, let's talk to the judge. He will have a better handle on law enforcement in Harris County and how to play this out. He will protect you, I'm sure of it. He adores you."

Joanne looked skeptical. "He might be able to help, but I

need a lawyer. Someone to go with me and make sure I don't get myself into this any deeper than I already am."

"Yes, we can work that out. Let's call the judge and go from there."

Joanne stared at him through tears.

Judge Bell took Quinton's call, and they spoke in code.

"Joanne is here with me in my office. She's been asked to come in for questioning by Detective Broussard. She's very nervous and knows more than we thought."

The judge swiveled in his chair and leaned back hard. "Everything?"

"Pretty much. She got a call from an old friend who wanted to meet for coffee. He told her what was going on but swore her to secrecy until they could meet. She says he didn't show up at the appointed time and place."

The judge began to rock back and forth. "Then, the detective called her after that?"

"Right."

"We'll have to read her in."

"I already did. Had to. She knew. I told her we'd protect her, but she's skittish and flustered. She says they think she might have had something to do with the incident."

"Of course she's nervous, but why do they think she was involved?"

"Maybe the phone call? I'm not sure. Broussard may just be fishing around for information."

"There was no phone at the scene to trace any phone calls unless they traced her phone backwards to the area. How would they even know to look at her? Let me see what I can do. I'll be in touch. Can you keep her calm until then?"

"I think so."

The judge disconnected the call and took in a deep breath. He rocked back and forth in thinking mode for a few more minutes, picked up the phone again, and dialed the chief of police of Houston.

"Afternoon, Chief. I need a favor."

21

The new Quinton called or saw Joanne every day as things went quiet with regard to Q's murder, and she calmed down and settled back into her routine. Detective Broussard had canceled his appointment with Joanne, offering an apology for wasting her time. She and Quinton guessed that Judge Bell's call to the police chief had worked.

Judge Bell had discovered from the chief and relayed to Quinton that what led Detective Broussard to question Joanne in the first place was a triangulation of burner phone calls in the area of the Top Value Motel. It seemed someone in the area had placed a call to Joanne's phone, but who or for what purpose Broussard could not be sure. It was disturbing to know that Broussard was still investigating the case.

Quinton was keeping tabs on Joanne to make sure she didn't get nervous and do something foolish, but he was also checking on her wellbeing and using that as an excuse to see her. Joanne seemed to find comfort in his presence. After all, he and the judge were the only ones she could truthfully confide in. Her family consisted of one brother, Alcott Wyatt, in San

Francisco, who had fled the oppression of the Houston social scene. Joanne enjoyed the lifestyle in Houston, but she always felt alone. She and Quinton had a strange family symmetry, he with a semi-estranged sister and she with a semi-estranged brother. The feeling of being the only fish in a vast ocean of fishes bonded the two, along with the shared secret of Quinton's true identity.

Soon, with the threat of Broussard's interrogation request fading away, Quinton became a fixture on the sofa of Joanne's River Oaks townhouse, and they eased into a relationship that neither had expected under the circumstances. He needed her to trust him, but he also couldn't stay away. She greeted him each visit with a smile and a peck on the cheek. She stocked his favorite foods and beer in her refrigerator, including pimento cheese and white bread, which she never ate.

After dinner, they usually settled on the sofa for a getting-to-know-you-better chat and romantic make-out session, which Quinton enjoyed immensely. So far, she hadn't invited him to stay over, but he expected, or maybe hoped for, the invitation any day.

After a particularly hard workday on the Dart Owens case, Quinton arrived at Joanne's townhouse with a bottle of red for her and a six-pack of Saint Arnold for him. They exchanged greetings, pecks on the lips, this time, and settled on the sofa with drinks in hand.

Quinton had never shared the story about Michael with anyone but decided to tell Joanne. She wept when he described how Michael had died on the hard, cold floor of his former office building. She touched his arm, in sympathy, when he described his feelings of the loss of his goddaughter, Sophie, and her loss of her father.

They sat and drank for a long while, neither saying another word. Eventually, Quinton went to the kitchen to pour another glass of wine for her and fetch a cold brew for himself. He returned, determined to lift the mood and move on.

Joanne pulled her bare feet up under herself. To Quinton, she looked like a co-ed in her tight jeans and pale pink sweater.

Quinton shifted on the sofa. "I bet you were a cutie when you were a little girl."

Joanne grinned. "I was a daddy's girl. I worshiped my father. Alcott is a lot like him, very protective and sweet, but distracted by work most of the time. I try to get out to San Francisco once or twice a year. Heaven knows he won't come here unless forced to for business or otherwise."

Joanne looked sad, then changed the subject by pointing to the bottle in Quinton's hand. "You know that beer is brewed right here in Houston."

Quinton admired her red toenails. "I did. A couple of Rice University grads started it, some say secretly on campus, then turned it into a full-on brewery."

"We should tour it sometime. It's right over on Lyons Avenue by all your favorite soul food restaurants."

Quinton smiled at her, looked into her eyes, and held her gaze. "We should. We should."

Joanne read his signals. "We should what? Tour the micro-brewery or do you have something else in mind?"

"I've been thinking of the something else for a while now."

"Oh, have you?"

"Yes, you know I have, and I think you've been considering it as well."

"Is that your lawyerly instinct talking?"

Quinton took her left hand and put it on his heart. "It's this talking. You know I've grown to enjoy our time together, and I adore you."

Joanne giggled. "Is that your heart talking?"

"Yes."

"Hmm. You have a lot on your mind." She didn't remove her hand.

Quinton pulled her in and kissed her, one long passionate kiss. They'd shared many before, but nothing this hot or urgent. "Are you ready, beautiful Joanne?"

"I am." She kissed him again.

He stood up and pulled her with him, then unbuttoned her blouse and pushed it down her shoulders along with her lacy bra straps. She unbuckled his belt and pulled it out of the loops, dropping it on the floor. He cupped her left breast and put his right hand on her behind. Within minutes they were naked and admiring each other between kisses and nibbles.

Quinton slid his arm around her bare waist and led her toward the stairs. "Let's take this tour to the bedroom."

"Let's."

22

The Owens trial started quietly and without much media attention. It was just another case of a gang member killing another lowlife in a drug deal gone bad.

Quinton and Mo sat at the defense table on each side of Owens, who dwarfed Quinton in size and Mo in size and height. He'd cleaned up pretty well considering his husky physique and numerous tattoos. No tie, but the black jacket did fit over his broad shoulders and white shirt.

Judge Blaylock, the magistrate who had appointed Quinton as Owens' counsel, conducted a shortened voir dire using a form, then allowing, but limiting, questions to six each per attorney. Quinton was not happy with the process, as he felt he often won a case getting to know the jury early on in a trial, but he had no choice but to comply. It did save a lot of time, but saving time was not in his plan, that was the court's goal. Saving Owens was Quinton's goal, and winning, always about winning.

After the jury was empaneled and settled in by Bailiff Grant, Prosecutor Carlos Diego put on the government's case. He spent two days using police officers and medical examiners to introduce evidence from the crime scene and the body. There was nothing in the state's case that contradicted Owens' story, but they could not know that there was a gun and what happened to it since, unbeknownst to them, Owens had tossed it in the bayou. Finally, after beating a dead horse for the last full day, at the risk of alienating the jury, the prosecution rested.

Now, it was Quinton's turn. He walked up to the jury box in his best new Armani gray suit, looked at each juror in order, then turned to the judge. "We have only one witness, Your Honor. The defense calls Officer Clayton Johnson."

Prosecutor Diego was on his feet. "Your Honor, we have no notice of this witness." The prosecutor's co-counsel tapped on a laptop, apparently trying to locate the witness list, or search the name.

Mo stood at the defense table and Quinton nodded at her. She pulled a folder from a stack on the table and said, "Your Honor, the prosecution has fifty-three police officers on its witness list. Clayton Johnson is number twenty-eight. We did not include him on our list because he's already on theirs. He was not called to testify by the prosecution, but that doesn't mean we can't solicit his testimony."

Judge Blaylock looked at his own laptop documentation. "Correct, he's on the list. Proceed with your witness, Mr. Bell."

Quinton turned and smiled at Owens and Mo, and Officer Johnson was called from the waiting area, outside the courtroom, where witnesses queued up before their testimony. Johnson walked into the courtroom in his dress blues, was sworn in, took his seat on the stand, and looked at Quinton.

"Officer Johnson, thank you for being here today."

Quinton knew that the prosecution had hoped to bury Johnson's name in their long list of police officers and hide the information he had to offer. *Nice try.*

Johnson grumbled, "Not my choice."

Quinton smiled. "Nevertheless, we are interested in what you have to say."

Johnson didn't respond.

"First of all, did you interview a witness called ChoirBoy, also known as Larry Boyd, in the process of the murder investigation of my client, Dione Arthur Owens?"

"Yes, I did."

"What were the circumstances surrounding the interview?"

"I was asked to obtain his statement along with a long list of those known to be a part of the drug and gang community here in Houston."

Quinton took a step closer to the witness. "And, what did he have to say about the encounter?"

"ChoirBoy described the interaction between Dart Owens and Jug, also known as Deshawn Brown, on the day of the murder."

"And did you file a report with the information obtained from ChoirBoy?"

The prosecutor was on his feet. "Your Honor, ChoirBoy was found deceased shortly after the murder of Jug Brown. There was no opportunity for us to depose him or obtain his video statement. His initial statement to Officer Johnson is incomplete and not evidentiary. It probably isn't even true."

Quinton approached Judge Blaylock. "Your Honor, that's a question for the jury. If I might continue, I think I can clear up any misunderstanding."

Prosecutor Diego stayed on his feet. "Out of the presence of the jury, please, Your Honor."

Judge Blaylock looked from one attorney to the other, then at the witness. "Bailiff Grant, remove the jury."

A couple of the jury members groaned as they stood to file out. They had just been seated and were ready to move on with their civic responsibilities and go home. Quinton used the moment to roll his eyes at a couple of them.

Judge Blaylock took note of the antics. "Mr. Bell, return to the defense table."

"Yes, Your Honor." Quinton sat down next to Owens and kept his facial expressions neutral.

Judge Blaylock called on Prosecutor Diego. "Now, what is so important that the jury can't hear it?"

Diego looked at the computer screen that his co-counsel pointed at, then up at the judge. "Your Honor, ChoirBoy Boyd was interviewed briefly by Officer Johnson on the day before his death. He was to give a video statement in our office the next day and never showed. That's when we found out he was dead. Apparent overdose. Since we were unable to establish a true accounting of his version of the incident, we did not include the statement to Officer Johnson in our case in chief."

"Mr. Bell, do you have a response?"

"Yes, Your Honor. It has come to our attention that ChoirBoy Boyd told Officer Johnson that he was initially in the meeting with Jug Brown and my client, went to the car with the drugs, then returned to the outside of the door of the room where they were arguing. That he saw Jug lunge with his gun at my client and that my client responded in self-defense to Jug's advances."

The judge turned to Officer Johnson, who was still on the stand. "Is this true, Officer?"

The witness adjusted his tie and cleared his throat. "In part, Your Honor. ChoirBoy Boyd told me that he returned to the door and saw Jug Brown and the defendant yelling and scuffling. He did not say whether the response by Mr. Owens was in self-defense."

Judge Blaylock looked at him sternly. "Did he say that the decedent pulled his own gun on Mr. Owens?"

"Yes, sir. He did, but he said he could not see all of the events that occurred after."

Quinton was still standing. "We were not given a copy of the statement or Officer Johnson's report. The statement, with or without the conclusion that my client acted in self-defense, and whether or not it is true or false, is exculpatory evidence. By definition, the information was required to be provided to defense counsel by the prosecution."

Prosecutor Diego looked exasperated. "Your Honor."

"Hold on, Mr. Diego. Continue, Mr. Bell."

"As you know, the Brady Rule, from Brady v. Maryland, requires prosecutors to disclose materially exculpatory evidence in the government's possession to the defense. Brady material includes any evidence favorable to the accused—evidence that goes toward negating a defendant's guilt, or that would reduce a defendant's potential sentence, or that goes to the credibility of a witness."

Prosecutor Diego interrupted. "We doubted the veracity of the statement from ChoirBoy, and he could not be a witness because he is deceased."

Quinton continued. "The fact that the possible witness is deceased is in and of itself exculpatory evidence. Was it an accident? Murder? Was it in relation to this case?"

Prosecutor Diego felt the case slipping away. "We had no duty to disclose and did not receive any request for further information."

Quinton protested. "We had no duty to seek information. In cases subsequent to Brady, the Supreme Court has eliminated the requirement for a defendant to have requested favorable information, stating the prosecution has a constitutional duty to disclose information that is triggered by the potential impact of favorable but undisclosed evidence."

Prosecutor Diego interrupted again. "The defendant bears

the burden to prove that the undisclosed evidence was both material and favorable. In other words, the defendant must prove that there is a reasonable probability that the outcome of the trial would have been different had the evidence been disclosed by the prosecutor. The statement was not exculpatory evidence because it wasn't vetted and could not be corroborated, even by the defense. Therefore, we were not required to provide it."

Quinton argued, "Your Honor, the defense has not had an opportunity to prove that there was a reasonable probability that the outcome of the trial would have been different, because we were not provided the information in order to evaluate it. It's the proverbial chicken and egg dilemma."

Judge Blaylock really didn't need Quinton to explain Brady to him. He was a well-respected scholar and judge, applying the law via precedent and rarely making new law unless fairness demanded it. "I agree with defense counsel. What remedy are you requesting from the court, Mr. Bell?"

Quinton retrieved a document from Mo and read from it, "If the prosecution does not disclose material exculpatory evidence under Brady, and prejudice has ensued, the case should be dismissed."

Prosecutor Diego argued, "Not so fast, Bell. Your Honor, now that the evidence has come to light, the defense must prove that the evidence is exculpatory and that it would have changed the outcome of the trial. We assert that even if we should have turned it over, which we do not believe to be the case, the defense must prove it would have changed the course or outcome here."

Judge Blaylock rapped his gavel to stop the arguing. "I've heard enough. I'll take briefs on the issue by ten tomorrow morning. Bailiff, let the jury go until after lunch tomorrow afternoon. Court dismissed."

After the judge left the bench, Quinton and Mo celebrated with a cautionary high five. Dart looked confused.

The next morning, Judge Blaylock had all the lawyers in the courtroom without the jury. "You may all sit down."

Everyone took a seat, but most remained on the edge, not relaxing until they knew where the court stood on the matter.

"I've read the briefs you submitted, and I must agree with the defense that the evidence is probably exculpatory. Mr. Diego had an absolute obligation to disclose it to Mr. Bell, and the cure for the error is dismissal of the case."

Mr. Diego was on his feet, trying to hold back the next sentence by sheer will. "Your Honor."

"Sit down, Mr. Diego."

Quinton smiled quietly at Mo.

The judge continued, "Since jeopardy has attached, the case is dismissed with prejudice. Court adjourned."

Prosecutor Diego sat with his mouth hanging open.

Owens turned to Quinton. "What's prejudice mean?"

"It means that they can't re-try you."

Mo patted Owens on the back. "You're a free man, Dart."

Owens couldn't speak for a moment, then the big man began to tear up. "Thank you. Thank you. I'll never be able to repay you for what you done for me."

Quinton smiled. "Just doing our job. This is how it's supposed to work."

Owens smiled too. "If there's ever anything I can do for either one of you, please call me. Please."

23

Quinton and Joanne were sitting in their usual places on her blue velvet sofa, in her exquisitely decorated townhouse. Quinton had turned on all his charm and was making romantic headway. Unfortunately, their blossoming romance and co-conspiracy hit a brick wall when there was a knock on the door.

Quinton, still in paranoid mode about the mob, pulled on his shirt, walked over, and peeked out the curtains in the entryway. "It's Detective Broussard."

Joanne jumped up from the sofa and buttoned her blouse. "Oh my God."

Quinton held up his hand. "Shhh. Let's stay calm. We don't know what this is about. Could be routine. More questions, anything."

"Right. Right. Give me a second." Joanne sat back down on the sofa, closed her eyes, and appeared to calm her breathing. "Okay, let him in."

Quinton opened the door and saw that Broussard was

accompanied by a female officer in uniform with L. Avery stamped on her nametag.

"Evening, Detective. How may I help you?"

Broussard stepped forward. "We have a warrant to search the premises. Is Ms. Wyatt at home?"

Quinton continued to block the entrance. "Yes, she is. May I see the warrant?"

Broussard started to hand it to him, then pulled it back. "Are you her attorney?"

Quinton paused, turned around and looked at Joanne, who was pleading with her eyes. "Yes. I'll review the warrant on her behalf."

Broussard handed it to him and pushed into the room with Officer Avery directly behind him, her hand on her holstered pistol.

After they looked around to make sure nothing was threatening, both gloved up and two other uniformed officers joined them, both male.

Broussard addressed Joanne. "Evening, Ms. Wyatt. This is Officer Louise Avery. We are here with these officers to execute a search warrant. Please remain out of the way."

Joanne, still sitting on the sofa, looked around as if to ascertain whether she would be in the way there.

Broussard and his crew started up the stairs. Quinton pushed air down with his hand toward Joanne indicating that she should stay put, then he climbed up behind them.

The officers began, on the second floor, in the bedroom as if they knew what they were looking for. Quinton followed them and pulled out his cell phone to video the search.

Avery saw what he was doing. "Please turn that off."

"No. There is no law against filming a search. I plan to stay with you during the entire execution of the warrant. There's nothing legal you can do about that."

Avery scowled at him, jerked open a drawer, looked inside, then slammed it shut.

Broussard saw her ruffled feathers. "Just go about your business." Then to Quinton, "As you can see, the search covers the house, any safe on the premises, and the garage. We'll be out of here soon."

Quinton continued to video. "Just what are you looking for?"

Broussard focused on the piece of paper Quinton was still holding. "Read the warrant."

Quinton juggled the warrant and his phone while trying to keep an eye on all searchers. "A handgun, knife or any other weapon, and clothing showing evidence of blood splatter."

"That's correct."

"Why? What's changed? You canceled the meeting. We thought she was clear."

Broussard shrugged. "Your contacts only go so far in protecting little Miss Wyatt. She's now a suspect in the murder of Byron Douglas."

Quinton blanched at the sound of his own name. It seemed a lifetime ago since he'd been called that.

Quinton continued to video. "She didn't know Byron Douglas."

Broussard looked disbelieving. "So you say."

When Avery finished with the dresser drawers, and finding nothing of interest, she went into Joanne's walk-in closet. She looked through dozens of pairs of shoes and took one pair of sneakers, with what appeared to be blood on them, and put them in a large evidence bag. Quinton shot a close-up of the running shoes before and after the bag was sealed.

Broussard ruffled through countless slacks, blouses, dresses, and jackets on the racks in the closet. Also finding nothing of interest, he began to open designer handbags on a tall shelf at the back, looking inside each one, then tossing them on the floor in a heap.

When Broussard had finished searching the handbags and a few pieces of luggage, Quinton said, "No handgun, eh?"

Broussard walked back into the bedroom. "You're pretty sure of yourself. How long have you known your new client?"

"Long enough." Quinton kept filming.

Broussard turned to the officer. "Let's check the living room and kitchen."

Both went back downstairs with Quinton trailing behind. Broussard addressed Joanne. "Please stand over there so we can search the sofa."

She moved into the kitchen, fighting back tears, and Quinton squeezed her hand as she passed him. He continued to record as Broussard and the officer looked inside and under each piece of furniture in the living area. Avery picked up Joanne's handbag from a barstool, dumped the contents on the round dining table, and sorted through the heap with a gloved hand. Joanne stood helpless, looking over the huge quartz island that separated the kitchen from the living and dining rooms.

After they finished, Officer Avery said to Broussard, "Nothing here." She left the purse on the table by the mess.

Broussard moved into the kitchen, and Joanne retreated again to the sofa. She put her head in her hands and appeared to be crying.

Avery followed Broussard's lead and opened each drawer and cabinet in turn.

The officers took all the knives with blades over four inches and put each in turn into separate evidence bags. When they were finished in the kitchen, Avery said, "I think that's all of them."

Broussard looked at Avery. "I agree." Then to Joanne, "Do you have a safe?"

Joanne looked at Quinton who nodded. "Yes, it's in the floor of the hall closet."

Broussard and Avery moved back down the hallway to a door they had opened earlier. Joanne and Quinton followed. "Where is it?"

Joanne pointed to the floor. "Under the carpet."

Broussard removed a square of carpet and a flat wooden cover to reveal a safe with a combination lock. "Open it, please."

Joanne moved around the group and into the doorway. As Quinton videoed, she spun the lock, turning it right, left, right, until the mechanism clicked. She reached for the handle.

Broussard pulled on her arm. "Stop."

Joanne froze.

Officer Avery moved in to take Joanne's place. "Step back, please." She reached down and opened the safe, revealing several envelops, jewelry, some cash, and a handgun. She photographed the contents, then picked up the pistol and handed it to Broussard who sniffed it, then bagged it in a plastic evidence bag. "It's a .38 caliber."

Broussard turned to Joanne. "Any other weapons in the house?"

"No. That's it."

Avery looked at Broussard. "Let's check the garage." He turned toward Joanne. "Where is it?"

Joanne pointed to a door down a short hallway through the laundry room at the back of the kitchen. Broussard passed through, followed by Avery, then Quinton, still videoing. Joanne trailed behind them.

When all six were in the garage, and Broussard had the lights on, the officers began to go through boxes on shelves lining the wall.

Broussard turned to Quinton. "Where are the car keys?"

Joanne responded. "Inside, on the table, but it's unlocked."

Broussard moved around the front of the sleek gray Mercedes sedan and opened the driver's side door. He leaned in and checked the console, the glove box, and under the seats in front and back. Finding nothing, he popped the trunk with the lever under the dash and walked around behind the vehicle.

Quinton grew impatient. "Finish up and go. This is all you're allowed to search and all you've found are a couple of soiled jogging shoes and the handgun from the safe."

Broussard rummaged through the trunk, moving around empty cloth grocery store bags, a tennis racket in a zippered case, and several empty refillable water bottles. Then he found it. In a compartment on the right side of the trunk, wrapped in a Whole Foods shopping bag, was a heavy metal object.

Broussard called the officer over. "Evidence bag, please." He unwrapped the bag, as all four watched, and revealed a sleek black M&P 40 Shield pistol with a hatched grip handle. It was rather large and masculine for such a tiny woman as Joanne, but there was no accounting for individual taste in firearms. "It's at 9-millimeter."

Avery opened and handed Broussard a plastic bag with a grid on the face for documenting chain of evidence. "Same caliber as the murder weapon."

Joanne gasped. "That's not mine."

Avery stifled a laugh at the cliché.

Quinton moved next to his new client as he looked at the phone screen. "Joanne, don't say anything else. Please."

Broussard bagged the pistol and peeled off the sealing strip, then secured the top and handed it back to Avery who took one last look around the garage.

The detective hit the button on the wall and the garage door began to rise. "We'll let ourselves out. Ms. Wyatt, you'll be going with us."

Joanne looked aghast. "No. I didn't do anything."

Quinton dropped the phone in his pocket and took Joanne's petite shoulders in his large hands. He turned her to face him and stared into her eyes. "Don't say another word, Joanne. I'll follow you down to the courthouse. It may take a while before I can see you. Just ask for your lawyer if they try to question you. Keep repeating 'lawyer.'"

Joanne melted into a puddle as her legs gave way beneath her. Quinton had to hold her up and practically carry her through the garage door.

Broussard stopped on the way out and almost spat at Quinton. "I thought the guy was your friend and now you're defending his murderer?"

Quinton helped Joanne into the back seat of the cruiser. "You don't know that's the murder weapon. Regardless, Joanne is no murderer."

"We'll see. Evidence doesn't lie. You should know that, Mr. Bell."

If you only knew, Quinton thought.

———

As soon as she was processed and allowed to meet with her lawyer, Quinton visited Joanne in one of the attorney-client rooms at the jail. He put his hand on hers on the metal table and she did not pull back.

"I'm so sorry, Joanne."

Her face was bare of makeup, and she was in a jumpsuit that sagged and draped around her body like a big orange bag. Still, her classic beauty, high cheekbones, and soft curves showed through. "I feel like I'm in a nightmare and all of this is happening to someone else."

Quinton looked sympathetic. "Let's be careful what we say in here and keep our voices low. It's illegal for them to listen or observe, but you never know who might be breaking the rules."

Joanne whispered, "I understand."

"The police will take a few days to see if the gun in your trunk matches the slugs from the body. If the blood drops on your running shoes are a matching blood type, DNA will take a little longer."

"I told you that gun was not mine, and I don't know how blood got on my jogging shoes, but I run in them frequently. It could have happened anywhere."

Quinton rubbed the day-old whiskers on his chin. "I need to know all the details, but not now. Let's discuss that when we have more privacy." For emphasis, Quinton gestured toward the camera mounted in the corner on the wall. It appeared to be off, but how could they be sure?

Joanne acknowledged the reminder.

"We need to decide how to proceed. I told Broussard that I was representing you for purposes of the warrant, but we should discuss your legal strategy moving forward. I hope we can get you out on bail to prepare for your trial."

Joanne went rigid. "What do you mean? What trial? You're not going to be my lawyer? I thought you were going to help me."

Quinton whispered. "I am going to help you in every way I can. I just don't want to harm your defense if the truth comes out about who was really dead in that motel room."

Joanne whispered back. "How would they find out?"

"We might tell them."

"Why would we do that? Wouldn't you have to leave town?"

"If it means you'd go free, we must tell the truth. I've hidden before. I can do it again if it means you'll escape prosecution."

Joanne turned her back to the camera and whispered even lower. "If we tell, will they then charge me with killing the real Q? Wouldn't that be worse? I did spread hate talk around town about him. I never met Byron, as far as they know. That should account for something. What if they think I knew it was Q and I shot him out of anger or revenge? What if they think I knew about you all along?"

Quinton paused to consider. "I've been thinking it through and I don't believe it would serve your case to reveal the secret, but it must be your choice. I can get you the best attorney in town. Judge Bell will help and make sure you're well represented."

Joanne put her head in her hands. "Oh my God. I don't know what to do, but I know I want you with me. I don't think I can get through this without you."

Quinton pulled her hand down and squeezed it. "I'm here. I want to be with you too." His heart ached for her. "It could still blow up in all our faces."

Quinton represented Joanne at her arraignment hearing where, after the charges were read, she pled, "Not guilty."

The case had been assigned to Judge Blaylock through the lottery system designed to rotate judges and limit forum shopping. Quinton was secretly thrilled, as he and the judge had become acquaintances, if not friends, and Judge Blaylock had assigned several cases to him after Dart Owens' trial.

Quinton and the judge had also bonded over swimming, as Judge Blaylock had excelled at the breaststroke and had tried out for the Summer Olympics during his senior year at the

Colorado School of Mines in Denver, back in the day. He still presented as a strong and impressive figure in his robe on the bench.

To Quinton's disappointment, on the question of bail, Judge Blaylock did not go for Quinton's argument. The prosecutor had described Joanne's extreme wealth and jet set lifestyle showing years of travel posts from her social media pages. Of particular note were those on private islands and villas where authorities would have limited access.

Quinton fought hard, stating that Joanne was needed to help prepare her defense and even offering that she wear an ankle monitor up to and during the trial. Judge Blaylock had a reputation to uphold and a long history of denying bail to those who could readily flee. He did not make an exception, but did offer to entertain the idea of bail again during the trial phase if the prosecution continued.

Quinton knew that future bail was probably not going to happen but did not tell Joanne his opinion on the topic. She looked frail and discouraged enough without taking away that tiny bit of hope.

His heart broke when she was led away in chains.

Joanne's brother, Alcott Wyatt, flew in to assist in her defense, but there was little he could do but offer moral support. The siblings had never been close, with a gap in age and an entirely different attitude toward Houston living. He saw it as provincial and redneck compared to San Francisco. The only things that really united them were history, their last name, and a shared trust fund.

Alcott moved into Joanne's townhouse until she could get bail, but once bail became a long shot, he flew back and forth to

San Francisco. He checked in with Quinton's assistant frequently and offered to come back, at a moment's notice, if he was needed.

———

Quinton went for a swim to get his mind straight around the topic of trial prep for Joanne's defense. He had very little time left to work with her before jury selection and he wanted to make it count. He'd constructed a list of questions and topics for discussion, and the swim allowed him to think those through and strategize how to approach her with each topic.

Joanne was privileged, but smart, and if he outlined the case too clearly at this point, she would see through his agenda and begin to wonder if she could win. He needed her to believe that she could beat the charges and stay positive in her own defense. Not only for herself, but for his precarious position as well.

Earlier, when Quinton had shared the latest with Judge Bell, the judge became angry and reminded him that his was not the only neck on the chopping block if the truth came out. Joanne, and the judge himself, would be harmed as much, or more, than the new Quinton. "You can always hit the road again, but Joanne and I are part of the fabric of the Houston community. Our lives and lifestyle depend on being respected and belonging."

Quinton reminded the judge that he'd become invested in not only Joanne, but in the judge as his father figure and mentor. "Judge, do you not realize how much I've grown to care for you? I'd be devastated to lose you. Joanne too. You're both my family now, along with my new firm. Mo is not only my second chair, but she's also my friend."

Judge Bell looked recalcitrant. "I know. I'm sorry. I'm just nervous about Joanne and her ability to stand strong. When it was only you and me, I felt we could control things, but the more people who know, the harder it will be to keep the secret."

"No one else will know, Judge. Joanne will not tell. It's in her best interest, as well as mine and yours, to keep quiet. I'm just keeping you informed."Although Quinton was more worried than he let on with the judge, he did not think it was likely that anyone else would find out the secret about Q. Even Broussard, after all his investigating, had not realized that the dead body was Q and not Byron. Judge Bell's state of mind was more worrisome. He was flying off the handle more and more of late, and sometimes zoned out when rocking back and forth in his thinking stance.

There were a few loose ends involving the judge. There was the forensic evidence that the judge had handled, and the calls he'd made to the chief of police, in an attempt to protect Joanne, prior to her arrest. But those were buried deep, and no one had a reason to question the fingerprints or be suspicious about Judge Bell's interest in helping his son's girlfriend.

All those involved had too much to lose as a co-conspirator after the fact. That alone should keep them quiet, along with the money Quinton was sure the judge was throwing around and favors he was calling in.

I hope.

24

That night Quinton drove around Houston trying to sort through the mess he had created. He had not felt this much stress since he planned and executed his pseudocide in New York City. It felt like a vise clamping down on his chest and restricting his breathing. He had left Manhattan to protect himself and now he was causing harm to those around him. Joanne was in jail and dangling by a thread. He was equally worried about the impact on Judge Bell if the secret about the switch with Q's fingerprints came out.

What was worse was the next time he met with Joanne, he was going to have to break the news that there would be no bail during the trial. He felt like a heel. Judge Blaylock had held the second bail hearing and ruled that she could be a flight risk because of the trust fund and international jet set contacts. Quinton didn't know if she could survive jail much longer, and he felt deeply guilty. He had caused all of it. Why did he ever come back to Houston and endanger all these good people?

Triggered by the recent events, he felt the pain of the loss of Michael as if it were yesterday. Quinton was unsure whether the Irish mob had read or seen the news about Byron's death in Houston, but if they hadn't, they certainly would soon. After being fooled once, would they take it for granted that Byron was really dead again? Did they kill Q, thinking he was Byron, and if so, had they realized their mistake?

Joanne's arrest was publicized all over the news and online and gossiped about in every bar and restaurant in Houston. There were pictures of her during the arraignment, and of him at the courthouse steps proclaiming her innocence. He was still sporting the Quinton haircut, and of course, the nose and face, but he felt naked and vulnerable as if it were just a matter of time before the mob found him and took him down. Imposter syndrome to the extreme.

Quinton had done all he could do for Joanne until court opened on Monday. It was late Saturday, and he wanted a drink. No, he wanted cards. He wanted to escape into a game and find comfort in betting hand after hand in a rhythm that soothed his tightly wound nerves and jagged soul.

Quinton had previously discreetly asked around the courthouse about local card games under the ruse of research for a client's case. He now knew where the best tables were set and how to get into them. Some were more public than others, and he would avoid the ones where anyone could walk in, buy a membership, and be dealt a hand. Those, he had learned, had been springing up all over town as the statutory definition of a private club had been relaxed. He was told that several of the attorneys he had spoken with often played cards and dice at them. He had found that there were also several private establishments around town. Quinton was concerned that word might get back to Judge Bell, Silver, or maybe even Bob

Sanders, his State Bar liaison. If he were seen gambling, it could put his law license at risk, so, he ran by Goodwill and re-created one of his Reno looks. Since his hair was so short and face groomed, he chose the computer nerd and duplicated closely the khakis, Google cap, glasses, and hoodie.

He drove down Memorial, past the loop, to T C Jester and West Tidwell Road, where he pulled into a small warehouse mall with parking in the rear. There were several dozen cars and trucks in the lot, all fairly high-end, no junkers. He parked, then took off his coat and tie, pulled out his shirt tail, and put on the rest of his new disguise.

He entered a business labeled *Spades Animal Boarding* and went into the empty reception area. The PI who'd told him about the place had given him specific instructions about how to enter. He continued through a room with wire cages and into a short hallway that led to a metal door in the rear. The business did smell like wet dogs, but the cages were empty, and there didn't seem to be any animals being boarded at the time.

Quinton tapped on the metal door and two eyes appeared behind a small rectangular plexiglass window. Quinton held up his fist then a peace sign with two fingers, and the owner of the eyes opened the door. Quinton was allowed to enter and, without speaking, was directed into a large room with five green felted tables, all occupied with men and women playing Texas Hold'em. A sign on the wall said: *Dog House Poker Club.*

"Thanks."

"Good luck."

He chuckled and looked around, but gladly, didn't see the private investigator who had told him about the place.

The room was sparse, but clean, with no frills. Generic elevator music was playing a familiar tune without the words. Something by the Rat Pack? No, it was Andy Williams's "Moon River." Quinton let his eyes adjust to the low lighting, found an open spot, and sat down. He placed ten one-hundred-dollar bills on the table in front of the dealer, who swapped the money for ten chips. Quinton nodded at the other players, and a waiter offered to bring him a drink.

"Beer. You have Saint Arnold in the bottle?"

"Yep."

Quinton did his usual slow buy-in until he had assessed the players at the table, then began to bet more heavily. The pressure eased as he became engrossed in the cards, chips, tells, and hands. For a short while, he didn't think about his former life as Byron, or the mob, or Joanne, or Judge Bell. The escape was freeing, and his stress diminished.

25

Quinton and Mo met on the thirty-ninth floor of the law firm to strategize the trial of Joanne Wyatt. Neither were very upbeat, and strictly business was the attitude of the day. They had less than a week until they would pick a jury. Judge Blaylock had established a deadline for pretrial motions which would expire in less than twenty-four hours.

Quinton took a big swig of coffee and turned to Mo. "How have you done on the suppression research?"

"Not great. As you know, the top legal grounds for the suppression of evidence start with unreasonable search, i.e., conducted without a warrant."

Quinton nodded. "Not applicable here."

"Right. Next, we have the police obtaining evidence in violation of the suspect's rights to a lawyer. Not so good on that one since you were there videoing the whole search."

"Yep. Go on."

"The suspect was not properly Mirandized. That one

doesn't work either, since that's the first thing they did at Joanne's door when they arrested her."

"Right. We're running out of legal grounds."

"I know. Hang on. Door number four is police failure to preserve the chain of custody of the evidence. I don't see that working here."

"Neither do I. What's left?"

"Lastly, and maybe our best shot, defective warrant."

"I don't know. So many lawyers have tried that. Maybe it works, maybe not."

Mo looked at the file in front of her. "It's a long shot, but this is different. Usually, the warrant has errors on the face of the document, such as the names and addresses. The warrant in this case listed the garage, not the car. Now, the car was in the garage, and the gun in the car, but technically, the warrant did not list the car."

"So, maybe we argue that the search went beyond the scope of the warrant?"

"It's all I could come up with. Failure of the warrant."

Quinton was quiet for a moment. "Okay. Let's prepare a brief. We could trot it out there and see if Judge Blaylock buys it."

"If he does, the case is over. They only have this one piece of real evidence."

"Right, the rest is all circumstantial."

Mo waited for Quinton to consider the plan.

"Worth a shot. Let's file the motion."

26

Quinton and Mo went to see their client in jail to break some bad news. When they convened in the attorney work room, the first thing Quinton noticed was Joanne's emaciated condition. She was handcuffed to a ring in the metal table. He bent over to hug her, and she felt like a skeleton.

In regular clothes in court, he had not clearly seen how much weight she'd lost, and with no makeup, her cheekbones and jawline stood out sharply on her sunken face. Both attorneys sat on the opposite side of the table with Quinton directly across from Joanne. "How are you holding up?"

Joanne looked at him and then at Mo. The couple's unspoken language said: *Be careful what you say in front of Mo.*

Joanne smiled weakly. "I'm doing a little better now that you're here. It's tough in court, not being able to hug you or hold your hand."

Quinton took her hand across the table and held onto it.

Joanne looked across at her co-counsel. "Hi, Mo. Good to see you, too."

"Hi, Joanne." Mo smiled then shrank back like a third wheel to give them a moment.

Quinton began. "We came to talk strategy and make some decisions about the trial."

"Okay."

"Tomorrow, we're going to try to have the gun evidence suppressed because of the wording in the warrant. It's a long shot, but if we're successful, that's the ballgame."

"You mean I'd be freed?"

"Yes, but it's not likely. I don't want you to get your hopes up."

"What about bail? Didn't the judge say he would revisit bond before the trial began?"

"I'm afraid we have some bad news."

Joanne looked stricken. "I don't know how much more I can take."

"I know. I'm so sorry, but the judge has denied bail during the trial."

"Oh no. Please."

"I know. I know."

"You don't know."

"One small bit of good news, we will be allowed extended time here to prepare for the trial. I will be here every hour that is allowed for work. Mo will come with me when her schedule allows." That was code for: *We will have time alone.*

Mo turned to Quinton. "Can we bring her some edible food?" Then to Joanne, "I bet you can't eat the shit in here."

Joanne perked up a tiny bit. "That would be so helpful. Some fresh fruit or maybe a salad. Everything here is cooked to mush."

Quinton jumped on the bandwagon of positivity. "Yes, absolutely. I'll bring something for you every time we meet. I'll also talk to the judge about extra fresh air time outdoors."

"I'd like to see my brother, if he can get back to town."

Quinton squeezed her hand. "Absolutely."

Mo suggested further, "We'll see if we can get you a tablet to read the documents we'll be filing. We can also load it up with books that you can read at night."

Quinton gave her an encouraging smile. "We will get your mind and health restored in any way we can."

Joanne tried to smile. "Thank you."

Mo opened her briefcase to get their work started. "We need you as strong as possible to help us prepare for the trial."

Quinton smiled. *Thank goodness for Mo.*

27

At the firm, Quinton climbed up the internal staircase and met with the partners of Jamail, Powers & Kent in the fortieth-floor conference room. The three women were already seated, and no one was smiling or enjoying the view of downtown. Mo partially hid behind her coffee cup and avoided eye contact with Quinton.

Silver started the meeting. "Quinton, we invited you here today to talk about the publicity the firm has been getting surrounding the Joanne Wyatt murder trial. When we brought you on as an associate, we knew there would be criminal law down on your level, but we thought there could be some separation between the civil floor and the criminal floor. We didn't expect to have news outlets calling here from opening until closing and at night after hours."

Quinton nodded. "It comes with the territory. By definition, criminal trials attract a lot of attention, especially when an iconic Houston family's fair-haired daughter is accused. This is what you hired me to do."

Buffy smiled her angelic smile from her round, friendly

face. "Well, we did, and we didn't. We needed someone to pick up the small white-collar crime cases and client transgressions. We didn't expect to have the tail wagging the dog. Your case has taken over most of the daily resources of the firm."

Quinton interrupted. "Our case. Joanne Wyatt and her family trust have paid a substantial retainer to the firm."

Mo came out from behind the cup to participate in the conversation. "That's true, and in all fairness, I've seen you in court and you are really good at what you do."

Buffy continued. "My point exactly. The firm has always been associated with business law and civil work. Now, our reputation is changing. Regardless of your high level of expertise, our other clients are not happy with the direction things are moving."

Quinton bristled. "I've gotten several of the firm's clients out of hot water since I've been here. They weren't complaining then."

Silver responded. "True, but we outsourced that work before you arrived and had a bit of distance from the criminal law side of things."

"It should all calm down when the trial is over."

Silver considered. "Yes, but what about the next case? We assume you are going to continue to pursue these criminal cases in the future."

Quinton sipped his coffee to give himself time to think. "I understand. I can't pull out of the case now, and yes, this is the type of law I came here to practice. I'm not some renegade intentionally harming your image. In New York, this type of case is actively sought after."

Mo looked up. "New York? What does New York have to do with Houston?"

Quinton realized his mistake and changed tactics. "Just a figure of speech. So, what would you have me do?"

Silver looked at Mo and Buffy and measured her words. "Of course, you have to see this through. No judge would allow you to withdraw at this stage of the case, even if we wanted you to, which we don't. Going forward, however, we're going to need to reevaluate how this impacts all of us."

"I understand. And, for now?"

"For now, we are placing a second receptionist here, on the fortieth floor, and she'll be directing all the incoming calls and correspondence related to the criminal cases downstairs to your floor. Your part-time assistant will go full-time for now and juggle all the calls for you. That should get us through the trial; then we can decide what to do after that."

Quinton knew it was probably the end of the line with the firm. His one-year anniversary with the firm would arrive soon after the trial, and his State Bar liaison, Bob Sanders, had given him every reason to believe he would be off probation on schedule.

He'd have a chat with Judge Bell, but he needed to start making plans as soon as the trial was over. He hated relying on the judge so much, as he was just starting to feel some independence from him, but he needed to stay in Judge Bell's good graces and get help from him in designing a plan of action.

He hoped he'd survive to need a plan. He would have laughed at the irony if it weren't so dangerous.

28

The next morning, Judge Blaylock heard the pre-trial motion on suppression of the gun evidence. Both Quinton and Prosecutor Wallace stood before the judge at the bench who rifled through the supporting brief before him.

"I'm a bit disappointed in you, Mr. Bell. Isn't this becoming your theme song? Cops can't get the warrant right?"

Wallace suppressed a chuckle.

Quinton cleared his throat. "Well, Judge, if the shoe fits ..."

Judge Blaylock leveled a look at Quinton that said: *Knock it off.*

Wallace started to speak.

"Wait your turn, Mr. Wallace. This is defense counsel's motion. Let's hear it, Mr. Bell."

"Thank you, Your Honor. As you can see from our motion, we assert that the search of the trunk of the defendant's car went beyond the scope of the warrant. It was technically a warrantless search."

Mo clasped her hands, almost in a prayer position.

Quinton continued. "As you can see, the search covered Ms.

Wyatt's home, any safe on the premises, and the garage. There is no mention of the car. The police should have had the car listed on the warrant, or added the car to the warrant before they opened the trunk."

Wallace looked flabbergasted. "So she'd have time to dispose of the evidence?"

"I said wait your turn, Mr. Wallace. Continue, Mr. Bell."

The prosecutor was fuming.

"She could not have disposed of the evidence because she was arrested and taken to jail."

The judge gave Quinton another admonishing stare. "Now, Mr. Bell. You know the reason she was taken to jail was because they found the gun in the trunk."

"Regardless, Ms. Wyatt's Fourth Amendment rights were violated and the gun evidence should be excluded."

Judge Blaylock turned to the prosecutor. "Your turn now, Mr. Wallace."

"Thank you, Your Honor. Courts have held that if a warrant covers an item that could fit in a particular container, then that storage vehicle can be searched. It's obvious that the gun could have been in the safe and, therefore, it was searched. It also could have been in the car, and that search is valid as well."

Quinton tried to interrupt. "You had your turn, Mr. Bell. I'll allow you to rebut after Mr. Wallace makes his point."

"Yes, sir."

Wallace added. "If Your Honor is seriously considering granting this motion to suppress the gun evidence, there is the exception of consent. Ms. Wyatt was in the garage with the police officers when they searched it and in response to their request for a key, she told them the car was unlocked."

Judge Blaylock looked at Quinton. "Anything further?"

"Yes, Your Honor. That is not consent. That's a statement of a fact in response to their request to violate her Fourth Amendment rights."

Wallace became animated. "Hardly, Your Honor. This is a trick by Mr. Sleaze here to try to circumvent the law."

Judge Blaylock frowned. "Watch it, Mr. Wallace. Keep it civil."

"Yes, sir."

The judge held up his hand for both to be quiet. "I see you've quoted Knowles v. Iowa in your brief, Mr. Bell. The Supreme Court did rule in Knowles that police officers cannot search a car during a routine traffic stop. That case is not exactly on point here, because law enforcement is allowed to conduct a warrantless search of a vehicle if the probable cause standard is met. Now, this is a parked car, searched during the execution of a warrant, which gets us to a higher standard, as the probable cause has been deemed existent by a judge signing off on the warrant."

Mo's shoulders dropped.

"In addition, there is de facto consent by Ms. Wyatt when she indicated to the officers that the car was unlocked. Therefore, the search was valid, did not violate the defendant's Fourth Amendment rights, and the gun is in."

"Preserve the objection, Your Honor." Quinton knew he wouldn't get the ruling overturned on appeal, but best to keep the record complete.

Judge Blaylock nodded at the court reporter. "So be it."

Wallace called to Quinton as the two defense attorneys left the courtroom. He caught up with them in the hall on the way to the elevator. Mo hung back and listened.

"Now that the gun is in, don't suppose Ms. Wyatt would

consider a plea bargain?"

"I don't think so since she's done nothing wrong, but I'll be glad to take your offer to her, as I'm required by law to do so."

"How about voluntary manslaughter, maximum fine, and fifteen years."

"That's not much of an offer."

"Okay. Maximum fine, since I know your client won't blink at that, and ten years."

"You must not have much faith in your case if you're willing to deal capital murder down to ten years."

Wallace scoffed. "I'm very confident with my case. You have forty-eight hours."

Quinton and Mo got into the elevator. Mo turned to Quinton. "What do you think?"

"I don't think she should do time for a crime she didn't commit."

"I know, but if she's convicted of capital murder, she could be facing the death penalty or life in prison."

"I'm aware, but if Wallace is willing to plead, he must not feel like he has a conviction in the bag."

"I know, but is she aware of how long her sentence could be?"

"Yes, she's aware. She's hanging her hat on the fact that she didn't know Byron and she didn't kill anyone. I'd like to talk to her alone about this if you don't mind."

"No problem. I've got plenty of work to do back at the office."

Quinton went to visit Joanne and was led into the same attorney meeting room that they'd been in so many times.

"Hello, Joanne. How are you holding up?"

"Not so great. I'm trying, but I keep slipping into depression."

He held her for a long time. "I asked Mo to let me visit alone today. I thought you might need this."

"It feels wonderful. Will we ever be together again?"

"I'm counting on it. Let's sit down."

The two sat at the metal table in their usual spots and Quinton took her hand in his.

"The prosecutor has offered a plea bargain."

"Why is that?"

"It's pretty common before a case gets fully rolling. Saves the taxpayers some money and ensures a guilty verdict. They count those over there like baseball stats."

"What's the offer?"

"Voluntary manslaughter, maximum fine, and ten years. You'd be under fifty when you got out."

"Fifty. No. No."

"I'm not recommending it, but we should discuss it. Capital murder carries the death penalty or a life sentence if you're convicted."

"But I won't be. You said they can't prove I knew Byron, and there's no motive."

"I know, but they aren't required to prove motive and anything can happen in a trial."

"Do you think I should take it? I can't go to prison for ten years."

"The only reason I'd recommend it is if you committed the crime and are afraid more evidence will come out."

"That won't happen because I didn't kill him. You know that's true, don't you? Do you think I should take the plea?"

"No, I think we should fight like hell, but it has to be your fully informed decision."

"No. No, I won't do it."

29

Quinton went for a swim at the gym and thought through the complaints that the firm had made in their meeting. He knew something was going to have to give soon. He wondered how the firm would feel about their image if the world knew he wasn't who they said he was. Maybe it was best if he did move away from the three lovely women. They had helped him when he needed it, but this whole thing could blow up and get all over them. The firm would surely be hurt if his secret came out and it could happen at any time, now or in the future. He hoped never, but it might be out of his control. What control? He felt that he had no control at all.

Quinton let the topic settle for a few more laps and decided he would discuss it all with Judge Bell. He wanted to slowly bring him around to the idea of separation from the firm. It might be a good idea if there was a bit of distance between himself and the judge, too. He was extremely grateful to Judge Bell for all he'd done for him, but the judge was getting clingier and more involved in Quinton's personal life every day. He called frequently and before the trial had asked intimate questions about his and Joanne's relationship.

The judge had even dropped by Quinton's apartment, unannounced, a couple of times after work. Most of the time, the attention and camaraderie were welcome, but occasionally, it felt downright creepy, especially the touching. Quinton recalled Judge Bell frequently putting his hand on his shoulder and calling him 'Son' in a way that felt invasive and inappropriate. It was more like a gesture of ownership, as if the judge had him in his grip.

Quinton had represented several women in litigation in New York who had described such a feeling to him during the course of trial prep and on the witness stand. They had spoken of the indignity of unwanted touching by men in their workplaces and the invasion of questions that were too personal. He thought he'd understood it before, but now it really hit home what they were communicating to him.

When he finished his swim, he was physically fatigued, but his thoughts had not settled and his mind was racing. It was rare that swimming didn't adequately do the job of calming and organizing his thoughts, but today, it was a miss. There were too many conflicting needs by too many people in his new life. Each deserved to be addressed, but, as a single man, he was not accustomed to putting others' needs ahead of his. He had always been single-minded, with succeeding for his client his only goal, and by way of meeting the client's needs, meeting his need to win at the same time. Split objectives did not play well in his mind. He went home, after a shower, with a bag of burgers from Beck's Prime and a six-pack of Saint Arnold beer from Midtown Market.

So much for rehab.

During the weekend break from the trial, and after a long Saturday of trial prep, Quinton drove by the Dog House Poker Club. The pressure was closing in. The swim had not taken the edge off, and he was looking for a game and some relief. The parking lot was packed, but his gut told him not to go in. He couldn't afford to take the chance of being seen, no matter how much he craved a card game. He couldn't go to the local legit clubs either, for the same reasons.

Tua Dannon could have the entire gambling community on the lookout, just like in Reno, and, although he clearly looked more like Quinton than Byron, any small thing could give him away. A gesture, a stray comment, meeting the wrong person at the wrong place and time.

What would be worse was if Judge Bell found out he was gambling and drinking. He was supposed to be maintaining the facade of a rehabilitated Quinton, on the straight and narrow. The judge would not be pleased to learn that he had risked their plan for a stupid card game.

He pulled into a parking spot and debated his options. He took out his phone, opened the map app, and checked the distance to Kinder, Louisiana, home of the Coushatta Casino Resort. It was less than three hours. Perfect.

He grabbed a Venti Starbucks at a drive-through for the caffeine, drove east out of town, through Beaumont and Lake Charles, and arrived at Coushatta just after 10 p.m. He parked in the garage and pulled on a Galveston Fishing Club ballcap from his collection.

He opened the casino website and took a quick look at the poker room rules. Pretty standard: table stakes, max of three raises, rake at ten percent or less, English speaking only, and so forth. All good. He walked up to the big glass doors and entered a sanctuary just like the others he knew so well. The casino had a huge central floor filled with machines, bars, restaurants, and gaming sections. Slot machines jingled as he passed through the main room and into the cards area, wondering if the machines were as loose as advertised.

He went into the poker room at the back and scoped the tables for a good seat at a no-limit Hold'em table. A blonde dealer with a nice smile and admirable assets caught his eye, so he joined the players at her table and exchanged twenty one-hundred-dollar bills for chips.

Quinton smiled at the dealer, tossed in the ante, and peeked at his two down cards. By the time the dealer laid the river card, he took a deep breath and began to feel better. He played all night, breaking only once for food and another time for the bathroom. His chips went up and down for most of the night, then finished tall as the sun came up.

He headed back to Houston about nine on Sunday morning. He needed sleep before going back to court on Monday, but he had settled his nerves and had added about three thousand dollars' profit to his pocket. He liked winning. He liked it more than just about anything, except the process of getting to the win. That was his favorite part, when he was in the thick of it and not sure which way it would go.

Loved it.

30

In New York, Dannon and Devlin had a strategy meeting at their warehouse office at the docks on the Hudson River. A printout of a *Houston Post* online article was on Dannon's desk, featuring a photograph of Quinton and Joanne in front of the Harris County Courthouse.

Dannon tapped the page with his perfectly manicured finger. "Why did we buy Byron's death in the Hudson, and how did he wind up dead in Houston?"

Devlin grunted. "Our contacts at the NYPD were convinced, as was Cronin. As you recall, I didn't totally buy the drowning back then and I'm not going to buy this murder story now without checking it out."

Dannon looked displeased. "I thought you were keeping an eye out just in case he surfaced somewhere."

"Yeah. We've had feelers out for him. That's how we came across the article. This guy, Quinton Bell, is Byron's best bud from high school. Maybe he went down to ask him for help."

"Okay. Let's get some eyes on him and see where it leads."

Devlin stared at the pic. "Good idea. Also, you know Byron

liked to gamble. Maybe he gave up the game, maybe not. We can check out the Houston gambling scene as well. See if he has been shooting off his mouth about anything."

"This means the guy discovered by the kid in the hotel room in Reno was probably Byron after all."

"Probably so." Devlin pointed at the page again. "This report came to our attention from one of our affiliates in Texas."

Dannon considered. "I guess we need to get someone down to Houston to work with them. Who is this Joanne Wyatt person and why would she kill Byron? This attorney, Bell, says she's innocent, but all lawyers say that."

Devlin looked at the picture of Joanne and Quinton. "If we didn't kill Byron, and this woman didn't kill him, who did? If he's dead." Devlin stood up. "If one of our guys took him out, without permission, he knows what will happen to him. I want to go down there myself. Put an end to this once and for all."

Dannon looked at Devlin and considered doing without him for a while. He had become more guarded than ever after Killian Tyrone's conviction and the aggressive pursuit by the RICO prosecutors. He also knew that Devlin didn't tell him everything and, so far, he assumed it was in his best interest. Now, he wasn't so sure he could believe that Devlin hadn't followed Byron to Houston from Reno and had killed the lawyer himself, or more likely, had someone follow and kill him on his orders. Dannon finally released his gaze.

"Okay, go down to Houston and sort it out, but get back here as soon as you can."

"Right, Boss."

31

At the office, Quinton took off his jacket, hung it on a hook on the back of his office door, loosened his tie, and dropped down in his chair.

Mo sat down in a guest chair opposite him and kicked off her shoes. "Whew, what a day. That's better. Joanne seemed to be improving a little."

"Yes. Having her brother, Alcott, here for a visit shored her up a bit."

"Let's shore me up. I'm starving."

"Me too. I've ordered delivery from H-town Noodles in Chinatown. While we're waiting, let's go over the alternative theories of the crime. I want to have at least two possible murderers to accuse."

"Just pick any old son of a bitch and trot them out there?"

"No, just pick a likely alternative suspect and test it out between us to see if it works. There's a difference."

"Hmm." Mo opened her laptop on her side of Quinton's desk and set up an Excel spreadsheet for listing alternatives to

Joanne as the murderer. The email notice on Mo's computer kept dinging an alarm that new email had arrived.

"Would you shut that off? It's distracting."

Mo quit email. "Happy now? Who's first?"

"Let's start with the Dannon Irish mob in New York. They already tried to kill Byron once, so it's not so farfetched to believe they'd try it again."

"Okay, got them on the list. Weakness in the argument is how they would know he was here. And, how did they find him at the motel?"

"True, and why would Byron be in Houston?"

Mo considered. "He was from here. Maybe he was looking for help? Maybe even trying to contact you or his father."

"We were longtime friends, and I would have helped him if he'd asked."

What Quinton didn't tell her was that Q was the one who was killed, so why would the mob go after him, knowing he wasn't Byron? It was an alternate theory, but one that didn't truly make sense. That was the great thing about alternate theories, they didn't need to make sense, just cast a shadow of doubt on the prosecutor's case.

"Biggest problem with this alternate theory, no evidence."

"Right. We don't have a witness to put up on the stand. I've left messages for the detective in New York who investigated Byron's disappearance, but no return call."

"Let's keep trying." Mo typed abbreviated comments into the spreadsheet's cells. "Who's next?"

"Let's put my Houston drug gang in there."

"Why? How would they even know about Byron?"

"I don't know. Maybe they thought I was helping him. Maybe he'd gotten into drugs and was trying to score."

"That's farfetched, but if he needed money, maybe."

"Right. Put them on the bottom of the page as a possible. Let's just spitball everyone who knew Byron."

"If you say so. If you're going to brainstorm everyone, how about Joanne, Judge Bell, and even you?"

Quinton laughed nervously. Of course, if Mo knew he was Byron, she could include all of those names on the list.

The noodles arrived and the famished two slurped and talked with their mouths open.

Finally, Quinton wiped his chin. "Sorry, bad manners."

Mo slurped in one last long string of noodles. "Me too."

She laughed and returned to the spreadsheet. "This doesn't make any sense. Our only real alternative theory is the Dannon cartel."

"I agree. Byron was on the run from them, so they must have found him."

"Right, and they aren't above planting evidence in Joanne's car and would know how to break into her garage without leaving a trace."

"Easy for convicted felons."

"Right, and it would be helpful if we could prove some of the members were here in Houston." He agreed for the sake of the case, but in no way did Quinton really want any Dannons in Houston for any reason.

Regardless of what he told Mo, Quinton had decided it was time to hire an investigator to look into Q's old gang and ascertain whether they had any involvement in the murder to either rule them out or start working that angle as an alternate theory.

He needed someone he could trust and who would get their hands a little dirty. Someone who could infiltrate the group without being suspected of spying. He also wanted to know if all was forgiven and if he was in any danger from them. He knew Judge Bell had paid them off, but grudges sometimes outweighed money.

He dialed Dart Owens' number and found it still working. "Hey, Owens, how's it hangin'?"

"Quinton Bell, you old dog, glad to hear from ya. It's hangin' long and loose." Owens laughed at his off-color joke. "When are you gonna start callin' me Dart?"

"Right now." Quinton recalled that Owens had not ratted out his former boss in the course of his trial and dismissal. As defense counsel, he was obligated to honor his client's wishes, but he had gone beyond that. He had kept Dart's secret. He hoped that might give him a leg up in gathering intel for Joanne's trial and for his peace of mind. "Any chance you're looking for work these days?"

"Diggin' ditches or runnin' drugs? That shit's off the list."

Quinton laughed. "Nothing illegal or that will cause you to break a sweat. I need you to snoop around my old drug gang and see who had it in for me enough to want me dead."

"Dat might be a long list."

"Well, you did say you owed me a favor, any time."

"What kinda idiot would say somethin' like dat?"

"My favorite kind of idiot."

"Now you talkin' trash tryin' to get on my right side, but you did good on my case so I hear you out."

"I need an investigator for the case I'm on. I have a theory that I can share with you, in person, once you're on the payroll for the defense. It's about attorney-client privilege and all that."

"Payroll? How much you gonna pay me?"

"My client will fund about a thousand a week until we get what we need, or when the trial is over."

"Dat's a lot of money."

"You in?"

"Maybe. What you want?"

Quinton met with Dart Owens at This Is It Soul Food, downtown on Blodgett. They settled in and ordered before they got down to business. The smell was too enticing to wait. When the food arrived, they tucked their napkins in at their necks, and Quinton dug into his fried catfish and okra and tomatoes, with a side of pimento cheese. Dart had ham hocks with lima beans and a double portion of macaroni and cheese. A bowl of steaming hush puppies and a brick of butter sat between them for sharing.

Dart eyed the pimento cheese. "How you eat dat cheap shit?"

"Love it. My mother made it for me all the time when I was a kid."

Dart smeared butter all over and shoved a hush puppy into his mouth. "You sho' you ain't black?"

Quinton munched a chunk of catfish. "I'm black on the inside. I really missed this food when I was gone."

"Where were you?"

"Oh, you know. Rehab and all that." Quinton would have loved to share the history of his many visits to Sylvia's in Harlem for fried chicken and greens.

"Yeah. Sho'. So, what's the big secret you wan' me to work on?"

"I need what's called an alternate theory of the crime in the Joanne Wyatt case."

Dart laughed. "I'm fresh out of alternate theories."

"Me too, so I'm trying to find one. I'm thinking that just maybe one of my old gang buddies thought Byron Douglas was me and killed him. It's the first place to look for a suspect. He had one of my old IDs on him."

"Hmm." Dart chewed slowly, but didn't blink.

Quinton had no intention of introducing the mistaken identity of Q as an alternate theory. But, if the drug gang had gone after Q and killed him, what if they thought they had killed the wrong guy and came after him? He was calling himself Quinton Bell. Or worse, what if they knew it was Q they killed and, therefore, had deduced Byron's secret identity? What if they had connections to the Dannons? His mind swam in the what-ifs. He needed to know what was going on in the seedy part of the world. Maybe Dart could find out.

If the gang had not killed Q, who did? Was Joanne guilty or innocent? He needed to know if she could actually have killed Q. If she was innocent, did Joanne think that Quinton had done it? Was she going through the trial to protect him? This had occurred to him more than once in the course of his representation of her.

Both men ate quietly for a moment, then Quinton said, "I have reason to believe that Byron might have made contact with someone in the drug world for some reason, same as he called Joanne from his motel."

"Why don' you just call the number and see who answers?"

"The burner phone was taken by the killer, so there's no way to trace the calls Byron made. The only reason we know he had a burner, or borrowed phone, is because he called Joanne and asked to get together with her. The police traced her phone backward to a burner, but no number. Also, Joanne told us that she received the call. No calls were made from the motel room phone, and Byron did not have a phone registered in his name."

Quinton didn't tell Dart that the caller had identified himself as Q.

"So, you wan' me to snoop around on our ol' gang buddies and see if any of them confess to murderin' yo' lawyer friend?"

"Something like that."

"You know how dangerous dat is?"

"I do, but I also think you're a smart guy. I think you can do it without calling attention to yourself or getting caught."

"There goes that jive talkin' again, tryin' to play me."

"No. I'm trying to get you to help me and my client. I have a healthy budget to spend, and I think you'd be the last person the gang would guess might be an investigator for a law firm since you didn't rat out your boss during your trial. It makes you a loyal gang member. No offense."

"No offense? You sayin' I don' look like a lawyer?" Dart laughed.

Quinton laughed too. "I bet you clean up nice, but I haven't met a lawyer as big as you are in my entire legal career."

"I bet. Let me snoop aroun' a little. If I think I can help you and your client, I'll take on the work."

"Thank you so much, Dart, and this stays between us."

"Then, we be even. Right?"

"Right."

32

Devlin flew from LaGuardia into George Bush Intercontinental Airport and was met at baggage claim by Shay Griff, a high-ranking member of the Houston Irish Mafia, or HIM, as it was called. He was a cousin of one of the Dannon gang members. There were no Dannons in Houston, only loose affiliates with the same corrupt goals and Irish connections, especially to drugs, shipping, and legal and illegal gambling.

Devlin could have rented a car, but why mess with that and parking when he could have someone drive him around for a change. He'd certainly driven Tua Dannon around New York long enough. It was his turn to be spoiled, and besides, the local gangs would be offended if he had refused the hospitality. He'd flown first class, in one of his best gray suits and monogrammed shirts, and felt like a big shot around Griff.

When they walked out to the curb, Griff's driver pulled up and hopped out to open the hatch of the big black SUV. Griff placed two suitcases in the hatch. "Devlin, this is my little brother, James Griff. We call him Jimmy." The two shook hands.

Jimmy opened the back door on the driver's side for Devlin, and Griff went around to the passenger side. When Griff slid in beside Devlin in the back seat, the entire SUV tilted, then settled, with the red-bearded Irishman's bulk. He took out a pack of Marlboro and offered one to Devlin. "Smoke?"

"No thanks."

As they headed into Houston proper via the Beltway and Interstate 45, Devlin said, "I want to get some info on this Quinton Bell lawyer. I need to find out if Byron met with him before he was killed and what he might have told him."

Griff nodded. "Easy enough. What else?" Griff flipped open a Zippo and lit up.

"I'd have someone check around the gambling places and see if Byron was hanging out in any of them. He had a serious love of poker tables."

"We can do that for you."

"I've got a guy who might have run into him in Reno. I'll have him come in and do it. He'll get better intel and faster."

"Okay. Where to? Hotel or courthouse first?"

"Let's get down to the courthouse. I want to get a sneak peek at the players before I settle in. Can we be a fly on the wall? I'm not ready to declare my presence just yet."

"No worries, we can slide in the back behind the reporters. There should be a boatload of them there today. Joanne Wyatt is a big socialite in town. Every news outlet around will have someone there covering the trial."

Devlin rolled down the window just a crack to air out the smoke from Griff's cigarette. The air felt swampy in the Houston humidity. "Perfect. Did you get those crime scene photos of Byron Douglas?"

"I'm working on it. I'm sure the prosecutors will show them

in court, but my usual sources haven't leaked them yet. Some judge is supposedly keeping a tight lid on them along with the autopsy report."

Devlin frowned. "Disappointing."

Griff blanched as white as his pale Irish skin would allow. "I'll get them. Just need another day or two. Today they're just picking the jurors, so we have some time before the jury is set and sees the evidence."

Devlin grunted.

Jimmy drove Devlin and Griff downtown, to the Harris County Criminal Courts building on Franklin Street. Griff placed his pistol under the seat of the SUV. "Can't get through the metal detector with that."

Devlin looked at the gun. "Right."

Jimmy dropped them at the door and went in search of parking.

Griff laughed. "He might be circling for a while."

Devlin laughed too. "Nothing like New York parking, I'll bet."

The two went inside and followed the crowd coming back from lunch to the fourth floor and the 180th District Court. As promised, the courtroom was a zoo, and they were able to find standing room only in the back behind a wall of reporters and onlookers. Devlin peeked between two reporter's hair-sprayed heads and sized up Joanne and Quinton.

Devlin didn't recognize any of Quinton's features or mannerisms as Byron's, but why would he? He had barely seen him in NYC. Tyrone might have known the difference, but he was dead and gone, thanks to Tua Dannon and the Portensky brothers.

Joanne was brought in by Bailiff Grant and sandwiched between Quinton and Mo at the defense table. The aggregate value of clothing, shoes, and jewelry on the three of them was close to a quarter of a million dollars. Quinton had not been sure how that would play with the jury and had reminded Joanne to plan on something understated for Mo to pick up from the townhouse. But even in her classic cream-colored suit, simple jewelry, and French twisted hair, money and prestige dripped off Joanne like honey from a comb. Her Stuart Weitzman shoes alone cost several thousand.

Prosecutor Derik Wallace strutted around in front of the jury like a peacock. He liked to win almost as much as Quinton, but he was an honest Christian man and truly believed the evidence pointed to Joanne Wyatt for the murder of Byron Douglas. He had carefully considered the file presented by police detectives, including Broussard, before bringing charges. His goal today was to pick a fair and impartial jury that would listen intently to both sides and reach a just verdict.

The second set of potential jurors were in the box and Wallace was conducting voir dire. Both Quinton and Wallace were seeking four more jurors and alternates, as they had finalized eight from the first set that morning.

With Judge Blaylock's permission, Prosecutor Wallace walked up to the jury box and asked his first question. "Have any of you formed a conclusion as to the guilt or innocence of the defendant? If you have, please raise your hand." If someone wanted off the jury, here was their chance to try, but no hands went up.

Quinton had been lucky to draw Judge Robert Blaylock again for this trial. He had been in his courtroom several times since the Dart Owens trial and had a growing respect for the magistrate. The feeling was mutual as Judge Blaylock had referred more and more cases to Quinton as he gained confidence in his ability. Judge Blaylock knew that Quinton was Judge Bell's son, but Quinton didn't believe he let that influence his decisions surrounding the referrals or outcomes in his courtroom involving the attorney or his clients. The judge was a straight arrow who believed in an eye for an eye, but also a fair fight.

As voir dire continued, Prosecutor Wallace asked about a dozen more standard questions, then turned to Judge Blaylock. "Pass the panel, Judge."

The judge turned to Quinton. "Your turn, Mr. Bell."

Quinton picked up his legal pad and took his place before the jury box, feeling as if he'd stepped into his favorite pair of shoes. "Prospective juror number twenty-three, how long have you resided in Houston?" The usual questions were asked and answered until both prosecutor and defense attorney were out of questions. When the challenges were all made, dismissing undesirable jurors on both sides, the attorneys were equally happy and unhappy and the jury was empaneled. Judge Blaylock set the calendar for the remainder of the trial, shutting down any protests from the lawyers.

In the back, Devlin had seen enough and gestured to Griff that he was ready to leave. Quinton had never turned around to look, so he did not know that the Dannon mob had come to town.

33

Quinton parked his Audi in the underground garage at his apartment building and went up the elevator to his unit. He was popping in for a quick change of clothes and a shower before heading back downtown to the jail to meet with Joanne, discuss the jury decisions, and take her some dinner.

He was running late, in a rush, and fuzzy headed from all the details that were swirling around him from the day in court. He needed a swim and would have really enjoyed a break from the Houston heat, but it would have to wait. He looked around for his jacket, grabbed it, but in his frazzled state forgot to grab his briefcase.

When Quinton came back down and walked into the garage, Detective Broussard was leaning over and looking in the Audi. The driver's window was broken and glass was scattered all over the concrete below.

Broussard straightened up. "I turned off your alarm."

"What happened?"

"You had a break in. Your neighbor reported it. Got the call about ten minutes ago."

"Couldn't a patrolman handle this? They have you on street duty now?"

Broussard laughed. "This is special treatment for you. You're on my notice list. I put you at the very top."

Quinton walked around the car, looked inside, and then addressed Broussard. "Where's your sidekick, Avery?"

"You'll see Avery in court soon enough."

"Thanks a lot. Who broke into my car?"

"You tell me. Some random stranger? Big coincidence don't you think?"

Quinton looked pensive.

Broussard waited for an answer. "Well?"

"Well, what?" Quinton knew exactly what Broussard wanted to know.

"Anything missing, smartass?"

Byron did a mental check of what was in the car. Clothing that might or might not be a disguise, which he wasn't worried about, but he had broken one of his cardinal rules. He had left his getaway briefcase on the back seat containing his laptop, extra ballcap and sunglasses, a change of clothes, and his gambling money, a banker's bag with ten thousand in cash. He was kicking himself. He had gotten too comfortable in his new life.

Quinton had wiped his browser history clean on the laptop, as he did every time he went online, and had no emails connecting him to his life as Byron, but the bag also contained a small notebook with everything inside written in code. It was the banking information of his offshore account and number for Lyle, the guy from the ferry in New York, who had arranged his fake credentials, and miscellaneous other contacts in the event he needed to run again.

All the information was written in an amateurish code with one digit off. Four for three, five for four, and so on. The names were a code word to remind him who the phone number belonged to. He had the bank account numbers memorized, but the rest of the information was now lost.

"Looks like my briefcase with my extra laptop is gone."

"What else?"

"Maybe a law book or two. Sweatshirt. Ballcap."

"Anything else?"

"Nope, I don't keep sensitive files and client information in my car."

Fuck me. I shouldn't have left that briefcase in there, either.

The security cameras for the building later showed a hooded man, probably young, who avoided showing his face and went only for Quinton's vehicle. There were a lot fancier rides in the garage than his Audi, but the thief had gone straight to his car and back out the way he'd come in through a metal gate.

What worried Quinton most about the break in was who would know to look for it. He doubted it was a random snatch and grab.

Who was watching him and why?

That night, Devlin, Griff, and Jimmy watched the Houston Astros play the New York Yankees on TV in Devlin's hotel room at The Lancaster with the AC blowing full blast. They were lined up on the only sofa, each drinking a Lone Star long neck, and Griff was munching on a can of peanuts from the mini bar.

Devlin was in a foul mood. "You know those peanuts cost ten dollars."

Griff looked down at the tiny can. "No way."

"Yeah, beer's five bucks a bottle out of that little fridge."

The game was tied at five-all at the seventh inning stretch. It stalled for a while with strike outs and foul balls, then the Yankees hit a home run, brought in four players, and won the game at nine to five.

Devlin swore. "Damn. About time."

Griff and Jimmy, who were rooting for the Astros, had stayed mum until the last inning when the Yankees won.

Griff smiled a fake smile. "You know, Minute Maid Park is just a few blocks from here. We can get tickets while you're in town."

"Maybe." Devlin moved to the edge of the bed, dumped out the contents of Quinton's Tumi briefcase, and looked at Jimmy. "Did anyone see you grab the case?"

"Nah. I was in and out of the garage in no time. Had my face covered for the cameras."

Devlin sorted through the notebook, cash, clothing, and cap. He folded the cash and put it in his pocket, then handed the laptop to Griff. "You have someone who can break into this?"

"Sure. Let me get somebody on it."

Devlin rifled through the paper notebook, but it only had a few entries that looked like they might be phone numbers. If they were, they didn't have any area codes he recognized. Odd names, too.

"Nothing here that makes sense. What do your guys say about Bell's law firm?"

"Seems like a normal workplace. No criminal clients going in and out. Mostly a lot of banker types and too many lawyers."

"Any FBI or cop types?"

"Not that we've seen. Should I leave them on it for another few days?"

"Yeah, can't hurt, if you've got the manpower."

"No sweat."

"Let's see what that laptop holds ASAP."

"Will do." Griff handed it to Jimmy who exited the hotel room, leaving the two gangsters to finish their beer and study the notebook.

34

Dart drove across town to the Steel Anchor Bar on the edge of the Houston Ship Channel. It was a rough area filled with oily jeans, hardhats, and blue collars. He felt right at home until he crossed over the threshold of the Anchor and saw a large group of members of his old gang sitting around high-top tables and shooting pool nearby.

"Hey, Dart! Long time, no see." Big Slick Warwick tipped his ballcap in Dart's direction.

"How's it goin', Big Slick?" Dart smiled, but inside his stomach churned.

"What you doin' down here?" Big Slick picked up a green cube and chalked his pool stick.

"Been missin' you guys." Dart laughed.

"Wanna shoot a round?"

"Sho. Let me get a beer." Dart put a dollar on the side of the pool table to indicate he was next in line for a game, then walked over to the bar and ordered a bottle of Budweiser. He walked back to the pool table, swigged his beer, and set it on one of the high tops. The other gang members moved over from the other tables and formed a circle around Big Slick and Dart at the pool table. Redeye, the big thug who had gotten Q hooked back in the day and talked him into getting the Q tattoo on his neck, looked at Dart with suspicion. Big Slick racked the balls and Dart broke, sending a stripe into the side pocket.

"You've got the big ones," Big Slick said as he walked around the table to the cue ball and lined it up on a solid. He pulled the stick back, but before he pushed forward to shoot, he looked up at Dart and held his gaze. "Way you disappeared, we wondered about you." CRACK! Big Slick let the stick fly.

Dart smiled a nervous smile. "I been layin' low waitin' for the law to get tired of watchin' me."

"That so."

"No need to bring the heat on the whole gang."

Big Slick looked appreciative as did several of the other gang members.

"You did right by us, so you're welcome here any time."

"Thanks. You don' never need to worry 'bout me."

Big Slick seemed to relax.

The gang members went back to their drinks and private conversations, and Dart felt a little better about the room. Redeye kept an eye on Dart from a distance.

"I hired Q as my lawyer. He been around lately?"

"You've probably seen him since we have."

"Yeah, he's all straight now. Mr. Quinton Bell. Got back in good graces with his daddy, the judge."

"Good for him, as long as he stays mum like you did."

"He told me he can't remember anythin' from the time he was strung out."

"You believe that?"

"Mostly, yeah."

Big Slick walked around the table examining it for his next shot. "Q's daddy, the judge, paid off his debt. We got no beef with Q, but you know nobody gets out of the gang alive."

Dart laughed as if it were a joke, but he wasn't sure if the double meaning was about Q or a warning to Dart.

Big Slick didn't laugh. "You need some stuff?"

"No, I can't take a chance sellin' anythin' right now, and I'm off it too."

"Good. No sense using up the profits."

Dart intentionally missed on his next shot, and Big Slick took another turn.

Dart laughed. "You hear anything about the lawyer from New York that got hisself killed? It was Q's buddy from school."

Big Slick looked around the room at the gang and laughed. "Yeah, we heard."

"Any idea who sliced him up?"

"Heard it was that blonde chick, Joanne Wyatt."

"Maybe, but maybe it was the New York Irish takin' another shot at him. Those Dannons got lots of friens around the world. I wonder if you know 'em?"

"Maybe we do and maybe we don't. Why do you care if I know them?"

Dart lowered his voice. "Maybe you did somebody a favor?"

"You're asking a lot of questions. Why do you want to know?"

"Quinton was worried you might have been sending him a warnin' by knockin' off his frien'. I wanna make sure we good so that don' happen to me or none of my friens." Dart was making up nonsense on the fly, but it seemed plausible enough, he hoped. Sweat popped out on his forehead.

Big Slick looked at Dart with suspicion. "No, we didn't, but if we did, you think we'd tell you or him about it?"

Dart laughed and took a long pull on his beer to steady his nerves. "Guess not." He missed his next shot at the corner pocket, and Big Slick cleared the table.

35

Quinton approached the courthouse on the opening day of the murder trial of Joanne Wyatt and saw a full-blown media circus before him. Every national news network and news outlet in the area had a reporter ready to interview anyone with a pulse. Content was king, and trials were a juicy source for dramatic material.

When a reporter from a local outlet shoved a microphone in Quinton's face, he waved it away. "No comment."

Once inside, courthouse security ran Quinton's briefcase along the belt of the x-ray machine and directed him through the scanners, allowing him to escape the throng who were unable to enter and secure a seat.

Inside the courtroom, the trial was well attended with reporters ready to summarize every word for their readers and listeners of their articles and podcasts. Judge Blaylock called the room to order. Joanne was brought in to sit between Quinton and Mo, the jury was empaneled, and the judge signaled the prosecutor to begin opening arguments.

Prosecutor Wallace, in his best Sunday church suit and

striped tie, stepped up to the box to make his opening pitch to the jurors. "Your Honor, ladies and gentlemen of the jury. Good morning. Thank you for being here and for giving your precious time to honor the long tradition of civic duty in our judicial system. Today, the people are trying Joanne Wyatt for violations of the Texas penal code, involving the willful, deliberate, first-degree murder of Byron Douglas. The people will prove beyond a reasonable doubt that Joanne Wyatt killed poor Byron Douglas with planning that is called malice aforethought. We will do so by calling to the stand witnesses who will make this assertion clear."

Joanne stirred in her seat, and Quinton placed his hand on her knee under the table. Her face appeared calm but her skin was pale and he could feel her trembling.

Wallace paced back and forth before the jury. "First, you will hear the testimony of Clive Broussard, an unbiased Harris County police detective, who was called to the crime scene at the Top Value Motel in north Houston. Detective Broussard will testify as to the condition of the murder scene, the body found there, and the subsequent investigation in search of the perpetrator of the crime, involving old-fashioned police work."

The jury was locked onto Wallace's every word.

"Detective Broussard will also testify, along with his partner, Officer Louise Avery and others, that a warranted search was conducted in the home of Joanne Wyatt. Such search uncovered a gun in the trunk of her car that was later identified through ballistic testing as the murder weapon.

"Several witnesses will be called to establish that Joanne Wyatt was in the vicinity of the motel where the murder took place, a far distance from her home or any other logical destination requiring her presence in the area. A waitress at a coffee shop will testify that the defendant was waiting for someone for over an hour and, when that person didn't show, she stomped out of the restaurant in anger."

The prosecutor held the gaze of each juror and allowed the information to sink in.

"Lastly, we will call the medical examiner of Harris County who will testify that not only was the victim, Byron Douglas, murdered in the aforementioned motel room, he was brutally mutilated and grossly disfigured postmortem, proving that the defendant fully intended the death of the victim and that she lashed out in anger against his dead body."

The collective jury sucked in a gasp of air at the drama before them as the prosecutor delivered his final line while pointing a finger at Joanne. "Today, the people will prove, beyond a reasonable doubt, that Joanne Wyatt is guilty, guilty, guilty."

Joanne jumped, causing Mo to jump. The spectators around the room rumbled and Judge Blaylock pounded his gavel. "Any more outbursts and I'll clear the courtroom. I'm sure your TV networks would not appreciate that." Then, he turned to Quinton. "Mr. Bell, would you like to present opening arguments?"

Quinton stood, a tall striking figure in one of his new navy-blue suits from Judge Bell's Galveston shopping spree. "Yes, Your Honor. Thank you."

Quinton had spent the prior night working on his opening argument and, after a midnight swim, felt he had thought it through and was ready for anything Prosecutor Wallace could launch his way. Mo had taken a quick look at his opening that morning and sent a couple of notes. He had to admit that being back on the battleground, since the Owens trial, was exhilarating. He felt a similar surge of energy to that he felt at the poker table, but much stronger.

"Proceed, Mr. Bell."

Quinton walked over to the jury box, knowing it was the

only time during the trial that the attorneys would be allowed to get this close to them, not through a witness or from the lawyers' tables. He looked into the eyes of each juror, then spoke directly to them.

"Ladies and gentlemen of the jury. I, too, wish to express my gratitude for your service here today and your willingness to listen with unbiased minds until the full story is laid before you. My opening today will be short because I plan to show you through facts, not assertions, the innocence of my client. Now, the prosecution would have you believe that Joanne Wyatt is guilty of a crime as heinous as murder but, during the course of the trial, we shall prove otherwise."

The jury was equally enraptured with Quinton's tale.

"First, we will also question, on the stand, Detective Broussard who will testify that during the search of Ms. Wyatt's home, she was open and cooperative. He will also testify that the murder weapon was not found in her home, but in her garage in her unlocked car, accessible to anyone with a motive to enter."

Joanne's skin turned pink again, and she appeared relieved to have someone taking her side, but the jury was fixated on Quinton.

"Next, we will call to the stand witnesses who will explain the circumstances under which Byron Douglas left New York City and came to be in Houston. The prosecution will not be able to prove that Joanne Wyatt ever met Byron Douglas, much less murder him, because she did neither. We will show you who really had a motive to kill the victim and what that motive was. And, there will be more. There will be so much more that you will have no choice but to find Joanne Wyatt not guilty, no matter how many times Mr. Wallace may repeat it."

What Quinton did not tell the jury was the fact that he himself was Byron Douglas. He hoped his theory and plan to create reasonable doubt about Joanne's guilt would not backfire and bring in his past. New York seemed far away, for now.

Hope is sometimes a dangerous thing.

During the next few days of the trial, the prosecution, true to their word, trotted out Detective Broussard and Officer Avery, a county ballistics expert, and Dr. Melvin Engle, the medical examiner. When the ME testified, he showed a series of photos of the crime scene, with splashes of blood around the room, and photos of Byron Douglas, who was almost unrecognizable due to the mutilation of the body and swelling of the corpse. Fortunately, Detective Broussard testified that Judge Bell had identified the body. Quinton was glad that Judge Bell did not have to appear and lie under oath. He also testified that follow up fingerprint testing confirmed the victim as Byron Douglas.

This testimony was not lost on Devlin, who was once again seated with Griff and Jimmy in the rear of the courtroom. It went a long way toward convincing Devlin that Byron Douglas was indeed dead. Devlin leaned over to whisper to Griff. "That bastard better be dead this time."

During the identification testimony, Quinton's skin crawled as he realized how powerful Judge Bell was to orchestrate that bit of evidentiary magic, and he was terrified that whoever had helped the judge pull it off could one day surface and spill the beans.

Quinton and Judge Bell had agreed it would be best if the judge did not attend and show himself at the trial. First, it would appear as if daddy was watching his son's first-grade play, and second, it would keep Broussard wondering just how close the judge was to the victim and Joanne. Lastly, Quinton had developed a good relationship with Judge Blaylock, and he didn't want him to be distracted or self-conscious with the oversight of another judge in the room.

Quinton asked that his cross-examination of the medical examiner wait until Monday morning, as it was late on a Friday, and he wanted to curry favor with the jury. He also didn't want the photos to remain on the screen any longer than was necessary before the break.

Judge Blaylock agreed and adjourned court for the weekend.

36

Over the weekend, Quinton and Dart met in Memorial Park. Quinton was already sitting on a park bench when Owens walked over from the parking lot nearby. Both were sweating in the humidity.

Owens wiped his brow with his arm. "Could you pick a more crazy place to meet up? It's over a hundred degrees out here."

"It's not the heat, it's the humidity."

"So, they say."

Quinton laughed. "I was getting worried that the soul food joints might draw some of the old gang. I don't want anyone to see us together."

Dart sat down beside him. "Well, I guess dat makes sense."

Quinton smiled. "You said you had some new info for me?"

"I nosed aroun' a little then wound up shootin' some pool with Big Slick at the Anchor."

Quinton made a mental note to look up the Anchor. "Yeah?"

"No one said they knew anything about yo' boy, Byron, except Big Slick. You remember him?"

Quinton was caught off guard. "Not really."

"I know you was dealin', so where you get your sale weight if it wasn't from Big Slick?"

Quinton squirmed a little. "Different people who worked for Big Slick. I know who he is, I just don't remember being around him that much."

Dart had a strange look on his face. "Hmm."

Quinton moved the conversation forward. "What did he say?"

"Says yo' daddy paid off all you owed him when you first came back to town."

"That's true."

"He say you off his books and out of his life."

"What about the murder at the motel?"

"Big Slick say he heard about it but had nothin' to do with it."

"Could he have been helping the Dannons?"

"He say he had no reason to help the Dannons. He barely knows 'em."

"Do you believe him?"

"Don't know fo' sho', but it felt right about the Dannons. Not sure about you. It's not generally accepted to leave the gang. I'm walkin' a fine line myself."

"I understand."

"I'm probably not goin' to find out anythin' else without making a stink. I think you safe, for now anyways. You sho' there's nothing else you wanna tell me? You know I can keep a secret."

"No. Let's let it drop for now. Keep your eyes and ears open and let me know if anything surfaces."

"Will do, Q."

"I asked you not to call me that."

"Right. Sorry."

After the weekend break, the circus began again with the murder trial of Joanne Wyatt. The courthouse was buzzing with regular business, which was heavy as usual, plus the added chaos of the trial which was covered most by media in the last decade.

Quinton headed toward the courtroom door, bumping his way through the throng. Everyone seemed to be in a rush to get somewhere, mostly to the Joanne Wyatt trial for a good seat. Unseen by Quinton, his co-counsel, Mo, assisted by a strikingly tall woman with cropped purple hair, hobbled off the elevator on crutches and down the same hallway toward the courtroom. Mo was careful not to slip on the shiny marble floor or bump into any attorneys, witnesses, or defendants.

Quinton, who was just going into the courtroom, held the door for Mo and her purple-haired friend. "What happened to you?"

"Tangled with an unhappy horse. Quinton, this is my partner, Abigail Page. Abby, this is Quinton Bell."

The two shook hands. "Nice to meet you, Ms. Page."

"Please, call me Abby."

The three slowly made their way to the defense table. When Mo was settled, Abby left after a quick goodbye.

Quinton looked at Mo. "Horse? Are you serious?"

"It's just a sprain. It'll be fine in a couple of days. I barrel race on the rodeo circuit. It's a hobby that sometimes gets out of hand."

The two opened their briefcases which were sitting on the table. Mo tried to get comfortable, and Quinton started unpacking his files.

"I'm still a little shocked. You were really in a rodeo over the weekend?"

"No. I keep a horse near Dayton. I go out there regularly and practice for the events. I usually don't have any trouble, but my horse has been ailing, and the vet can't put his finger on the problem."

"Are you pulling my leg? Rodeos and ailing horses and barrel racing. Not to be insulting, but I'm not sure I believe you."

Mo was exasperated with Quinton's disbelief and the strain of getting to court. "What don't you get? The horse was ailing and threw me off. Don't you remember, it's Houston. Texas? We rodeo here. A lot. I like to ride and I often win my events. Practicing law is not the only thing I do."

"Okay, okay." *I guess I was in New York too long*, he pondered.

"I thought you'd be more surprised that my partner is a woman."

"That's none of my business, and why would I be surprised?"

Mo smiled. She was sitting back in her chair causing Quinton to turn back toward the courtroom to see her face. That's when he saw Devlin, at first out of the corner of his eye, then when he repositioned himself, in full view, just to make sure. It was him alright, trying to be low-key, sitting in the left corner of the room in the back row behind a gaggle of reporters and lookie-loos. He was whispering with a red-headed guy who looked like Irish muscle. Quinton was careful not to catch his eye.

Mo stopped smiling. "You look like you've seen a ghost."

Quinton turned, looked down, and opened a file. "All good here."

He didn't have time to dwell on Devlin, because Joanne was brought in and the bailiff called the room to order. After Judge Blaylock settled the room and started the trial for the day, Quinton looked back again, and the two gangsters were gone.

It was Quinton's turn to cross-examine the medical examiner, and a lot of effort had gone into preparing for the questioning.

"Dr. Engle, you testified on direct examination that after the victim was shot, the corpse had been mutilated in two places. Correct?"

The doctor straightened in the witness box and focused on Quinton. "Yes, after the shooting in the back, the body was dismembered in part, the head removed, and a small cut and scrape on the thigh."

Quinton grimaced. "Now, you said the thigh wound may or may not have been a previous wound. Correct?"

"That's correct."

"So, let's focus on the head and neck wound."

"Okay."

"The murderer took a few parts of the body with him, is that correct?"

"Yes, part of the neck and shoulder, two fingers, and parts of the thigh muscle were missing from the scene."

"Do you have any idea why the perpetrator would take parts of the body?"

"They may have been taken as trophies, or they may not have come to the lab from the crime scene."

"Did you examine the body at the crime scene?"

"No, I only did the autopsy. Another doctor was on duty at the time of the discovery of the body. It's highly doubtful that the parts were misplaced, but I was not there so I cannot testify to their disposition."

"Okay, so the body parts may or may not have been taken. Why would someone cut up a corpse?"

"Most likely, she intended to move the body in smaller pieces in order to dispose of it. Maybe she was interrupted or didn't have the stomach for it."

"Or he?"

"Or he."

"In your experience, Doctor, are men or women more likely to desecrate a body?"

"More men than women, but there is the exception."

"Were you able to examine the instrument that was used in the mutilation?"

"No, it was reported not to have been left in the Top Value Motel room. Regardless, it was not brought to the lab."

"Now, you testified that the gun was a 9mm. Did you develop a theory with regard to what type of knife was used?"

"Yes, it was most likely a professional butcher's knife."

"So, Dr. Engle, this was not a chef's knife like one used in the average home for preparing dinner? This was a specialty knife used by butchers to cut meat?"

"Correct."

"Why could it not have been a military or tactical weapon like a ka-bar knife?"

Dr. Engle looked at the jury to explain. "A butcher's knife has a curved blade that allows butchers, hunters, and professional chefs the ability to get under the skin and around bones. The ka-bar is usually straight and shorter. It often has a jagged edge whereas a butcher's knife has a long smooth edge from hilt to tip. Plus, butcher's knives tend to be super sharp, thick, and made of heavy-duty steel. Most have textured handles to prevent slipping."

"Now, Dr. Engle, where would one find such a knife if they wanted to purchase one?"

"The most popular butcher's knives are made by Wusthof, Dalstrong, Mercer Culinary, and Victorinox. They're sold at specialty shops and high-end kitchen stores."

"And, based on your experience, which knife do you think was used to mutilate the victim?

"Probably the Wusthof."

"And that's a very expensive brand, correct?"

"Yes, their eight-inch Artisan butcher knife is about two hundred dollars. The blade curves in and then out like the hip of a woman. That's what allowed us to identify it as the most likely weapon."

"Is this the type of knife someone would go to a fancy cooking store to purchase, like Williams Sonoma or Sur La Table?"

"Correct. It would not be carried at Walmart or Target." The doctor chuckled at his joke, then regained his solemn demeanor.

"Okay, so we have a fancy knife that can only be purchased at a fancy store or be in a fancy kitchen, a restaurant, or butcher shop. Right?"

"Right."

"As far as you know, did the police search Ms. Wyatt's home for such a knife or a set of knives that would have this particular blade included in the set?"

"Yes, they did search, and no, they did not find such a knife or a set. They brought several knives, but not this particular knife or brand to the lab for testing."

"Okay, so after they came up empty on the knife from Ms. Wyatt's home, as far as you know, did the police visit the fancy stores in the Houston area that carry the Wusthof Artisan butcher knife to see if one had been purchased recently by my client, or anyone else for that matter?"

"Yes, they did."

"And?"

"No evidence of a purchase by your client was found, and others who had made a recent purchase were cleared by alibi or other circumstances."

"Thank you, Dr. Engle. Now, one last thing, with apologies

to the jury for the graphic questions. Was the mutilation of the victim jagged and sloppy or professional and surgical?"

"It was very neat and tidy, almost like filleting a pig."

Female juror number four made a small gasping sound.

"And who would be able to make such neat and tidy cuts?"

"Someone with butchering experience, such as a professional, a hunter, or trained military or militia personnel."

Quinton looked over at the pale and petite little Joanne Wyatt for emphasis, then at the jury. "No further questions."

After the trial wrapped for the day, Quinton met with Joanne in the attorney-client meeting room. He placed his briefcase on the metal table across from her and dropped down hard in the chair.

"The mob is here. They've found me."

Joanne looked startled. "What?"

"I saw a guy named Devlin in court today. He's Tua Dannon's right-hand man from New York. He's the guy who chased me down to the Staten Island Ferry and sent his goons to finish me off."

"Oh my God. Are you sure it's him?"

"Positive."

"How could he know you are Byron? You look nothing like your pictures from those days."

"Maybe he does, maybe he doesn't. But he's here for some reason, and Byron is the only thing that makes sense."

"Maybe they think Byron shared some sensitive information before he died, with you or me, or the cops for that matter."

Quinton scratched his chin. "Or, maybe it's a case of fool me once, shame on you; fool me twice, shame on me."

"What do you mean?"

"Maybe they want to make sure Byron is really dead this time."

Joanne's big green eyes got even bigger. "You're scaring me."

"I'm scared myself."

"Maybe you better leave town. I don't want anything to happen to you. Could you hide again? What would occur at the trial if you left and Mo took over?"

"If I disappeared, it might cause a mistrial or Mo would have to find another first chair. She's not capable of handling a full-blown murder trial. And the Dannons would start to chase me again. They'd either guess that I'm Byron or that Byron told me enough to make me want to hide."

"I didn't think of that."

"But it's a moot point. I'm not leaving you." He took her hands in his. "I caused all of this, and I have to see it through. I'm not running again."

"If you stay and they kill you, it will be worse than if you disappeared, and if they identify you, I'll still be tried for killing Q. They'll just say I knew he wasn't Byron and I was in on the whole charade with you and Sirus. There's just so much evidence against me. Even more if it's Q who's dead."

"I know, but Judge Bell would be charged too, for tampering with evidence and probably worse. I'd be abandoning him as well, after all he's done to help me."

Joanne hung her head. "It all feels so hopeless."

Quinton realized he was tending to his needs more than hers and needed to prop her up. "Don't give up. We are going to find a way out of this mess. The momentum always shifts. It looks bleak now, but don't forget your second wind. I'll find a way around or through." He looked into her eyes. "I promise."

What Quinton didn't tell her was that he didn't know for sure that he would find a second wind, or a way out, or even that she was innocent. He was in love with her and his instinct was to defend her, but for all he knew, she'd killed Q and made up the story she'd told him. He knew from long experience with his fellow man that on any given day, anyone was capable of anything and everyone lied at some point.

On another level, Quinton knew in his heart if he left the practice of law this time, he'd never get another chance to be in a courtroom and he'd always be alone. He thought back to those days of loneliness and fear in Reno. Always being on guard and not trusting or knowing anyone. Moving from one card game to the next in more disguises than he could remember. He didn't want to go there again. He gambled that between his courtroom skill and Judge Bell's connections, they would find a way.

37

Quinton met with Judge Bell for fajitas at Ninfa's
Uptown on Post Oak, one of their favorite restaurants
in Houston. The eatery was a Texas icon as was its
owner, Ninfa Rodriguez. The fajita recipe was originally a
Mexican ranch hand dish from the 1930s, but Ninfa made it
popular when she opened her restaurant in the early 1970s.

Quinton was seeking a sounding board for strategizing the
predicament with Joanne, as well as an understanding father
figure with whom to sympathize about the Dannons. The
tequila and comfort food wrapped in fresh tortillas were also
desirable.

Quinton wanted to know how his sister in California was
doing. She had decided not to attend the trial after gentle
coaxing from Judge Bell and was communicating with him
regularly to keep abreast of the progress on the prosecution of
Byron's murder.

Quinton took a scoop of guacamole. "How is my sister
doing? Is she distraught?"

The judge took a sip of his margarita, then looked at Quinton. "She's doing alright. I've told her I don't think Joanne Wyatt is guilty and that we may never know who murdered Byron. She seems to be getting used to the idea of moving on without closure. It's been so long and drawn out, I don't think she has much choice."

Quinton rubbed his eyes. "Thank you. Please let me know if anything changes with her."

"I will."

Quinton took a slug of margarita. "Now for some bad news. Tua Dannon's right-hand man, Seamus Devlin, is here."

The judge looked startled. "Didn't you bury the lead? What is the mob doing in Houston?"

"Obviously looking into Byron's death. Devlin and some goon were in court watching."

"You may be able to use this to your advantage. Proof that the mob is in town and could have been here earlier to kill Byron. It's a tight rope to walk between the two viewpoints."

"I've thought of that, but don't see a clear path yet."

"How is the trial going? Is Joanne going to keep the secret that you're not Q?"

"She's become very invested in keeping quiet. She knows her best bet to win at trial is if the victim is Byron and not Q because she'd never met Byron and had no beef with him. Plus, she really wants me to defend her. The only way I can do that is if we keep the secret between the three of us."

The sizzling iron skillets of flank steak, peppers, and onions were served and the two grew quiet until the waiter left. Judge Bell reached for a fluffy flour tortilla. "And?"

Quinton took a big whiff of the steam coming off the entree and his mouth watered. "And, she loves me. The only hope of a future for us is if I remain Quinton."

Judge Bell grinned. "Thought so. Now, the question is how

to exonerate her at trial with all the damn evidence pointing to her as the murderer."

The judge wrapped steak, onions, and peppers in a tortilla, smeared it with guacamole, and said, "Anyone could have accessed her car, as it was in the garage and always unlocked."

"Right, and when it's boiled down to the basics, they only have that one piece of physical evidence, the murder weapon from her trunk."

The judge swallowed and washed it down with the icy beverage. "There is the issue with the phone call from Q at the motel to her mobile and the witness testimony from the coffeeshop where they were supposed to meet."

"Right. They've obtained her phone records and found a call from a burner in the area earlier that day. They have no proof it was from the deceased, but it adds to the circumstantial evidence. We haven't decided how to handle that. Why would Byron have called her if they had never met?"

The judge agreed. "No proof they spoke, since the burner phone was missing, and no calls were made from the motel room. Right?"

"Exactly, and the prosecution hasn't introduced motive. In fact, they've skirted motive in all the testimony from every witness. I don't know what they have up their sleeves, and I can't imagine what motive they could attribute to her, since she didn't know Byron. They've given us no discovery at all about motive. No witnesses, no documentation."

"Right, but what if they are assuming she knew Byron because she knew you and me, as Quinton?"

"That could be the play, but if they're going to bring that in, they better step it up. Of course, they don't have to prove motive at all, but I've never seen a murder conviction without one, either express or implied."

"Neither have I."

Quinton scratched his chin. "A tougher issue is opportunity."

"How so?"

"They're asserting opportunity because she went to the coffeeshop in the area and she has no alibi. We know Q didn't show, but unless Joanne testifies, they'll never know that, and she sure as hell isn't going to testify that she was going to meet him. The waitress can verify that she was there, but it doesn't connect her to Byron, only to the general area."

"Right. She could have been waiting for anyone, or no one. Just having a cup of coffee. She didn't answer any questions about where she was that night, did she?"

Quinton swallowed a big bite. "No, she repeated 'lawyer' just like I instructed."

"Smart woman."

"We caught a break on the blood on her running shoes. Thank goodness they found it to be animal blood. She could have picked it up on a run in Memorial Park, or anywhere for that matter."

Judge Bell patted his chest as a small burp popped out. "Excuse me. All sketchy and circumstantial except for the gun. Can you get the gun excluded from the trial?"

"I've asked Mo to do some research. It wasn't Joanne's pistol. She has a .380 Ruger, and Broussard took it from the safe when they searched her townhouse."

The judge wiped his hands on his napkin. "But it begs the question, if she had a safe, why wasn't the murder weapon in it?"

"And, if she had a gun, why didn't she use it instead of the 9mm?"

The judge rocked a bit. "They might assert that she was planning to get rid of the 9mm and hadn't done so yet, or maybe she didn't believe she'd be connected to the murder and was careless."

Quinton licked the salt on the rim of the margarita glass and took a big gulp. "That doesn't sound like the Joanne Wyatt I know. But, of course, murder doesn't seem her style either. We'll have plenty of character witnesses to say so, but that still leaves the gun in her trunk, pointing straight at her as the perpetrator. They have no proof that she bought the gun, or that it belonged to anyone she knows."

"And no fingerprints."

"No, but the gun was wrapped in a cloth bag. Easy to remove prints with it or explain how they may have been rubbed off, or she wore gloves. The prosecutor has already used that excuse at trial. Since there were no fingerprints or physical evidence at the motel, the murderer obviously used gloves there."

The judge pushed his plate away and began to rock harder, back and forth, in thinking mode. "What if we can show the connections Q had to his old drug gang? What if they thought Byron was Q and shot him?"

"True, but that's a double-edged sword. It would call more attention to me, maybe even trigger a DNA test."

"I have that handled, along with the fingerprints."

Quinton swallowed a mouthful of fajitas. He wanted to ask how the judge had handled that but didn't really want to know.

The men had avoided the elephant in the room, but Quinton finally said it. "What if she knew it was Q, was angry that he stood her up again at the coffeeshop, and in a rage, killed him?"

Judge Bell nodded. "I've thought of that, I must admit, but the killer had a gun, something to cut up the body, and the motivation to make it happen."

"True, and the crime scene lends itself more to a gang slaying. It's not a female trait to mutilate a body like that."

The judge looked stricken at the thought of his son's body being desecrated.

"Sorry, Judge. This is starting to make me dizzy."

Judge Bell patted Quinton's arm. "It is a merry-go-round of information, Son. I think your best bet is to assert that someone else did the crime and planted the gun in Joanne's unprotected car. It wouldn't be that hard to break in."

"Right. I've hired an investigator, Dart Owens. Remember him from the trial in Judge Blaylock's court? The one that I got off on self-defense?"

"Right. Is he an investigator?"

"No, but he knows Q's old gang, Houston like the back of his hand, and seems very sharp about people. Has good instincts. I just want him to check and see if any alarms go off that would cause us to question Q's old gang as the murderers."

"Good idea."

"So, the murder suspects are Q's old drug gang here in Houston, the Dannons from New York, and Joanne, his disgruntled ex-girlfriend, but no one knows that but us."

"Can't think of anyone else, can you?"

Quinton tilted his glass and drank down the last of his margarita. "Well, now that you mention it, me. If it comes out that I'm not really Quinton, that I had access to Joanne's garage and car, and I didn't want it revealed that I'm still alive, I'm a better suspect than Joanne. The police could come after me."

"That's not going to happen, Son. Remember? We were together at your office all that night." The contrivance gave little comfort to Quinton.

"Right. Right. What better alibi than a sitting judge."

38

Devlin and Griff sat in a booth at Dot's Coffee Shop, near the courthouse, and pored over a manilla folder with twenty-three eight by ten glossy pictures with 'Byron Douglas Autopsy' stamped on each one. Some photos were of the torso with parts attached and others were of the head, hands, and loose flesh.

When the waitress approached, Griff flipped the top picture over to hide the rest. She was wearing a too-short skirt for her age, a polka dot apron, and dark rouge on her cheekbones. She handed the men a couple of menus. "What can I get for y'all?"

Devlin pushed the menu away. "Coffee for now."

"Same."

"You got it, Darlin'."

The men waited for her to finish the pouring ritual and leave, then Devlin returned to the photos. "It could be him. There's really no way to be sure, the face is so swollen."

Griff agreed. "It could be anybody."

Devlin pulled out the autopsy report and scanned it. "Anybody that was male, fit, tan, over six feet, with brown hair and blue eyes."

Griff took a sip of the acid brew and jerked. "Coffee's hot. Was Byron Douglas fit, tan, over six feet with blue eyes?"

Devlin avoided the coffee and set down the report on the table. "Yep."

Griff flipped through the rest of the documents he'd brought. "Says here the fingerprints were those of Byron Douglas. Confirms the ID."

"So, it does. Any luck on the laptop?"

"Nothing there. Just some lawyerly stuff that doesn't seem to be confidential. Research and such."

"Email?"

"Bunch of lawyers' email addresses and the contact list has offices, restaurants, gym. Nothing about Houston or Quinton Bell. No New York Byron Douglas. It's looking more and more like Douglas is really dead this time."

Devlin was almost gleeful. "Yes, it does."

39

Quinton and Dart took a short walk along Buffalo Bayou on Allen Parkway, leaving their cars in the Texas heat in the parking lot. As always in July, it was sweltering with the high humidity. Quinton was reluctant to involve Dart further. He sensed Dart's suspicions about him, but he didn't have anyone else he could call on for help.

"I've got another assignment for you."

Dart wiped his forehead with his handkerchief. "Okay, but this is the last time I'm meetin' you outside."

"I'll figure something out for a better meeting place. For now, I need you to sniff around the local gambling places and see if a Dannon member named Devlin is still in town. There's also been a big, red-headed, Irish-looking thug with him in the courtroom. Find out who he is and what they might be up to. Be very discreet. They are dangerous."

Dart got out a small pad and pen and jotted down a few notes. "Okay. What am I lookin' for?"

"Mostly general info. There's another Irish-looking guy, a kid, about twentysomething. Light strawberry-blond hair. He's a real card shark and won't be too far from a poker table if he's in Houston. You play a little cards, right?"

Dart took more notes. "Yeah."

"See if you can spot him anywhere around town. He'll know all the off-beat gambling places. Don't waste your time on the membership clubs. Keep track of what you spend and expense it to me."

"Gotcha. You know I can come to yo' office. I bet you got good air conditionin' in that fancy building of yours."

"I haven't put you on the firm's list. I'm paying you off the books, through Joanne's brother, to make sure you remain a secret."

Dart laughed. "You ashamed of me?"

"No way. You're my secret weapon."

"Uh-huh."

"If you should run across any of them, try to follow and see if you can tell who they're talking to and where they're staying."

"What does this have to do with Joanne Wyatt?"

"It's part of the other alternate theory. We know Byron was in trouble with the Dannons in New York. If they found out he was here, maybe they killed him."

"That seems like the best alternate theory you got."

"I hope so."

"What if yo' client girlfrien' decided she had enough and there ain't no alternate theory at all?"

Quinton paused. "Then let's create one."

———

Quinton and Dart met again, but this time in a Starbucks in the underground system consisting of six miles of tunnels running under downtown Houston. Having begun as a walkway between two movie theaters, it now connected ninety-five city blocks and included restaurants, retail and service establishments. One could pick up his dry cleaning, get a haircut, have his shoes shined, and eat lunch all without venturing out into the Texas humidity. Quinton thought it was unlikely that anyone in Q's old gang would have reason to be in the tunnels. Unbeknownst to Quinton, they were seated exactly two blocks over, below Devlin's hotel.

Dart was already seated at a cafe table with a cup wearing a cardboard wrapper in front of him. "Now this is better. Air conditioning and hot coffee. Want a cup?"

Quinton took off his jacket, hung it over a chair, and sat down. "Nah, I've already had about four cups. What you got?"

Dart spilled the beans. "That red-headed muscle you saw in court with Devlin is part of the Houston Irish Mafia called HIM, connected to gun runnin' in Ireland. They're a really small outfit compared to the Tango Blast and the Texas Mexican Mafia, who basically run the state as far as organized crime goes."

"Hmm. I'm sorry to hear that, but not Dannons?"

"Not Dannons, but friens' of the family, so to speak. The red-headed tough guy is named Shay Griff. He and his brother, Jimmy Griff, have been showing Devlin around for a while now. They've been roaming through the gambling spots, just like you said."

"Did you follow them?"

"Just until the Griff boys dropped Devlin off at his hotel. He's staying at The Lancaster, downtown. Living it up while he's here. Tipping big and buying drinks in the bar for anyone who'll kiss his ring."

Quinton blanched white, looked around the shop and out into the tunnel walkway. "You mean The Lancaster, above ground, just two blocks over from here?"

"Sorry. I didn't think of that when you said to meet here."

"Let's hurry up and get out of here. What about Dannon?"

"He's still in New York, best I can tell."

"Okay. Good work. Anything else?"

"One more thing. That young gambler from Reno you ask about. I think I foun' him. Someone match his description was askin' 'bout Byron and you 'round the gamblin' clubs. The most activity was at The Dog Pound."

"Yeah?" Quinton had told Dart he'd been there for a night of cards. Just once.

"I threw around some cash and made up a story 'bout him. No one seemed to know anythin'. If they remember Byron or you, they didn't say anythin' to me, and I'm guessin' they told the same thing to the Reno guy."

"Good work. I have another job for you." Quinton was still keeping an eye out. "I need you to go up to New York and sniff around the Dannons."

"New York? I got no contacts in New York."

"Make some. Just hang out. See if the drumbeats tell you anything. While you're there, see if you can locate a convict named Cronin. Declan Cronin. He was convicted for the attempted murder of Byron Douglas."

Dart got out his pad and a pen to jot down the name. "He still in the joint?"

"He was in Rikers last time I checked. Should be public record but verify. Those searches are usually out of date. Give me a call when you find him, and we'll go from there."

"If I find him."

40

Devlin got a call from Tua Dannon just as he was picking up the phone to call him.

"Hey, Boss. How's New York?"

"About the usual. You moved to Houston or are you coming back?"

"I was just about to call and give you an update."

"Glad to hear it."

"The Reno kid has been sitting on all the gambling places for days now and there has been no sighting of Byron Douglas before or after his alleged death. He was told Douglas might have been in one place called The Dog Pound a while back, but he can't be sure, and that may or may not have been before the date of death. It's a long shot that it was even him."

"What else?"

"The laptop showed us nothing of interest. Just a work tool. The notebook in the briefcase makes no sense and, even if it did, what use would it be? There's nothing to tie it to Byron Douglas. The lawyer, Quinton Bell, is probably the only one who can decipher it, and we certainly can't ask him without calling attention to ourselves."

"Agreed. Bring it with you just in case, but let's assume that it's a dead end."

"I've been monitoring the Joanne Wyatt trial and the cops are convinced that it was her that killed Byron Douglas. Regardless of who did it, he seems to be dead this time."

"Looks like you've done all you can. Ready to head home?"

"Yes. I'm tired of this cow town and all these local wannabe gang members. Time to get back to the big boys."

"Let me know when your flight's coming in."

"Will do."

Jimmy knocked on the door of Devlin's hotel suite, alone.

"You got a minute?"

"Where's your brother?"

"Griff doesn't know I'm here. I'd like to have a word alone if that's alright with you."

Devlin stood back from the door. "Sure, come on in."

The two settled on the sofa in the living room portion of the suite. Devlin could smell the stress sweat on Jimmy and he was still damp from being outside. He looked like he didn't know what to say.

"You called this meeting. What's up?"

"I know you're going to be heading back to New York soon, and I was wondering if there might be a place for me there. In the Dannons, I mean."

"You see yourself a mobster, Jimmy?"

"I could learn. My brother is always on my butt here. I can't do nothin' he don't know about."

Devlin chuckled inside. "Want to make your mark?"

"I do. I know I got something to offer, Devlin, and I'm loyal to a fault. You won't regret taking me on."

"Let me consider it and I'll let you know before I leave."

Devlin had no intention of taking Jimmy Griff anywhere. He could find a hundred Jimmy Griffs in New York without trying very hard. What use would he be in the five boroughs?

41

Quinton was driving his rented Audi home from the office in a pack of traffic when he got a call from Dart in New York. He pushed the speaker button, then put his hands back on the wheel, on guard against possible lane invaders.

"Hey, Dart. Glad to hear from you. I was starting to get a little worried."

"Calling from New York. I'm okay. Enjoyin' the sites on yo' dime."

Quinton laughed.

"Yo' boy Cronin is still in Rikers, but his trouble got worse. While he servin' a short for going after yo' frien' Byron, he got jammed up."

Byron put his blinker on to change lanes. "How so?"

"Seems he got tangled up with some other gang in prison and somehow somebody got killed. Might have been self-defense, might not."

Some driver in the next lane blasted a horn. Quinton

started to flip him the bird, then thought, *what's the point?* "Cronin go down for the killing?"

"Don't know yet. He got a hotshot lawyer, like you, and they goin' to trial soon. Word on the street is he done the guy. Don't think he'll ever get out. Might get the death penalty."

Quinton wondered if it might have been the Dannons who sent somebody after Cronin. Tying up loose ends.

"The death penalty only if it's a federal case."

"Oh yeah. They don't string up murderers in New York."

"Can you find out his lawyer's name and get a copy of the docket sheet from the courthouse? You know how to do that right?"

"Go to the courthouse and ask for it?"

Quinton laughed. He was beginning to realize how smart Dart was and what an asset he could be to his work. "Right. Also, can you check to see if an FBI agent named Frank Purvis is still in the New York office? Don't contact him, just locate him, and get his phone number. I lost it."

"Is your new alternate theory that the FBI killed Byron Douglas?"

Quinton laughed again. "No, it's still part of the theory that the Dannons killed him. We're going to stick with that one for now."

"Ten-four."

The next morning, as Quinton was getting dressed for work, he got another call from Dart in New York.

"Seems that a hotshot lawyer named Jeremy Robledo is now lawyer for Cronin. He mighta been hired by the Dannons. Not sure, but that's what my gut says."

"How else would he be able to afford a hotshot?"

"Right. I've got his firm name, phone, all that, if you need it."

Quinton pulled on his tie and spoke into the speaker as he arranged a knot. "Good. What else?"

"I found that FBI agent Frank Purvis. He was promoted to Washington, D.C., and somebody took him out."

"Damn. Killed him? Dannons?"

"Some say. His replacement is a guy named Timothy Tyler. I've got his address and digits."

Timothy Tyler. Quinton remembered the puppy dog who was fawning after Purvis when he, as Byron, had asked for help in New York.

"Word around town is that Tyler is out for blood to avenge his mentor and frien'."

"That could be useful. Please put all the contact info in an email and send it to me. If you think that's all you can learn, get on a plane back to Houston."

"That's probably all I'm goin' to find out without callin' attention to myself. I'll be back tonight, but if you need anythin' else, call me."

"When you have time, send your invoice and receipts for the trip. I'll get you paid asap."

Later, when it came across his laptop, Quinton forwarded the email from Dart to Judge Bell with a note that said: *Let's discuss. Reasonable doubt back on the menu, and maybe some help too.*

42

Quinton and Judge Bell met at STAT Coffee Shop near the medical center for a quick chat. Judge Bell, in a well-cut black tux, sunk down in a booth across from Quinton who was already seated and drinking an espresso. "Hey, Judge, want a cup?"

"No, thanks. I have an event with Silver. Got your email. You wanted to discuss some New York crook and the FBI? What's up?"

"My investigator has discovered that the FBI agent, Frank Purvis, who was in charge of the Dannon task force, has been murdered. Probably by the Dannon gang. Purvis's protege, Timothy Tyler, is in charge now and out for revenge."

"How does this help us?"

"Cronin, the second guy on the ferry, during my fake drowning, is in jail and up for a possible life sentence. It's a chance for Agent Tyler to turn him on Tua Dannon. I'm sure he's either done it already or trying to."

"Good for crime stopping in New York, but what's that got to do with the trial here in Houston?"

"I'd like to subpoena Cronin to testify about how badly the Dannons wanted Byron. That's my alternate theory of the crime, if I can get some evidence to back it up."

"Will he know you're Byron?"

"I don't think so. I was never in the same room with him, but he was watching me for a while. It was always at a distance."

"I see. Finally, a witness who can be put on the stand. Reasonable doubt and a bribe for the FBI?"

"Something like that. Joanne's brother, Alcott Wyatt, is willing to put up a large reward, through the FBI or Crime Stoppers, if Cronin testifies or anyone else comes forward."

"I remember Alcott. Bit of a weasel, if you ask me, but money talks. Might give Cronin the resources to hide from the Dannons. He won't be able to go back to jail."

"True. He'd be dead in a day. The FBI will probably offer witness protection, but the money could make it sweeter."

Judge Bell considered. "Hmm."

"If Agent Tyler can escort Cronin down for the trial, maybe he can scoop up Devlin, if he's still here. Get him off my back. Finally put Dannon away for good."

"That's a lot to hope for."

"If you can get the ball rolling with the FBI, I'll have Mo make all the arrangements. I'm hopeful you can convince them. It will come across better from a sitting judge than a defense lawyer like me."

"Might Tyler recognize you?"

"I only met him once, and I'm sure he has photos of Byron, but I don't think he'll recognize my new look in court."

Quinton was inviting to town the very men he'd been running and hiding from.

Crazy.

Quinton and Mo met with Joanne at the jail for what Mo called the reasonable doubt summit. Mo kicked off her shoes and sat at the metal table. Her injury had been healing nicely, but a long day was still uncomfortable, even sitting at her desk or in court.

Quinton put down a bag of food for them to share, as usual.

Joanne looked at Mo. "Looks like you're healing up."

"I am, thanks. You hungry?"

Quinton sat down with the women. "Let's talk for a minute first."

"Okay." Joanne looked a little better with the upgrades in food and fresh air.

"Judge Bell has contacted an FBI connection. We found a man named Declan Cronin who is vulnerable to a bribe or deal. He is the surviving pursuer of Byron Douglas on the ferry in New York."

Joanne's eyes flew up and at Quinton.

He patted her hand and held her gaze. "It's okay."

For the first time since she was denied bail, Joanne looked hopeful.

"If we can't prove the Dannons killed Byron, at least we can muddy the water. If we can get Cronin to testify, I think we can establish reasonable doubt for the jury."

Mo smiled at Joanne. "Your brother has put up a million bucks for information leading to information or the arrest of the real killer."

Joanne began to sob softly. Quinton went around the table and held her while Mo turned away to give them some privacy.

Quinton's receptionist buzzed him on the intercom. "A Detective Broussard is here to see you."

Quinton reached across his desk and hit the button on the phone. "Send him in."

Quinton did not get up when Broussard entered but pointed to one of the guest chairs. "What brings you here?"

"Don't get your panties in a bunch, Cher. My boss got a call from a Timothy Tyler from the FBI. Says you're bringing in a witness for the trial. My Lieutenant wants me to coordinate, escort him to court and all that. Big waste of time if you ask me."

"Well, no one asked you. Why can't you see that Byron was being hunted? Did you even try to find out if the Dannons were involved after we talked?"

"Why can't you see your girl is a murderer? All the evidence points to her. Seems love is blonde and blind."

Quinton fumed. "We'll see when Cronin testifies in court. You'll be eating Cajun crow."

"Why would the FBI comply with a warrant from you and bring him here to testify?"

Quinton figured that Broussard would find out anyway, so he told him. "Two reasons. It puts Cronin on the record while the FBI builds their case in New York against Tua Dannon. The witnesses have a way of disappearing, so it's insurance in case the Dannons take Cronin out. And, Joanne's brother, Alcott Wyatt, has put up a million bucks as a reward for anyone with information leading to information about the real killer of Byron Douglas."

"Oh, I get it now. All you rich and fabulous are bribing a witness."

Quinton scowled. "Only pressuring him to tell the truth and rat out Tua Dannon, not to lie for my client. There's a difference. It's no secret Cronin was on that ferry after Byron

Douglas. The Dannons kept tabs, just in case he wasn't dead, and found Byron in that motel room here in Houston."

"That's all circumstantial. You have no witness that the mob killed him."

"Well, isn't that the proverbial pot calling the kettle black. You have no witness against Joanne, and all your evidence is circumstantial."

"Touché."

"Look. Just open your mind for one minute, then I'll leave you alone to think what you do. Byron Douglas lost the trial in Manhattan involving the Irish mob. Tua Dannon threatened him and tried to kill him on the Staten Island Ferry as he fled. Joanne never locked her garage, just used the garage door remote to automatically close it. She never locked her car in the garage. She had a gun that she didn't use, to kill a man she didn't know, and had no motive to harm. She can barely cut up a steak, much less a body. Why are you so keen on putting her down for this?"

"You know as well as I do that she's fit and works out. She could have cut up that body or had some help doing it."

"Even if that were true, what about all the rest of it?"

"Okay. Since you want to have a heart-to-heart, I'll tell you. It's you. Something has been hinky about you since the first day we met at the morgue. You and Judge Bell been doing a fais do-do that set off my silent alarm that night and it's only gotten louder since. You're seeing this Joanne Wyatt and all of a sudden, she's in the neighborhood of a rundown motel and has a gun in her car that's matched as the murder weapon of your childhood friend. I think you and Daddy Bell have been protecting her all along. What would you think?"

"I understand. I'd probably think what you're thinking, but you've got it all wrong. Joanne is not a murderer."

I hope.

Griff and Jimmy knocked on the door of Devlin's hotel room. When Devlin opened the door, he frowned at them.

"I'm almost finished packing. I told you I'd meet you downstairs. We have plenty of time before my plane leaves."

"We need a minute. You might not want to go to the airport after all."

Devlin stood back and let them enter. Jimmy walked over and stood by the window playing with the blinds, obviously agitated.

Griff got down to business. "You've got a problem with the Wyatt murder case. Seems a guy named Declan Cronin has been subpoenaed to testify that he, you, and your dead buddy, Jim Breslin, were hired by Tua Dannon to hunt down Byron Douglas and kill him."

"What?" Devlin threw down the shirt he was folding.

"The assumption is that the Dannons missed him in New York on the ferry and found him here in his motel room."

"Yeah, well, why am I here making sure he's dead if we killed him?"

"Maybe someone went around you?"

"I've considered that, but who?"

Griff shrugged.

Devlin sat down on the bed. "I told Dannon we should take out Cronin, but he didn't want any more attention at the time. Now, we can't get to him."

"Word is Cronin says he knows who killed Killian Tyrone in prison and who paid for that too."

"Shit. We'll have to take him out before he can testify."

Jimmy piped up. "I'll do it for you, Devlin. Just give me the word."

Griff gave him a look that said: *Shut up.*

Devlin got up from the bed and started pacing. "He's probably already given info to the Feds about Dannon. The sooner we find him, the better."

"My guys can't find where they're stashing him, but they've verified that Detective Broussard and the FBI are hiding him here in Houston."

"Well, look harder."

43

The next day, Judge Blaylock ended a long day on the bench, dismissed his court reporter, and was escorted to his Cadillac in the municipal garage by Bailiff Grant. It was a weekday ritual for the two; they caught up on family, sports, the weather, and politics as they walked. Never religion, sex, or money. Those were taboo topics and both men liked it that way.

Today was like every other day, except for one thing. When the judge was secured in his car and waved goodbye to Grant, a hooded man, wearing jeans and boots, ran toward the bailiff and clobbered him from behind with a tire iron. Judge Blaylock honked his horn, drove up to Grant, and almost rammed the mugger. He would have if it would not have caused him to run the Caddy over Grant as well. The mugger scurried away and others in the garage came running.

The judge jumped out of his car and rushed over to Grant, lying on the concrete, and checked for a pulse as he yelled, "Someone call 911." The judge covered Grant with his jacket as blood pooled around his head. "Help is on the way, George. I'm here."

He was still alive. Barely.

Quinton, Joanne, and Mo sat at the defense table for the biggest day of the trial to date. The defense attorneys had prepared for hours, laying out a series of questions to lead Cronin, and the jury, down the primrose path to the logical conclusion that the mob had killed Byron Douglas. Not Joanne Wyatt.

It was a full house with the usual reporters and observers sitting in the gallery, packed cheek-to-cheek on the wooden benches. The new temporary bailiff cautioned several onlookers to find seats and settle down. Unseen by Quinton, Devlin, Griff, and Jimmy slipped in the back, as usual, and parked themselves on the right on the last bench in the row.

After Judge Blaylock went through the preliminaries and settled the jury and courtroom, Detective Broussard and FBI Agent Tyler brought in Declan Cronin. When he took his seat on the witness stand, Cronin almost looked like a model citizen. Clean-shaven, neat haircut, dressed in a well-fitting suit, all his mob tattoos covered by clothing except one peeking out on the back of his neck, and another on his wrist, that were too large to hide. It was all Quinton could do not to jump over the defense table and strangle him. He was fairly sure, although never proven, that Cronin had killed Michael in New York, widowed Nina, and orphaned Sophie. Quinton hated depending on him for anything, especially since he would get away with any number of crimes in exchange for his testimony today and later against Tua Dannon.

The last time Quinton had seen Cronin was on the ferry in the Hudson River where the mobster tried to shoot him. Mo sensed Quinton's unease and smiled at him. The lawyer part of him was not nervous to question Cronin, he relished it, but he let Mo think what she would.

Judge Blaylock gestured to the temporary bailiff. "Swear in the witness."

Cronin raised his right hand, and the show began.

After the mobster was settled, Judge Blaylock looked at Quinton. "Your witness, Mr. Bell."

"Thank you, Your Honor."

Quinton approached Cronin who showed no signs of recognition. *So far, so good.*

"Please state your name and state of residence for the record."

"Declan Cronin, Rikers Island, New York."

"You said that you reside in a prison. How did that come to be?"

Declan told the tale of working many years for the Dannon mob, leading to the day he tried to take out Byron Douglas, on orders from Tua Dannon. "I was ultimately convicted of attempted murder and sent to Rikers."

"Have you had further charges brought against you since that conviction?"

"Yes, I was involved in an incident at Rikers that led authorities to believe I murdered a fellow inmate. I have not been convicted of that crime and have turned state's evidence on the Dannon cartel in order to avoid prosecution and possible conviction."

"So, Mr. Cronin. You are a convicted felon, possibly a murderer, and a member of the most notorious gang in New York. You'd do anything to save your own skin. Why should we believe a word you say?" Quinton knew the prosecutor was going to bring out the entire history, so he got it on the record himself so he could control the narrative.

"You don't have to believe me at all. I'll just tell you what happened, and you can let the activity speak for itself."

"What activity?"

"Well, I was arrested when the ferry docked, convicted of attempted murder, and I've been living at Rikers. That's not my word, it's the State of New York's. The FBI has evidence linking me to the Dannon cartel going back over ten years." Cronin pointed to Agent Tyler. "I understand he's going to testify next."

"Are you pointing to FBI Agent Timothy Tyler?"

"Yeah."

"What else?"

Cronin pointed to the back of the courtroom where Devlin, Griff, and Jimmy sat. "That man in the gray suit in the back row on the right side is Seamus Devlin, Tua Dannon's right-hand and mob lieutenant."

The temporary bailiff quietly moved behind the court reporter and, unnoticed, toward the door to the judge's chambers. Devlin slid down in his seat and pointed at Jimmy, giving him the signal to action.

Broussard and Tyler turned in unison to look at the mobsters in the back of the room. At that moment, Jimmy stood, pulled a Glock from his jacket, and shot Cronin between the eyes. Griff seemed as shocked as Broussard and Tyler. Devlin didn't blink, just slumped farther down in front of the bench onto the floor.

Quinton dropped and squirmed on his belly under the defense table where he and Mo pulled Joanne down. Judge Blaylock ducked behind the judge's riser as spectators and reporters screamed and pushed toward the left side aisle of the courtroom and jammed the exit door.

Broussard crouched near the center aisle, pulled his gun, waited for a clear shot, then peeked out, took aim, and fired at

Jimmy, who dove behind a bench, causing the bullet to miss him by inches.

Cowardly, Devlin crawled under the benches and between the legs of those exiting the side door, pushing to get out.

Jimmy turned the Glock toward Agent Tyler who had pulled his own Glock and returned fire, missing, while trying to avoid hitting a reporter who was moving to get out of the way. Unfortunately, Jimmy's shot hit another reporter who was moving toward the side door. He went down, moaning and holding his leg.

At that moment, Judge Blaylock slid on his belly, around the side of the witness stand, took careful aim with his courtroom piece, a .357 magnum Smith & Wesson, and blasted Jimmy's chest wide open.

Griff grabbed Jimmy's fallen gun and fired ten shots blindly into the courtroom, wounding two observers and splintering wood on the benches and walls.

Broussard counted four shots left, assuming the Glock held the usual fifteen rounds. Tyler fired at Griff again and missed. Broussard took a deep breath, popped up, and fired at Griff, taking him down, but not out, with one shot to the gut. As he fell, Griff emptied the last four shots, splintering more wood, breaking glass, and causing bullets to ricochet off metal medallions on the walls.

Broussard flew across the aisle and harbored between two benches, waiting to see where the next bullets might come from. When he saw the slide lock back on the Glock, indicating it was empty, he held his gun on Griff and yelled, "Drop it." Griff dropped the pistol to his side, bleeding from the gut shot, and passed out. Tyler joined Broussard, holding his 9mm on Griff, while they assessed the room. Both were dripping with sweat.

Devlin, who had made his way out the side door, disappeared along with the crowd of reporters and courtroom observers.

Quinton was still crouched on the floor, holding Joanne and Mo in one large circle of his arms, halfway under the defense table. He felt something wet and warm on his legs. He looked down to see his bloody pants and a puddle forming on the floor. When Quinton let go of her, Mo looked at Quinton, then down and saw the blood. She patted herself and then Joanne. Quinton released Joanne from his grip, looked down and realized the blood was coming from her chest.

Quinton looked down into Joanne's eyes as she succumbed while he held her. At first, he was in shock and froze. As Mo began to get up, Quinton was brought back into his body. He realized what had happened, looked back at Joanne, and wept during waves of loss, guilt, regret, and love.

44

The next week, Quinton, Wallace, and Broussard met in Judge Blaylock's private office at the courthouse for a post-trial wrap up. The judge and other men wore their usual work suits, but Quinton had on a pair of jeans and boots. His white shirt had the sleeves rolled up. He could care less what they thought of his attire.

Judge Blaylock sat at the head of the table. "Just move that stuff out of your way." Wallace and Broussard took a seat around a conference table loaded with law books and file folders. Quinton cleared a chair by placing a stack of folders on the only empty corner of the judge's desk, then sat down.

Quinton had been working his way through the five stages of grief over Joanne's death and had cleared denial. He was stuck in anger for the time being, with bargaining and depression coming up next. Acceptance was not in the foreseeable future with guilt and regret his primary emotions most days. His anger often turned to rage when he allowed it to fully bloom. Something in him knew he was most angry at himself.

Joanne would be alive if not for him. Michael would be alive if not for him. Q would be alive if not for him.

Broussard turned to Judge Blaylock. "How's Bailiff Grant?"

"George's recovering from a severe concussion from being hit with the tire iron in the garage. Big scar across his scalp, but no brain damage. I hope to have him back in a month or two."

"I'm glad to hear that. Excellent shot in court, by the way. Didn't know you had that .357 cannon under the bench."

"Always have it handy. Never know when I might need it."

Broussard nodded. "Hopefully never again."

"Amen to that."

"We've located the temporary bailiff who smuggled in the guns for Devlin and the HIM. He's turned state's evidence, but we haven't been able to locate Devlin yet. Agent Tyler is pulling out all the stops to find him. It's just a matter of time, they think."

Quinton woke up to the conversation and the update. "What about Tua Dannon?"

"Agent Tyler got enough on tape from Cronin, combined with their other evidence, to arrest Dannon. They took him into custody in New York the day after Cronin was shot in court. It's up to the FBI now to make the charges stick. If they find Devlin, he may be able to help with that if he'll turn on the big man. Either way, both are going down."

Judge Blaylock nodded. "Good. I assume you'll be clearing the murder case now that Ms. Wyatt is no longer with us, Mr. Wallace."

"Yes, Your Honor."

Quinton stared at Broussard. "Don't you have anyone else you can falsely accuse?"

"We follow the evidence, but I am sorry that your friend was killed."

Quinton jumped up with eyes flashing at Broussard. "Her

brother wants a public apology and a full statement clearing her name." He turned to Wallace. "If you provide that, he has agreed not to sue."

Wallace seemed pained but agreed. He had been fully expecting a lawsuit. "I can do that. I'll have my co-counsel draw up some type of agreement and draft a press release and send it over."

"Fine." Quinton, having gotten what he came for, acknowledged the judge, then stomped out.

Broussard followed Quinton out the door. "Bell, wait. I really am sorry for your loss, and for the way things turned out."

Quinton almost spat at him. "I'll bet you are."

"I mean it. I'd do it differently if I could. A lot more security in court for one thing, but mostly checking more carefully on the Dannon angle. We still don't know who actually killed Byron Douglas at the motel, but there are a thousand thugs who could have done the deed for hire."

"So, you finally accept it was the mob? It only took four dead bodies in a courtroom to convince you."

"I'm not truly convinced of anything. I know you're still hiding something, but I'll assume it's wrapped up for now. Truce?" Broussard stuck out his hand.

Quinton didn't want to drop the anger that was shielding him from going too deeply into his grief. To do so would mean actually admitting that everything that happened was put into motion by his own actions. He wasn't ready to fully face it. He swung back and forth between blaming himself and then law enforcement. He didn't shake Broussard's hand, just hung his head, turned, and walked down the hall toward the elevator.

45

Quinton and Judge Bell met at the Victorian beach house in Galveston for a long weekend. Both men needed time away from the press and craziness in Houston that followed the horrific courtroom shoot-out that took Joanne's life. Judge Bell had preordered a grocery delivery, including plenty of shrimp, steaks, and fixings for grilling.

Quinton went for a long swim in the Gulf while Judge Bell did a run to Spec's for beer and booze. When they both returned to the beach house, the judge had the beer chilling in the fridge and coals burning down in the Weber. The smoke smelled like the end of summer. Palm trees were waving gently, and it seemed to Quinton as if there might be hope of some peace after all.

Inside, Quinton opened a beer, and the judge poured his second bourbon, over a single cube of ice, and took a sip. Quinton put Pandora on the sound bar with a vintage Beach Boys and Jimmy Buffet mix, then perched on a barstool at the kitchen island to watch the judge's chef skills.

The judge laid out ribeyes on a cutting board so that they

could come to room temp. He pulled a long curved blade from the knife block and began to shave the hard edge off the fat rind. He used the curve of the knife to precisely and expertly cut away about half of the fatty rim.

Quinton hummed along with the music as he watched, then froze with his beer halfway to his lips. The butcher knife had a long curved blade like the hip of a woman. The metal icon on the knife block said 'Wusthof.' Quinton had seen Judge Bell fillet fish with the knife many times over the years. He'd also seen him sharpen it on a whetstone in the garage.

Quinton's mind swam in memories as he floated out of his body. Small details swept over him. Of course, Q would have called his father before or after he called Joanne to set a meeting. The judge could have gone to the motel room. Q may have told him he'd called Joanne. The judge could easily have known about Joanne's garage and car from his visits over the years to her townhouse for social events. Everything clicked and Quinton knew who had murdered Q.

Quinton stared at the knife, still not wanting what he knew to be true. "Judge?"

"Yes?"

"That butcher knife. It's a Wusthof."

Judge Bell put down the knife, took a long swill of his bourbon, then looked at Quinton. He walked around the island and sat on the stool next to him. His shoulders slumped and his body sagged.

Quinton leaned away from Judge Bell. "Why?"

When the judge looked up again, he seemed almost relieved that Quinton had figured it out.

"For you, Son."

"Me?"

"I didn't want to kill him, but he was insistent on outing you and showing the world that I was a hypocrite. He said I used the law to fit my purposes and to punish everyone else. After all I had done for him, years of worry and hundreds of thousands in rehab and bribes. He looked like a bum in that filthy motel room. I offered him money. He took it, then said he was going to go public anyway."

"But he was your son. He was my friend."

"He wanted a shrimp boat. How ridiculous is that? My son, a shrimper? He stopped being my son long ago. You are my son. The son I always wanted. The one he could never replace by coming back into our lives."

"But you must have planned it. You had an untraceable gun and a butcher knife. You must have had gloves, trash bags, and all manner of other items with you. That's premeditation, not anger in the moment."

"I gave him one last chance, but I knew it would never end with him. Once a junkie, always a junkie."

"But why did you mutilate him? He was already dead from the gunshot according to the medical examiner."

"I was trying to protect your new identity. I got rid of the Q on his neck and the tattoo on his calf, but I didn't have time to finish the hands and fingerprints. I never completed the search of the room or his clothes, either. I missed my business card and his old ID. The guest down the walkway called the police, and I had to grab the flesh from the neck and calf, along with his burner phone, and run."

"But, why?"

"My plan was to take the head and fingers and leave the body for the police to wonder who he was. I assumed he would have drugs in his system, and they'd never spend the time to find the killer of a deadbeat addict."

Quinton was bewildered. "But, Joanne. You wanted her to be convicted of killing him? I thought you loved her."

"I did. She was going to be the mother of my grandchildren. She would never have been convicted."

"You couldn't know that. What you put her through was cruel. That's not love."

"Q told me he'd called her and that they were meeting for coffee. I had to get leverage over her because she knew you weren't Quinton. I had to throw suspicion somewhere for Broussard. It also worked to keep her quiet, don't you see?"

"That's why you wanted to provide an alibi for me. It was really for you. And, all the while, poor Joanne was twisting in the wind."

"I would never have let her go to jail. If you hadn't gotten her off, I would have found another way to exonerate her. I swear. Even if I had to confess, I'd have protected her."

"But you didn't protect her. You threw her into a fire that she didn't survive."

Judge Bell rocked on the barstool for a moment. "Don't you mean we? We threw her into the fire. You were as much involved as I was."

"Yes, I lied. But I did not kill or frame anyone."

"No, but you went along for the ride and benefited at every step. You might as well have pulled the trigger. Look how sought after you are now. Every high-priced criminal in Texas will be calling. You can write your own ticket. We got what we wanted. Don't you see?"

Quinton shook his head. "No. It's not what I wanted. You're no different than Tua Dannon or any other gangster."

Judge Bell rocked a while longer. When he turned back to Quinton, the look in his eyes was vacant. His mind just slipped away.

Quinton went into the guest room and packed his bag. It was too much to bear. He had gambled with the life of someone he loved. He was now trapped. He couldn't out the judge without putting himself in danger and obscurity. He was in a jail of his own making. How could he live with Quinton's name now that he knew the truth? He had to get out of the house and away from the judge. He needed to think. Decide what to do next.

Judge Bell did not go after him. While Quinton packed, the judge poured one more bourbon, neat, and downed it all in one gulp. He took the butcher knife, wrapped it in a kitchen towel, walked out of the house, and down to the beach. He should have thrown it away before. Did he want to get caught? Did he want Quinton to know? He didn't know anymore, and he didn't care. His mind had lost touch with reality. He had no son. No daughter. No grandchildren.

When he got to the water, he avoided the tourists and walked out about waist deep, then began to swim. When fatigue took over and he could go no farther, he unfurled the knife from the towel and let it go in the water. The undertow grabbed the blade and sucked it out to sea.

He took the wet towel and stuffed it deep into his mouth and throat. He gagged and coughed, but did not pull it out. When he breathed through his nose, water went into his lungs, and he gagged further. It felt like torture. The waves tossed him about.

Back at the house, Quinton came downstairs with his bag and car keys in hand. He did not see Judge Bell, but wasn't planning to say goodbye anyway. When he went outside, he looked around. Not seeing the judge, he threw his bag in his Audi and checked to see if the judge's car was in the garage. It was.

He sensed the danger, realized what was happening, and ran toward the beach. When his feet hit the sand, he could see

Judge Bell out in the wave swells. He kicked off his shoes and ran into the surf, then dove into the waves and swam out.

Judge Bell's arms began to fail him, and the salty water was soaking his throat and lungs. He stopped swimming as he passed out in the sea just as Quinton reached him. Quinton turned the judge over onto his back and pulled the towel out of his mouth and throat. He grabbed him in a dead man's tow and started swimming to shore. When he reached the sand, he pulled the judge out of the water, tilted his chin, and checked for breathing. Finding none, Quinton began to pump the judge's chest and breathe air into his lungs. Others on the beach came running and called 911.

Quinton pumped and breathed until EMS arrived, but it was too late. Judge Sirus Bell was gone.

46

The heat of summer broke, and beautiful fall days allowed Houstonians to enjoy outdoor activities and take a breath of relief. Quinton received a call from Judge Bell's estate planner advising him that he was the primary beneficiary of Sirus Bell's estate. A lot had been bequeathed to charities, including several colleges and law schools, along with a local legal clinic to be founded in his name. There was a small, but nice donation to the rehab clinic that had helped clear Q's record, and the high-rise condo in River Oaks was left to Silver.

Everything else, including the Galveston Victorian house, several investment properties, and several million in cash was left to 'my only son, Quinton Lamar Bell.'

Quinton knew he couldn't keep the money and wouldn't enjoy it if he did. He had the estate planner redistribute all of the cash and proceeds from the sale of the real estate to an entity he named the Sirus Bell Trust. Quinton and Silver were named as co-trustees and had equal votes in administering the assets.

Most of the cash went to a new wing at the South Texas College of Law. It was to be named the Sirus Bell Criminal Justice Education Center, and would open in about two years, post construction. A yearly scholarship for a deserving student was also established. A second scholarship was set up at the University of Houston Law School.

The only thing that Quinton kept was the Galveston Victorian beach house. He knew it was safer if he didn't keep anything that was not legally his, as he was not truly Judge Bell's son, but he couldn't part with it. Instead, he put it in the trust with a life estate for himself, to be relinquished upon his death.

Quinton and Silver Jamail parted well, and he found a new office in a building near The Galleria off Westheimer near Post Oak. He was now a loop lawyer, as attorneys were called who located outside of downtown around the 610 Loop that circled the city.

The location provided some distance from his old firm in hopes that if he was ever discovered, there would be less danger and damage to Jamail, Powers & Kent. He did strike a deal to do all of the firm's criminal work, and they happily expanded the banking section into the thirty-ninth floor after Quinton moved out. No more criminal lawyers for them.

Quinton felt he was safe, but he couldn't be sure. The only people who knew of his deception as Quinton Bell were dead. He knew Dart Owens had suspicions, as well as Clive Broussard, but neither could be sure, and he hoped any ideas about him would soon fade. There were the loose ends surrounding the fingerprints and DNA swaps that Judge Bell had paid for, but he was sure those contacts did not know who the new fingerprints or DNA really belonged to. Besides, they had committed criminal acts and had a lot to lose by coming forward.

Judge Blaylock still depended on Quinton to take on an occasional pro bono case when a worthy candidate arose, but Quinton no longer hung out in court seeking referrals. He didn't need them. His phone had started ringing immediately after Joanne Wyatt's trial and hadn't stopped since. He could afford to be picky about who he represented and planned to stay a solo practitioner, only hiring office personnel. He would not grow close to, or endanger, another lawyer in his business.

He did make an arrangement with Mo at the old firm to sit second chair with him when he needed help. He liked working with her and she was a real asset to have around, but he planned to keep her at arm's length.

Quinton paid Dart a hefty bonus, courtesy of Joanne's brother, Alcott Wyatt. After Dart used some of that money for a vacation, and some to attend a PI school and obtain his license, Quinton put him on the firm's payroll as the chief and only investigator.

Quinton's last hire was a temp office worker named Lacey Brooks. For the time being, she would serve as receptionist, answering the phone and opening the mail. Quinton wanted to hire an assistant, office manager, and paralegal all rolled into one. He planned to run an ad in the *Texas Bar Journal*.

The only thing left was to get out of his apartment near downtown and find a house close by. The traffic was killing him. He had a realtor looking in the Afton Oakes area, between The Galleria and downtown Houston, near River Oaks.

Quinton sat at his desk and looked out over The Galleria from his big picture window. Houston was a lot greener and prettier than outsiders realized and it had a world-class cultural scene, international vibe, and intercontinental airport that could get him to any city in the world in record time. He was glad to be here and establish his new life. He smiled inside as he prepared for a meeting with his first major client in the new Law Office of Quinton Bell.

Lacey brought in the mail and dumped it in a box on the corner of his desk.

"The client will be here in about half an hour."

Quinton looked up. "Right."

She had opened everything that came in that day and tossed the advertisements in the recycling bin. Per Quinton's instructions, she paper clipped the envelopes to the back of each piece of correspondence. The envelopes were saved to verify mailing dates in case of a dispute around deadlines.

Lacey rolled her eyes. "Hard to believe people still use snail mail."

Quinton laughed. "Lawyers will always use snail mail. Old habits and old laws still on the books. Less and less all the time though."

She walked back out, yelling over her shoulder, "I'll put on some fresh coffee."

"Thanks."

Quinton rifled through the stack of mail, looking at documents, notices, and State Bar materials. He found an envelope the size of a greeting card marked: Personal and Confidential. Lacey had not opened that one. He put his feet up on his desk, ripped the back flap, assuming it was an invitation to some social event, and found a one-page postcard with a photo of the

Staten Island Ferry and the skyline of New York on the front. His stomach clutched. He turned it over and read.

"Hello, Byron. I know who you are, and I know what you've done. Be seeing you."

THE END

Will Quinton outrun his past, or will he be trapped by it? Hold onto your seat, and check out Hunted By Proxy, the next page-turner in the Proxy Legal Thriller Series !

Sign up for Manning Wolfe's FREE newsletter and get a FREE book. Claim your copy:
www.manningwolfe.com/giveaway

LEAVE A REVIEW!
Thank you for reading **Dead By Proxy**. Please leave a review to help future readers find their way to this series.
Click here, or go to Amazon and Goodreads. Thank you.

ALSO BY MANNING WOLFE

Merit Bridges Legal Thrillers

Proxy Legal Thriller Series

Bullet Books Speed Reads

MANNING WOLFE, an award-winning author and attorney, writes cinematic-style, smart, fast-paced thrillers and crime fiction. Manning was recently featured on Oxygen TV's: Accident, Suicide, or Murder, and has spoken at major book festivals around the world.

* Manning's Merit Bridges Legal Thrillers features Austin attorney Merit Bridges, including Dollar Signs, Music Notes, Green Fees, and Chinese Wall.
* Manning's new Proxy Legal Thrillers Series features Houston attorney Quinton Bell, including Dead By Proxy, Hunted By Proxy, and Alive By Proxy.
* Manning is co-author of Killer Set: Drop the Mic, and twelve additional Bullet Books Speed Reads.

As a graduate of Rice University and the University of Texas School of Law, Manning's experience has given her a voyeur's peek into some shady characters' lives and a front-row seat to watch the good people who stand against them.

www.manningwolfe.com

Visit Manning Wolfe's website:
www.manningwolfe.com

Follow Manning Wolfe on Social Media:
www.facebook.com/manning.wolfe
www.twitter.com/ManningWolfe
www.instagram.com/manningwolfe/
www.tiktok.com/@manningwolfe

Sign up for Manning Wolfe's FREE newsletter and get a FREE book.
www.manningwolfe.com/giveaway